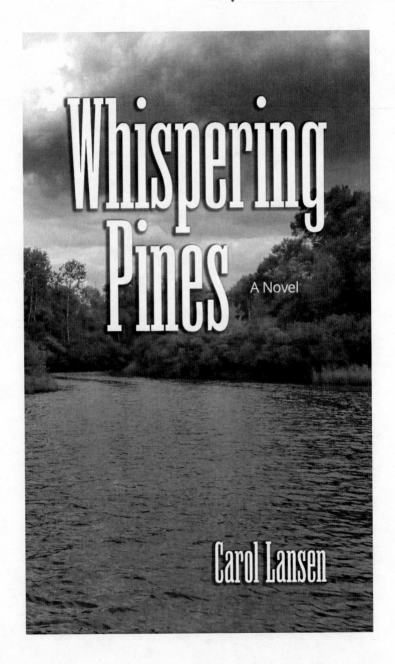

Whispering Pines

A Novel

Carol Lansen

Whispering Pines

A Novel

Carol Lansen

ISBN: 978-0-9972085-9-7
Library of Congress Control Number: 2020915000
First Edition

U.S. Copyright Registration Number TXu 2-185-282
Published by Spumoni Books. Contact at spumonibooks@gmail.com.

Cover photo by Carol Lansen

Cover/interior design
Mark E. Anderson
AquaZebra™
Web, Book & Print Design
www.aquazebra.com

Printed in the United States of America

Dedication

For my family, especially my Dad—thank you for everything.

Spring

The sound of a lawnmower plucked Bryn from a deep, dreamy sleep. She lay there listening to the rotary blades as a breeze sucked the gauze curtains of her bedroom window in and out against the screen. The entire house was inhaling and exhaling the late spring air. Bryn's mother Charlotte called those days between spring and summer the Chaldean of spring—Bryn thought it sounded romantic. The drone of the mower, the smell of fresh-cut grass and the rising heat gave Bryn the momentum to start the day. She sat up and peeked outside. It was the neighbor's teenage son Gary mowing the strip that ran parallel to Bryn's ground floor window. Gary was an odd guy—the kind who'd wear sweat pants with penny loafers—their neighborhood version of Napoleon Dynamite. She shrugged and swung her legs over the edge of her bed, feet touching the cool hardwood floor. She didn't put much on: a two-piece swimsuit in pale yellow and a pair of cut-offs. The temperature was already unseasonably high. She checked herself in the mirror, straight on and then sideways, stared at her Roman nose, voiced the compulsory "yuck" and walked out her bedroom door.

As she passed Gary on the way to the dock at the front of her house, he took a hand off the John Deere, waved and leered at her as if she were a nice, juicy lamb chop simmering on the Weber. Bryn waved back, but caught herself shaking her head in resignation. Whenever Bryn mentioned his attention to detail on the patch of lawn next to her bedroom window, her mother would say, "Oh no, I'm sure Gary Jensen is gay." Her mother was wrong. Bryn had seen him look toward her window on many occasions, focusing to get some small peek; she often thought he'd lose a foot on the mower's blades for lack of concentration.

Bryn's mother was an enthusiastic flirt and by her standards, if the guy didn't flirt back, he must be gay. She flirted with the mailman, the UPS driver, the manager at Piggly Wiggly, even the pimply kid who dropped off the cleaning and perhaps Gary Jensen. But mostly, she loved to flirt with Bryn's older brother's friends—a rub on the back, a touch on the knee or a playful tousle on the head. It drove Jack crazy, especially because they usually reciprocated and it didn't seem as innocent as the UPS guy. On one occasion, Jack asked his friend Nick Henkel point-blank: "Hey Henk, you ever screw my mother?" Henk hesitated just a second before calling Jack a pervert. It was the hesitation that haunted Jack. She understood her brother's frustration. Jack was several years older than Bryn and it wasn't hard to imagine their mother carrying things too far with Henk or any number of other young men. Charlotte was different and it was an attractive difference. She had her hair washed and blown dry every Friday like clockwork—at noon on the dot, she would walk through the door of Studio 213 waving at the salon girls like the Duchess of Cambridge. Her nails were always manicured and she threw catered parties and wore tailored pants with cashmere sweaters. Half the neighboring moms wore overalls with Green Bay Packers jerseys underneath. She knew about Frette linen and Jimmy Choo and the art of Modigliani and architecture of Holabird, but not in a superficial search engine kind of way, but in a bona fide "I know what I'm talking about" kind of way.

Charlotte Bolandz Wilson grew up in Tappanook, Wisconsin, a small hamlet hugging Lake Michigan. Bryn Googled it more than once, and although bordered by the Lake on its east side, it looked depressed rather than picturesque. Everything looked old—old houses, old train trestles, abandoned factories and downtown buildings that were growing weary from neglect. It didn't look like the kind of place that would have a Target, let alone boutiques selling Frette linen and thousand-dollar shoes. On the rare occasion when Bryn asked her mother about extended family in Tappanook or anywhere else, the questions hung there, unanswered. Bryn knew her grandparents were dead and she had an aunt who lived in Washington, DC, but that was it. There was a quiet understanding that her mother did not like to talk about herself or where she came from.

It was a beautiful morning with the sun glistening off the lake's surface. Bryn made her way to the end of their pier and lay down against the uneven cedar planks, knees bent at the edge of the dock with her feet dangling in the cold water. She listened to the small splash of water against the pylons until she heard a speedboat and laughter some thirty yards out on the lake, to her right, toward The Trading Post. The Post was a local institution. Everyone who lived on the 90 acres of Crane Lake's shoreline fueled their boats and got their snacks, bait, suntan lotion and other sundries at The Post. The owner was Josie Porter. She was just shy of ninety, and every Porter (and there were a lot of them) had worked at The Post at some point during their adolescence.

In Bryn's age group, there were about thirty or forty kids. Everyone knew everybody, but Bryn spent all her days with Claire Porter and by association, with Claire's brother Wally and Wally's best friend Jon Wright (a.k.a. Midnight). Wally and Midnight were the lake's nerve center. Mischievous, quick-witted, ingratiating—like a Sunday morning televangelist, they attracted followers.

Feet still touching the cool water, Bryn propped herself on her elbows and lifted her head to watch a speedboat haul a solo skier out of the water. She sat propped, neck craning until it ached, drinking it all in. She was smiling at the water-skier, at the crystal-clear water and the hot sun warming her skin as a breeze drifted across her midriff. The speedboat belonged to their neighbors, the Brandts. It was Nora Brandt who was driving. The woman sitting shotgun and spotting the skier looked like Nora's mom, but Bryn couldn't be sure who the boy they were towing out of the water was. He looked about her age. How nice it would be to have someone new living on the lake or, at the very least, visiting the Brandts for a few weeks. He looked cute. He had long red nylon swim trunks that flapped in the air along the hemline as he came out of the water on a slalom ski. His hair was dark and stuck to his forehead in a pattern of quarter moons. His smile was broad and white and his stature was confident as he leaned back against the pull of the Evinrude. From Bryn's perch, she could see his arms were firm and his legs were muscular and well defined. As they rounded the opposite side of the lake, it seemed like the boy began to shake. The water was always freezing and Bryn figured he was hamming it up for his audience, but he was not steady on the ski and his body tumbled a couple of times, legs akimbo, before he went down hard on the water with one big splash. Nora circled around to either retrieve him or let him have another go at it. Oddly, she and her mother were both standing and, at least from

Bryn's view, Nora turned the boat in ever-decreasing circles. Bryn could see the neon-colored bootie of the slalom ski, but not the boy. Then she heard Nora scream. Bryn couldn't make out anything but "HELP!" and instinctively looked toward the Post and saw Wally on his cell phone. Bryn fumbled for her footing and ran inside to call the water patrol, leaving wet footprints the entire length of the cedar dock.

She would later find out the boy's name was Davis Brummell. He was Nora's cousin on her mother's side visiting for the week from Dubuque. He was 18 years old when the boat pulled him out of that cold water and he proceeded to have a grand mal seizure. People guessed that his ski vest was shaken off when he tumbled, because no amount of trawling or dragging the bottom was successful in retrieving him. There were miles of freshwater seaweed, long tendrils that reached up from the bottom like aspens reaching to the sky. It could cage his body forever. That lake was well over 100 feet deep in some spots. No, it was clear to everyone, except maybe Davis's mother, that he was not going to see nineteen.

For over a week, the water patrol went up and down, back and forth, grappling hooks dragging, trying to latch onto Davis's body. The entire time, Charlotte reminded Bryn and Jack to stay out of the water. The weather was hot and humid, but she asked that there be no swimming, no diving, no laps, no water polo, no dangling feet and especially no water-skiing. Jack asked, "What do you think is going to happen if we go in the water?" Charlotte responded by saying, "What if anyone were to accidentally brush against that poor boy's body? It's gruesome to even think about." When Jack said he didn't think drowning was contagious she went silent. When he continued to ride her for an explanation, all she said was, "I can't bring myself to talk about this anymore. Can you do as I ask? Besides, I can't imagine the sheriff would let anyone out on a motorboat. The whole thing makes me sick. Imagine that poor boy."

Jack responded, "You are a complete reactionary. We're not talking about going out boating or joy riding. We're talking about taking a nice cool dip. You act like you knew him or something. Quit dictating like I'm a kid and stop acting like you're concerned about someone who is a complete stranger to you. And can you also please stop saying 'that poor boy'? I feel like I'm in a Tennessee Williams play."

With that, he headed toward the bathroom to grab a beach towel, still talking at his mother, obviously ignoring her request.

"He can't get any more dead. He's been somewhere under water for nearly a week. I think the fish have probably begun to pick at him by now. It's boiling outside and I'm going in."

"Oh my God! The fish. There's a grim thought."

"That's nature. That's how it works, Charlotte. There's always some giant musky or walleye that mistakes the aglet on your trunks for a minnow."

"Jack, stop being so graphic and for the umpteenth time, stop calling me Charlotte."

At that, she walked into her bedroom and slammed the door while Jack headed to the dock.

Bryn whispered, "I will never eat pike from this lake again."

Then she walked out the back door of the house away from the lake and toward the road. She figured a nice walk around the back of the lake would be a diversion from her mother and brother's disagreements, which usually ended with Jack bringing up his version with their father and the two of them sharing a rib about Charlotte. Jack was his father's golden boy and he strained a relationship between Charlotte and Richard Wilson that was already taut. They lived atop their own version of the San Andreas Fault. You couldn't spend every day waiting for The Big One, but you knew it was coming just the same.

When Bryn asked Jack to explain why he was so hostile toward their mother, he'd said she treated their father badly and he didn't appreciate how she acted around his friends. He would usually add that Richard should leave her and get the hell out while he was still young and could meet someone who might actually love and respect him. Bryn would inevitably ask him to elaborate, but Jack would shrug his shoulders and tell Bryn he didn't want to talk about the details. No amount of coaxing could change his mind. Bryn could never figure out why her brother had moved back home after college. Boulder seemed like a nice enough place. Better than Andover, Wisconsin. She knew he was looking for a job and couldn't afford his own place out west, but always thought he would have preferred to live on the street in a cardboard box. Their bickering made Bryn anxious. The dueling mother and son—parry, lunge, feint, counterattack. Bryn tried her best to keep out of their arguments, avoiding crossfire. She couldn't count the number of times she'd opened her bedroom door, only to close it just as quickly, as the sound of arguing wafted down the hallway.

She needed fresh air and quiet. She considered heading toward Claire's, but wasn't sure. As she aimlessly walked she thought about Claire. Most girls didn't want to associate with her— she was too pretty. She looked like a teenage version of a Victoria's Secret model. Bryn would see her after classes walking down the hallway smiling wide, waves and swirls of thick blond hair swaying. She often wore it with a headband along with a ponytail to keep it harnessed, because it was big and beautiful and wild. Claire's hair *was her*. She was five-foot-eight at the age of sixteen and her mother was convinced she had some more growing to do. No doubt about it, Claire was a classic beauty, but there was an underlying vulnerability that maybe only Bryn understood and Bryn loved her for it or maybe despite the illogic of it, coming from someone so attractive. She pretended to be unflappable, but she was not. The one place Claire was completely confidant was the outside lane of an Olympic pool. There, she was like a Mako— ready to dart through the water and take home first prize. There she could shut off mean girls and catty classmates.

Lost in thought, Bryn walked a good two miles before realizing she was well past the Porters' house and headed in the direction of the Argent River. When she finally stopped walking she was at the river's mouth and Chris Bello was about ten yards from where she stood. He was in a canoe and paddling toward her.

Chris was dark-skinned and dark-haired, with brown eyes as deep as hickory and a nose that was too small for his face, unlike Bryn's prominent, aquiline feature. He wore glasses and stood five feet, eleven inches tall. He was broad-shouldered and he was solid like a California sequoia, sturdy and unwavering.

He held down several summer jobs, one of which was as a sweeper for Argent River Excursions. A sweeper canoed down the river at the end of the day picking up any equipment, sometimes including a canoe or two that people had abandoned or lost when faced with the more difficult whitewater portions of the river. Bryn figured Chris was on his way down the river to begin his day as others had finished theirs. Chris smiled, gave a wave and sidled up to the shore where Bryn was standing and asked if she'd like to join him for the rest of the afternoon. She jumped at the chance. She hadn't really noticed much of him that spring. He didn't hang out at the Porters', frittering away his days or his money. The rumor was that his father was very strict. Chris was expected to work and study hard and realize the American dream as his grandfather had done, having fled Cuba many years earlier.

Bryn teetered slightly getting into the canoe, but Chris took her hand. A rush of goose pimples ran along her arm when he touched her and she shook for an instant.

"You cold?"

"Not really, I just got a chill."

He took his shirt off and handed it to her. It was warm against her skin and the long sleeves smelled like suntan lotion. The late afternoon air was getting cool and all she was wearing was a sleeveless tank top and shorts. She welcomed the gesture.

Staring at his bare chest, she asked, "You're sure you're going to be OK?"

"I'm fine."

His torso was long and his pectoral muscles pronounced, not showy like a weightlifter, but smooth and rounded. He had no chest hair to speak of but a few black strands of hair jutted out around his nipples, which were pigmented a deep rose color and hardened by the fast rush of cool air.

Bryn began, "Canoeing isn't much in my wheelhouse. I'm more of a spectator when it comes to sports and I'm afraid I may not be much help to you."

"Don't worry about that. I've been down this river a million times by myself, but I saw you walking and thought it'd be nice to have some company."

"Well, company I can provide."

Despite her lack of any preparation—no makeup, no small bag with a comb and lip gloss, Bryn was immediately comfortable with him. They headed down the river. Bryn awkwardly rowed at the bow while he steered at the stern. Conversation came quickly and easily. She felt good about him, about herself, and about how a day with no special promise was turning out pretty well.

The river was secluded and beautiful under the afternoon sun. Its headwaters were freckled with shallows, where you could easily see the bottom through the clear, cold water. The sun glistened on its sandy belly. Schools of minnows darted by. Their silver skin reflected the sun and created an underwater string of sequins. Long reeds grew along the shoreline, providing shelter for chub and small perch. The river curved and twisted and as it got slightly deeper and darker, it was pocked with jutting boulders, which created great streams of white water on either side. They were completely alone. The last rafting group was long gone and nature was returning to the river. They heard the occasional fish jump to scoop an insect hovering too close to the surface and listened to the birds caw above. They stopped to watch a beaver running along the roof of his wooden dam searching for leaks or holes, and listened to the steady slap of water against the canoe. A dome of trees shadowed overhead, shielding them from the late afternoon sun and the outside world. There was no one to watch or overhear and Bryn said softly, "Only good things could happen in a place as beautiful as this."

They talked about school. Chris talked about football and how much he loved to play. He was excited his junior year was coming to an end and he'd be back on his varsity squad as a senior. It was more than a sport to him. Every year it started with the Packers draft, then summer training through the Pack's season and the University of Wisconsin's, his own season at Andover West High School, and then to the Super Bowl. It was all peppered with his fantasy league, which apparently took the dedication and discipline of a Trappist monk. It was his religion, his solace during bad times and his joy during the good. As he continued to talk about his team's prospects for the upcoming season, their coaches, who had talent and who did not, Bryn nodded in agreement, pretending to understand. She silently vowed she'd watch games more often and actually pay attention.

She talked about her family and the ongoing battles—the fencing match that she explained was her home life. At first she felt guilty divulging so many intimate details, but the stories gushed, stories she hadn't even shared with Claire. She told him about one Saturday evening after her parents had argued about one of their car leases. Her mother had thrown a plate of lasagna at her father's chest like a hard Frisbee toss on a long stretch of beach, red sauce and mozzarella pooling on his khakis. She confessed it embarrassed her to admit it, but that was pretty much routine at her house. Bryn became aware of how much she was talking.

"I'm talking too much, aren't I?"

"No. It's all really funny."

"Thanks, I think. The really funny part is that it's all true, and I'm guessing with my mother pitching the plate, the lease they were arguing about was probably hers."

Bryn said her parents had to have been in love once too. They got married, after all. She told him she remembered seeing them slow dance in the living room to Eric Clapton's "You Look Wonderful Tonight" and they looked happy, but that had been a long time before. She supposed time and circumstances whittled them into something else. She didn't know why tears were welling in her eyes and she brushed them away before Chris could see. She didn't want him to see her crying. She was not an attractive crier.

"Eric Clapton's a little old-school, don't you think?"

"Well, they are a little old-school."

"What kind of music do you like?"

"I'm into lots of music. I like Jay-Z a lot and some country and I love all the girls: Pink, Gaga, Lorde, you know."

"Yeah, girls like the girls. I'm not a huge country fan."

"Who do you like?"

"I'm like you. I like a lot of different stuff. I like Mark Ronson and Kanye, and people like that, but I also like more obscure bands like Jane Jam. Hey, can I ask you something?"

"Sure."

"You've told me lots of stuff about your family, but do you, like, know anything about mine?"

"Oh, everybody gossips about everyone around here. I don't know much of anything except that your mom died."

"Yeah, and I have a pretty awful stepmother married to Mr. B."

"You call your dad Mr. Bello?"

"Stands for Brute, not Bello. He can be really tough. You know my mom isn't just dead either. She killed herself when I was ten."

Bryn didn't have the heart to tell him everyone knew about his mother. She swiveled in her seat to look at him and said, "I'm so sorry."

"Yeah thanks. The thing is, every family's got their stuff, you know?"

Faced with his candor, she felt better about divulging family gossip, a practice her mother frowned upon, but all she said was, "I guess so."

Chris said he'd rather change the subject if she didn't mind and she didn't, so they talked about other kids they both knew, mostly kids from around the lake who went to the same school as Chris. She envied that he went to the town's large public school, Andover West, endearingly called Wild West. She liked many of her teachers, but disliked the parochial, provincial environment, the hideous uniforms and mandatory theology classes, which she had little interest in. She and her friends jacked up the plaid skirts of their uniforms, snuck an occasional joint outside the gym and faked menstrual cramps to get out of Mrs. Lowell's biology class, but no matter the amount of minor rebellions, they were geeky, conformist, nerds who went to St. Agnes.

They talked about their siblings. Chris's older sister and Bryn's brother Jack knew one another, although they weren't close friends. The conversation got around to Midnight and

Wally, whom Chris knew pretty well but didn't hang out with much anymore. When she asked why, he explained his three jobs, which his father made him keep so he wouldn't have time to get into any trouble with Wally and Midnight or anyone else.

Bryn turned in her seat again and smiled wide. "I have heard your dad's a bit of a nightmare."

"Yeah, he's legend around here. The only way to get Mr. B's attention is if you get into trouble and that's the beginning of a long lecture about disappointment, family values and how hard everyone had to work for me to be where I am. By the way, I'm not so sure where I am is so great. Anyway, my grandfather came to the U.S. from Cuba and if I have to hear the story one more time, I think I'll bust something. The journey gets more perilous at each telling. When I first heard it, he left Cuba on a sailboat. The last time I heard it, I think he was traveling on a piece of driftwood."

"You're funny."

"It's not a joke."

"Ha! You know, I try not to get into trouble for the obvious reason, but I never know whether the reaction from my parents will be even remotely appropriate to the offense. A couple months ago my father found out Claire and I went to an R movie. I mean, come on, we're sixteen not six. Anyway, he grounded me for two weeks and used the F bomb twice when he was yelling at me about it. You get where I might be confused, right?"

"You're pretty funny yourself."

"It's not so funny if you're the one doing time. I just want to be, or stay invisible, which is more often than not what I am to both of my parents."

"I doubt if you could be invisible."

"It's pretty true."

"Well I should maybe try that, because I get my dad's attention all the time, and the stepmother's. I feel like she's all over me and it comes off real fake."

"Maybe she really cares."

"I don't think so. I think she'd prefer if we all went away. Well, 'all' really meaning me."

There was quiet for a time and he moved forward in his seat, toward the middle of the canoe. He reached his hands toward her shoulders in an attempt to draw her back to him. It took Bryn by surprise and she was pulled off balance and see-sawed with the canoe, but he steadied it.

"Sorry," he said.

In a second attempt, he moved to the middle of the canoe, saying, "Come and sit with me in the middle. There's no rough water for a while and we can drift with the current." He pulled Bryn to him with more determination and coordination. The small of her back rested against his stomach. They sat like that for a long time and it felt good to rest her head back against his strong, warm chest. That's when he told her more about his mother. She had taken an overdose of sleeping pills. He was the one who found her. He had come home after hockey practice and called for her. When no one answered, he assumed no one was home. He was on his way to his room to start his homework, but stopped in the kitchen to call his dad to ask if he knew where his mom was. After a scolding about interrupting him at the restaurant while getting ready for the dinner rush, his father told him she should be home. He hung up the phone, walked upstairs to his mother's room and knocked on the closed door. When no one answered, he opened it.

She was sprawled facedown across the bed, wearing a pink terry cloth bathrobe. The fingers of her right hand were just touching the floor and he noticed her nails were beautifully manicured and painted a deep cherry red. There was a thin line of spittle dripping out of her mouth. He gently pushed at her shoulder, then shook her a little harder hoping to wake her up, but in his heart he knew. And out the corner of his eye he saw an envelope propped against the mirror of her dressing table. A thick snow had begun to fall. He did not stop to take in the falling snow or read the note. He was racing along the hallway and down the stairs two steps at a time, to get to the kitchen phone and call an ambulance.

He confided to Bryn that he had never asked his father what the note said and his father had never offered to tell. He added that he had stopped caring about it, but Bryn thought that could not be true. How could someone stop caring about a thing like that? The curiosity would eat at you. You would wonder whether you were mentioned in the note. And what if you were mentioned in a bad way? What if you had been part of their wanting to die? And quite suddenly, Bryn was crying and she didn't care if Chris saw it. Her heart was breaking for him and for all the screwed up families everywhere.

They let the river take them along and as he wrapped his arms around Bryn's chest, she cried with total abandon. The tears ran freely down her cheeks. He said, "I'm sorry. I probably shouldn't have told you about that. I guess it's not the kind of thing you talk about when you first talk to someone. The really, really shitty thing is that I loved my mom and thought she loved me."

"I'm sure she did."

"Hell of a way to show it."

"I'm so sorry."

"Yeah, well, it was a long time ago, but I guess it's always there, you know?"

In a soft and sympathetic voice, Bryn said, "Of course."

Chris squeezed her gently. "Shit, let's talk about something else."

"I can't believe we haven't talked about the drowning."

"What drowning?"

Bryn's mouth was open when she said, "You're kidding, right?

"Yes, of course I'm kidding. I may work three jobs, but everyone knows about the Brummel guy."

"He was Nora Brandt's cousin from Dubuque. He had a seizure while he was water skiing. I was on our pier and I saw the whole thing happen. My mother doesn't want us in the water, so this little trip is a nice departure. I kind of agree with her. It's creepy to think about going in."

Chris paused, but then said, "Yeah, I guess I was a bit freaked out setting off down the river today, but then I saw you and figured we could go together. I mean, think about it. What if he drifted down here?"

"Could that really happen?"

"It's unlikely, but I am less freaked out with somebody else coming along."

"Thanks a lot. Now I know why you offered."

"No, no. It's been fun talking and stuff."

They didn't speak for a long time. They sat and held their embrace. When hearing the rush of white water, they assumed a position for rowing out of it, but would return to that warm cuddle, to aimlessly drift again as they cleared the rocks. The sun was getting lower and the air began to feel cooler. Bryn asked Chris how long they had been gone. He said it usually took him three hours and pointed to a bend about fifty yards ahead of them, telling her their pick-up point was right around it and that would make it around six o'clock.

The van driver could not conceal his surprise at Chris having company. Chris ignored the guy's stare and without a word they loaded the canoe and equipment, along with two extra life preservers, an abandoned oar and a Styrofoam lid from an ice chest they found en route. The driver smirked as he asked Chris how the trip was and how the day had been. He didn't acknowledge Bryn and Chris hadn't introduced her. They rode in virtual silence after Chris said, "The day was fine, man, like always."

They dropped her off at the Argent River Excursions office before they went to unload the van. Chris asked her if she was okay to get home and when she said she'd be fine, told her he'd call her.

Since no one knew where Bryn was and her cell was on her dresser, Richard was angry by the time she walked through the front door just before seven o'clock. Bryn had feared as much when Chris told her how long they had been on the river. She quickly said she had been hanging out with Chris Bello for the afternoon.

Richard began. "He's from that Mexican family with the crazy mother, isn't he?"

Charlotte defended Chris. "Well, come on, it certainly is not the young man's fault that his mother had problems."

Bryn added that his family was not Mexican but Cuban.

Richard quickly added, "Whatever, the old man is a loser."

The subtle racism captured in Richard's *whatever* was a reminder, despite all the class work and student rallies about gender and race equality, there was a very long way to go. Maybe *To Kill A Mockingbird* should be required reading for parents.

Charlotte defended Samuel Bello as well. "That is most definitely not true. Why would you say that? He's not the most successful…" Charlotte's voice trailed off, but Bryn heard her father say, "Ha! About as far as you can get from successful."

And so it went for fifteen minutes—true to their family recipe—parry, lunge, feint and counterattack. And, as often was the case, the barbs were completely unrelated to the original topic.

The only thing they agreed on was that it was unacceptable for Bryn to be gone the entire afternoon and into the evening without explanation or at the very least, a quick phone call. It riled Bryn that their debate was ruining the end of her lovely day. As her anxiety grew, her day withered. She nervously picked at a small chip in her fingernail.

"And where in the hell have you been hanging out all this time? Jesus, all you have to do is read the news and there's a missing person every day. Someone's found in the deep woods or in a mall parking lot with fifty stab wounds."

Bryn mumbled under her breath, "Well that would have been inconvenient."

"What did you say to me?"

"Nothing. Sorry."

"And what the hell are you wearing? Is that a boy's shirt?"

"Yes it is." She tried to assure him nothing sinister or subversive was going on and told both of them exactly what happened that afternoon, starting with the disagreement between her mother and Jack and the need for some fresh air. Her father's expression could have melted rock and she felt herself getting more nervous and anxious about her explanation even though nothing had happened that was out of the ordinary. She wasn't so naïve that she couldn't tell the direction his mind was going. She assured him being out on the river gave them no access to a phone. Chris never brought his cell on the river, having lost two to the rapids on prior trips, and her phone was kept dry on her night table, where it was left behind for what was meant to be a short walk. She left it there on purpose. Her school had recently promoted a movement called "Digital Down for the Day"—Bryn was embarrassed to admit that she actually liked it. She had stared at the phone and continued to struggle with leaving it behind, but she didn't want to talk to anyone or text anyone or feel the need to reply to anyone. All she wanted was to be alone.

They said they had seen it lying on the nightstand, which created even more alarm. But for some inexplicable reason, Richard was completely fixated about Bryn wearing Chris's shirt. She explained that it had gotten chilly and he offered her the warm shirt, which she found touching, but Richard seemed suspicious about his motives. Bryn thought about saying if Chris had been sexually motivated, he would have removed clothes rather than adding more on, but wouldn't dare. Richard was on a rant. He was lashing out at her and her mother as well for defending Bello. Was this going to be the Big One? She thought she was going to witness the tectonic plates smashing into smithereens, but then there was a lull and Richard's face returned to a healthy shade of rose, so Bryn went off to her room. She wanted to be alone to reconstruct every second of the day: the smells and the sounds of the river, the feeling of the soft cotton of his shirt, the smell of sunscreen on his strong arms. She had been unkempt and uncombed and knew he liked her for herself, and not what she looked like, good or bad—a feeling that was rare and extraordinary, in equal measure. She closed her eyes and pictured the river and felt the warmth and strength of his arms wrapped around her.

Behind her closed door, she could still hear her parents bickering in the living room. She shut her eyes tight and tried to expel them from her mind. How contrary they were. They never told one another they loved each other, but Bryn would occasionally glimpse her father patting her mother's rear end or wrapping his arm around her waist while she stood rinsing dishes and loading them into the dishwasher. Her mother would one minute be furious with her father for driving home

after he'd been drinking with co-workers and the next she'd
be in the crook of his arm, her own glass in hand, watching
Late Night or an HBO movie.

They had spoiled her lovely day and made her feel guilty about nothing. It was like the night when Jon Wright got his nickname. Almost everyone called Jon Wright "Midnight." The nickname came from a small caper that morphed into legend within their circle of friends.

It had been back in 7th grade. Claire had come up with the idea to sneak out of their houses long after everyone had gone to sleep. It was January and it wouldn't be much fun to go anywhere in the middle of the night unless it was back into a warm bed, but they decided to do it anyway and Claire insisted they include Jon. When Bryn suggested Wally join them too, Claire said she didn't want to do it if the plan included her brother. Bryn acquiesced and it was Jon and Claire and Bryn walking down a dark, quiet street sometime around 1 a.m., laughing with pride at their escapade.

Bryn was wearing a parka that made her look like a bloated beetle. It was completely unattractive, but she didn't care—it was purely utilitarian. Well, she didn't care until she saw Claire. Her cheeks were flushed from the cold and her hair was wound up in its customary topknot and she had on a navy blue ski jacket that cinched at the waist. Bryn would never come straight out and say it to Claire, because Claire would tell her she was crazy, but sometimes Bryn felt her most unattractive being around her.

When the temperature dropped below 15 degrees, their shenanigans seemed less brave and more idiotic. The trio walked down the middle of the snow-covered road and finally admitted it was too cold to stay outside. Bryn's house was the closest, so that's where they went for shelter. They sat in the family room talking very softly, trying not to giggle or give themselves away, but after a short time Claire said she was going to go home. She asked if Jon was going to head out with her, but he said he was going to hang out for a while if Bryn didn't mind. She didn't. She was having a good time. They were munching on popcorn and watching a horror movie on FX with the volume turned low. Midnight had asked Claire if she'd be all right walking home alone. Claire mumbled that it was only a few blocks and left quietly out the back door. She had been gone a few minutes when Jon confessed he was still freezing, so Bryn suggested they build a fire. While pulling a log off the log rack, it slipped from her fingers and dropped to the floor with a thud. It didn't occur to either of them that the noise might wake someone. They were preoccupied with their conversation about the brutal amount of homework they were both getting and the movie, but the thud did wake someone. It woke Richard.

It had been a little after two in the morning. With one hand, Richard gripped Jon's shirt and shoved him out onto a snow-covered lawn, followed by his jacket and scarf, and proceeded to call Kevin Wright, Jon's father. All Bryn heard Jon say was "oh, shit" as his back hit the snow. The cold created a thin layer of ice on the top, crusty enough to make a sound. It looked like satin sheets, but she was sure it didn't feel like it.

"Mr. Wright, I don't know if you remember me from last year's lake association party, but I'm Bryn Wilson's father. Bryn is an acquaintance of your son, who, by the way, was just sitting in my den watching some movie on TV, munching on a bowl of snacks. He was looking really comfortable on my sofa, which would all appear pretty harmless, but it's after two o'clock in the goddamn morning."

Mr. Wright had been woken from a deep sleep, but raising two boys gave him a built-in restlessness, so his response was clear and lucid. "Mr. Wilson, I understand you're upset. Jon being over there at this hour is crazy. Can you remind me of your address? I will be there in a few minutes to fetch him."

"I'm at 1907 Harbor Lane, about a mile down the road from the Trading Post. For all I know, he's already on his way home or he'll be waiting on the front porch!"

"Mr. Wilson, it has to be ten below zero."

"That didn't stop him from making his way to my house in the middle of the night and you can tell him he isn't welcome here, ever, no matter what time of day." Glaring at Bryn, he added, "I think I've made myself loud and clear with my daughter."

Mrs. Wright asked who it was and what was wrong. Mr. Wright said, "There's nothing to worry about, no one is hurt or dead, but Jon is grounded for the rest of his life. He's fine. I'll explain it all when I get back, but mark my words, he is grounded for life."

"Hold it, where are you going?"

"He's at some girl's house."

"What?"

"I have to go look for him. I'll be back in a while and we'll talk about it then."

With that, Kevin Wright grabbed a pair of sweats, a fleece and his car keys and drove off to pick up Jon or at least fetch him en route. He found him a few blocks from home, feet dragging, his head buried in his jacket, protecting his neck and face from the cold. Kevin Wright stopped the car, leaned across the front seat and opened the passenger door. Jon got in, but before he could say anything his father said, "We'll talk when we get home."

"Dad could you…"

"Jon, not a word. I'm too angry right now."

"I only wondered if you could turn the heat up."

Despite himself, Kevin Wright smiled.

Jon relayed the story to Wally, who dubbed him "Midnight." It stuck like Gorilla Glue.

As promised, his father grounded him. It was a stiff two-week punishment: no video games, no TV, no cell phone, nothing but homework and one hour of music and plenty of chores to fill any down time. There was no complaining on Jon's part. All he said was, "OK. I understand you're mad and I get being grounded, but can you call Bryn's dad and tell him she shouldn't be punished? It was all my idea."

"That's very generous of you to take the blame, but it doesn't really sound like something you'd concoct, and either way Bryn clearly went along with it. More than anything, I don't want to get involved in parenting beyond these walls. Get my drift?"

"I guess so, but it seems unfair that Bryn should be punished. To tell you the truth, it was really Claire Porter's idea."

"Ah, now that sounds more like it."

Midnight smiled at his dad and said, "Now you see why I think it's unfair."

"Yes, I do and it's very kind that you'd try to take the blame. I have a feeling you will become very popular with the ladies someday."

"Yeah, right."

"I mean it."

"Well, thanks, I guess."

The mood at the Wilson house wasn't as jovial. Bryn's father asked for an explanation, but the one she gave, the honest-to-God truth, was completely implausible to him. He was angry and he stayed that way for weeks.

Bryn was embarrassed the next morning as she walked into the kitchenette and heard her father repeating the episode to Jack, who was home on a break. He hadn't heard the thud of the log or the scolding and slept, uninterrupted.

"Christ, I was awakened from a deep sleep to find some stranger in my den."

It bothered Bryn that her father was exaggerating what actually happened and felt the need to tell Jack at all. Sure, she and Jon had screwed up, but they hadn't done anything really terrible and no one had gotten hurt. And he had known Jon and the Wrights since they had moved to the lake. Jon was no stranger.

According to Richard, she was going to have plenty of time to think about her behavior. She was grounded for a month and forbidden to see Jon during that duration. The punishment was ridiculous since she could not possibly avoid Jon. It was a small community with few places to go, but she wouldn't point out the obvious to her father. She sat somberly and didn't say a word about the length of her punishment.

Charlotte jumped in. "I have to get going to the salon for a quick trim and then I'm going to do some shopping."

"You're leaving in the middle of this situation with Bryn?"

"Richard, this is not a crisis. This is misbehaving—a dare or a prank. I don't think you should get yourself so worked up. You'll make yourself sick."

"Finding some kid in my den at 2:30 in the morning is not misbehaving. I'm concerned. These are twelve year olds for god sake."

"It was Jon Wright, Richard, not Son of Sam."

"I understand that, but I am worried about the behavior."

Bryn considered jumping into the discussion, telling her parents once again that it was a small prank and nothing more, but it wouldn't do any good, so she sat silent. She didn't want to get into any more trouble than she was already in. Staying quiet was usually her best option.

Jack, who rarely credited his mother, said, "Good one on Son of Sam," then looked at Bryn and said, "lame stunt."

As Bryn thanked her brother for his unconditional support, Richard gently asked Jack to stay out of it.

As she guessed about the unenforceable punishment, she saw Jon that very afternoon at Claire's house. He and Wally were watching a snowboarding event on ESPN. She sat down with them before heading up to Claire's room.

"So, how did your dad react, besides throwing me out into the cold?"

"I'm grounded for a month and not allowed to see you."

"That's not working out too well for him."

Wally began laughing, but Bryn told him it wasn't funny and that thirty days was a long time to be doing dishes and coming home right after school and having homework done before dinner.

Jon added, "I think my dad thought it was a pretty harmless

prank but feels like he had to be strict. He gave me two weeks, but he seems OK and he'll put it behind us pretty quickly."

"Ah, so you have a father who is sane," Bryn said.

Bryn's cell rang, jogging her from the memory of that night. It was Claire. Bryn was thrilled since she was bursting to tell Claire about her day with Chris.

"So, my mother and brother were arguing about Davis Brummell and I decided to take a walk and was actually thinking about heading to your house, but lost track and wound up near the mouth of the Argent River and ran into Chris."

"So? He works over there."

"Yeah, I know, but he paddled over and I guess he wanted some company and we went down the river together."

"Sounds riveting."

"Well, actually, it was."

"Oh yeah? What happened?"

"Well nothing exactly happened, but he's so sweet and cute and I am hoping he calls me."

"I guess he's OK. I never paid much attention to him. I feel like he sticks to himself a lot and there's some kind of rift between him and Midnight."

"What kind of rift?"

Claire paused, but then said, "No idea."

"Well, good, because I'd like him to like me and not you and if he's never around Wally and Midnight, then he's never around you."

"That's harsh. I'd never like him if you did. You know that!"

"Yeah, I guess."

"What do you mean, you guess?"

"It's not important, OK? Let me tell you what's important.

We spent half the trip cuddling."

"You said nothing happened."

"Nothing did. We didn't kiss or anything, we sat together and he held me around the waist and we talked the whole afternoon. Which reminds me of my parents' awful reaction, which I don't want to go through again."

"Why not?"

"It's the same old Richard and Charlotte reaction. No substantiation, completely tangential and lots of random conclusions."

"Ha! Are you in trouble?"

"No. Well, I don't think so. I think they're going to get over their initial outrage, then Richard will stay mad at me for his standard two weeks and then they'll be on to the next thing."

"I'm sure Chris will call you. If you feel so strongly, I'm sure he feels the same."

"I don't know. He said he would. I hope so."

"I'll keep my fingers crossed."

"That's never worked for me, but thanks."

Two weeks had passed since she and Chris had gone down the Argent. Not a day went by when she didn't think about him. Despite all the wishing and finger crossing, he hadn't called. Claire continued to tell her that he would, but she sounded less confident as they neared week three of radio silence.

During that time, Bryn had taken to borrowing Jack's kayak and paddling until her arms ached in the hope she might catch a glimpse of Chris heading to work or out with a friend. At first she struggled with the boat, but she quickly got good at the simple draw, paddle and pry strokes until it became second nature. She kept her promise to Jack and initially stayed close to shore, but in a short time felt confidant enough to venture onto deeper waters and was commandeering around Crane Lake and its tributaries with little effort. She would bring a paperback and a small lunch wrapped in saran and stow it at her feet in a larger Ziploc bag. When she was hungry she'd nestle at the shoreline under the overhang of a willow's tendrils and eat her bagged lunch and devour her book. She sat quietly and listened to the sound of the water, hidden from anyone going by. Occasionally she'd lean back and take a nap, but inevitably would wake to her hand touching water or small splashes coming into the boat from the wake of large boats passing by.

One day she got caught in a heavy rain and sat under the hanging leaves watching the fat droplets hit the water around her. The force of the rain hitting the surface of the lake sent up tiny splashes and created thousands of ripples across the water. The rain slid along the tree's tail of leaves, weeping on the water. The long branches protected Bryn and she barely got wet as she watched the world get drenched. She had been gone a long time that day while she waited out the storm. It wouldn't matter. Her father was away on business, Jack was in Colorado with his girlfriend and she knew it would never occur to her mother to wonder where she was.

She didn't understand her mother very well and she knew her mother didn't understand her. Did she love Bryn? She never said, "I love you." It was always "I love you too," said with a palpable lack of sincerity—yeah, sure, whatever, I love you too. Nothing more than an involuntary reflex, like a blink or a yawn.

She understood why Jack was her father's favorite. Jack was handsome and smart and a great athlete. But since it was clear her mother didn't like Jack much at all, then why wasn't she her mother's favorite? Bryn thought it was because she wasn't pretty—at least not pretty to her mother. Bryn saw herself plodding through life with a big nose, small boobs and no chin and she was discounted for it.

She was lonely. It wasn't for lack of friends or acquaintances living around the lake, but her heart ached for someone special. As the long days of summer neared, there was the promise of vacationers and weekenders coming to the lake, increasing the likelihood she might meet someone new—maybe someone for her. Then her mind would travel to Chris and she brooded about all the things she wanted. She wanted a big, loud, wonderful family like the Porters. She wanted to be pretty like Claire. She wanted someone to love her like she was special.

Knowing those things would never happen made them all the more real and painful. She stared into the water at her muddled reflection. The sun had come out and she shook it all off—the rain, the disappointment and the heartache.

Summer

Bryn heard a knock at the back door and yelled out to her mother, "I'll get it," but wasn't fast enough to beat her mother to the door.

"Hello, Chris! How can I help you, honey?"

"I'm here to see Bryn."

Before Chris could finish another sentence, Bryn was at the door guiding him out the doorway. "We're going to go sit outside."

"It was nice to see you, Chris. Say hello to your father for me."

Chris replied, "Nice to see you too. I'll definitely say hi to my dad." Bryn rolled her eyes reflexively.

They walked outside and sat side by side at the end of the long pier. A shiny half-moon reflected against the rippling water.

Bryn was nervous and the silence between them was making it worse. She began the conversation. "So where've you been, stranger?"

"You do remember I work three jobs, right?"

"Sure I do."

Chris put his hand on her knee. "You know I've been thinking about the day a while back when we went down the Argent."

"Yeah, I've thought about it too. I had such a nice time."

"I did too."

He stood up quickly and grabbed her hand. "I have to get going. I have to work tomorrow, naturally."

"So soon?"

He pulled her up from the dock and they walked a few feet back toward the house. There, illuminated by a light coming from a patio window, he embraced her. He enveloped her and his strong, young arms held her tight. And then he kissed her. If the earth had swallowed her whole on that spot, she would have died happy with Davis Brummell paving her way.

He stopped kissing her and held her chin in his right hand, her eyes forced to look into his. Bryn stumbled, slightly off-balance. His other hand was wrapped around her waist and he grounded her against his chest. As they stood there, brushing against one another, he confided that before they went down river, he had seen Bryn water-skiing on the lake a few times with Midnight and Claire. He thought she was cute, so he'd asked around. Everyone told him she was really nice and didn't have a boyfriend, and he promised himself he'd say something to Bryn when the time was right. He'd figure out some way to approach her.

Yes, she could have died happy right there.

From some distant window in some distant house, she heard Cat Stevens singing "Wild World." That old tune from the '70s instantly became her favorite song.

He asked Bryn, "Was that your first kiss?"

"No, Billy Reider in the sixth grade was."

"How do I compare to Billy?"

"I don't know."

"Uh-oh, that's not much of a confidence builder."

"I didn't mean it like that. Everything is perfect."

He smiled and turned her toward the house. His hands held onto her shoulders as he walked behind, navigating their path.

He stopped and took her hand and spun her in a tight circle, so she was facing him again. "Bryn, do you want to go out with me this summer? I'm not saying we get all serious or anything, but we should go out, don't you think?"

Leaning into him, she said, "You mean just see each another and no one else?"

"Yeah."

"Thank you."

"That's a funny thing to say.'"

"I'm not sure why I said that. It came out sounding lame. I don't know. I feel like it's been a really long time since anything good has happened."

"I know what you mean. Maybe I should thank you too."

"No, it's more than that. It's like you're so out of my league."

"What? You are not. You're cute and smart and you're funny and, I don't know, you seem great."

"I can't explain what I mean in the right way. I don't know. Forget it. I'm talking too much."

How could Bryn ever explain it? When he noticed her—no, maybe when he kissed her—he gave her value. He went to the popular school and he played football and was easy to talk to and she knew he'd be the kind of guy to pay for movies or dinner or even a concert. He wasn't like any of the dorks that usually liked her. The coolest boys liked Claire. Bryn acted funny or self-deprecating around boys, acted like she didn't care, but she did care. Boys made fun of her small chest, her long nose. Well, now she existed. She was important to someone. He had said she was cute. No one ever said that to her before. He kissed her forehead. She smiled and held his hand so tight she felt pins and needles in her fingertips, but she didn't want to let go. As she struggled to say exactly what was on her mind, he was already becoming her nucleus. Like an electron, she would revolve around him with complete abandon, unable to defy gravity's pull.

She sat on the steps and watched him get on his bike and head home. She tilted her head back and looked to the night sky. It was white with stars. Bryn prayed she would always feel this way. The night was quiet except for a breeze winding through the top of the pine trees—no crickets, no birdsong, only the wind. As the needles brushed against one another it sounded like a thousand hushed whispers—whispering pines peering down on the earth.

She picked up her cell to call Claire and tell her she'd been right. Chris had kissed her and even asked her to be his girl-friend. They agreed to meet the next day at their secret spot to talk all about the details.

The secret spot was an abandoned boat mooring on a tiny cove adjacent to Crane Lake. The water of the inlet was thick with surface algae, water lilies and cottontails. Cars and boat trailers couldn't make it down the overgrown path, nor would they want to since the lake was clogged and murky, but Claire and Bryn could make it through on their bikes. It was only thirty yards or so from the road, but seemed hidden and a million miles from everyone.

Bryn told Claire every detail of the previous night, Chris holding her and kissing her and making plans for the summer. Claire interrupted, saying she was happy for Bryn and that it looked like a promising summer. And then, in that guarded spot, she told Bryn something she said had been on her mind a long time, but had never confessed to anyone.

She began the conversation innocently enough asking, "So, I've been thinking a lot about something. Bryn, do you think Midnight likes me?"

"Of course he likes you. You're wonderful and he's your brother's best friend."

"I don't mean it that way. I really like him and I don't think he notices me at all."

Bryn stared at Claire with her mouth slightly open. "You mean you *like him* like him? When did that happen?"

Claire couldn't suppress her smile. "I think I've been in love with him since I was in third grade."

"I can't believe I'm hearing this."

Claire was twisting a strand of her long blond hair around her index finger and gushed. "He's funny and fun to be around and he's smart and interesting and he treats girls really well and… I don't know there are a million things. His smile alone is worth loving him."

Bryn interjected. "Yeah, I guess he is all of those things and he does have a great smile, but I never thought you thought so."

"Well it's been a secret crush, obviously."

"Yeah, obviously. You make me laugh."

"Why's that?"

Bryn nudged her shoulder into Claire's upper arm. "You could have any boy you want, but you pick one that seems almost related to you."

A gust of air blew across the pond, moving the lilies and cottontails with its force.

Claire replied without acknowledging Bryn's comment. "The night we all snuck out of the house I was going to tell him I really liked him, but then he stayed at your house. I thought he liked you."

"Midnight likes everyone."

Claire stared down at the water. "I'm not so sure about that."

"Well, I've known him and your brother since I was eight, so he's had time to tell me, don't you think?"

"I guess you're right. He just kills it and I'd like to tell him how much, but I think Wally would be pissed."

Bryn paused and thought before responding, "Wally would

be surprised and maybe a little annoyed with you, but I don't think Midnight would be. You're pretty special, Claire."

"Thanks, but I don't know. I see him around Nora Brandt a lot."

Bryn looked up at the passing clouds before saying, "Well that's a different story. I don't know what to say about that."

Claire untied her right sneaker, pulled off her sock and dipped her toe in the water. "Yeah, I think they're always on again/off again. Ha! Maybe I could off her and trap him in a bungalow somewhere."

"So you've got a plan."

Claire laughed, smiled at Bryn and then added, "I think I should see how the summer goes. Maybe I'll find a good time to let him know how I feel."

"Like when?"

She shook her head and played with the strands of hair again, pretending to look for split ends. "I don't know, let things happen naturally. Hang out more at his house and have one thing lead to another and… God, I don't know, naturally."

"Yeah, I guess."

"Well, you don't seem to have any other suggestions."

"Well let me think about it. It's only now I'm finding out about it. I can't believe you kept this from me. I'm with you all the time."

"I don't know how I kept it from you, or anyone else for that matter. It's never felt right to tell anyone."

"I guess I get that."

"Maybe I should forget about the whole thing. Maybe it's like you said. It's like he's practically related to me."

"Oh, don't pay any attention to me, it shouldn't matter and

it won't matter once he starts to see you in a different light."

Claire took off her other sneaker and slid both feet into the water. "I guess, but it doesn't help me feeling weird about it—weird enough that I've never told anyone, including him or you."

"I think you're right. See how the summer goes and this time, will you keep me posted?"

Claire smiled wide. "Now that you know, of course I will."

Bryn and Claire parted on the turn toward Bryn's house. Bryn smiled about Chris and about Midnight. She was excited at the prospect of Claire and Midnight together. Maybe they could double date. She went into her house and walked directly along the hallway and into her room. She picked up a drawing pad and some colored pencils to start a sketch of the cove while it was fresh in her mind. She sat on her bed thinking about how Claire could have kept her crush on Midnight a secret for so long. It had been four years since that night they snuck out in the cold. Bryn would never have been able to keep such a secret, but conceded Claire could be guarded, even secretive. Claire freely admitted it. She loved the idea of keeping something to herself, even if it was her own thoughts and ideas. Usually exasperated by one of her younger siblings, Claire would tell Bryn how frustrating it was to have nine brothers and sisters. She rarely had new clothes, she would always share a room and there was never one blessed moment of solitude and silence at her house.

The two had met the week before the start of third grade. The Wilsons had moved from Chicago to the shoreline of Crane Lake, which was part of the town of Andover. A new family was news. Claire stopped by the Wilsons' house on moving day and introduced herself. She had felt uncomfortable, but her father insisted that she make the first effort, having seen that the Wilsons had a daughter who looked her age. They sat out on the pier talking about Bryn's life in Chicago, about their parents, Claire's grandmother Josie and a host of other topics. Their birthdays were on the same day of the month, exactly half a year apart; Bryn's on September 3, Claire's on March 3. Bryn liked riding her bike and reading and art class; Claire liked swimming and modern dance. An hour had passed and Mrs. Wilson called for Bryn to come in the house and help with the unpacking. Claire said, "I guess that's it, then. I'll see you in school next week. I'm glad we're in the same grade and that you'll be going to St. Mary's."

After that day, they spent countless hours with one another, doing homework together, sharing lunches, gossiping after school. Unless Claire had swim practice, they would see one another every day, and on those rare 'off' days, they would talk on the phone until their parents insisted they get back to their homework or off to bed. As the years passed, they talked about their future, more and more—it was unfathomable that any part of their plans wouldn't include one another. Bryn would smile and stare at Claire as they pranced around her bedroom listening to pop music—all that enviable height and hair flashing about. Claire dismissed Bryn's admiration, but had to concede she was never the last man standing in a schoolyard pick.

Were all the Porters fashioned from platinum and precious stones? Maybe Midnight felt about Wally the way Bryn felt about Claire. In the conga line of life, there is always someone in the front, dictating all the steps, while the stragglers toward

44

the back look awkward and out of rhythm. Bryn thought Midnight might have been somewhere in the middle, while she was trailing near the dreaded end of the line.

Bryn lay on her bed and pulled her pillow to her chest. Thinking about Chris, she kissed it. She reached for her cell on the nightstand to phone Claire.

"Claire, will you answer one question for me?"

"Sure."

"Forget all this stuff about letting things just happen. Sometimes they don't just happen."

"That's not a question."

"Why don't you say something to Midnight? Just do it."

Claire paused. "I don't know. Not sure I have the nerve."

"You should do it, because he will like you back."

"Yeah, you say that, but you don't know."

"Well you're right. No one absolutely knows, but that's what my gut is telling me."

"And mine is telling me the opposite."

"I don't understand your lack of confidence. If I looked like you…"

Claire cut Bryn off. "I don't like the way I look at all. I'm too tall and gangly and have no curves. I look like a boy, for god sake. My hair is out of control and there's nothing I can ever do to it to make it look pretty or sophisticated. I don't know how to put on makeup and I never have any good clothes. It's always hand-me-downs."

"But you must know you're beautiful."

"I do not know that. I'm sandwiched between all my brothers and sisters and no one ever tells me I'm pretty or special, although in their defense, I'm not sure they have any time to."

Bryn laughed, but meant it when she said, "I don't think they need to tell you since it is so obvious."

"Thanks, Bryn."

"It's true. Now think about talking to Midnight."

"I'll think about it, but can't promise anything."

"You don't have to promise anything. It's usually my experience, at least in my family, that people don't deliver on their promises anyway, so let's keep it at 'think about it.'"

Throughout the summer, Chris and Bryn spent all their free time together. Even when he was working, Bryn would sometimes surprise him with visits to The Rendezvous, his family's restaurant, or the Clear Water Café, where he held his other job. She would plop down on a stool and order a cheeseburger and be content watching him flip burgers and grilled cheese sandwiches. He'd take his break and they'd go to the back of the café and sit down in the cool grass. They'd talk about the day and their plans for that night, whether it was a movie or a walk along the lake or a boat ride or hanging out on the dock in front of one of their houses.

Their progress as a couple was swift. She encouraged Chris and more often than not, it was Bryn who reassured him of going one step further each time they had moments alone, but they never went "all the way". More than anything, she was afraid of getting pregnant. If not for that, she might have let Chris do almost anything with her. There were a handful of pregnant girls in school the previous year and they might as well have been lepers. Even their boyfriends shunned them— the genuine walking dead.

One night in particular, she had little else on her mind. They were swimming under the glow of a full moon and they were teasing and laughing. Chris would touch Bryn's leg pretending something swam underneath them. He'd feign looking startled saying, "What was that? I felt something grab at my foot." Even though she knew he was kidding, swimming at night freaked her out. She still thought about Davis Brummell even though his body had been retrieved from a shallow between Crane and Willow Lakes weeks earlier. Two fishermen in a small V-hull had been up with the dawn and spotted his body lying face down near their favorite fishing nook.

Chris and Bryn treaded water under the watchful eye of her father who walked by the patio windows every ten minutes and peered out at them. They were talking about the upcoming Fourth of July celebration at the municipal park. She wanted them to go with Claire and Wally and Midnight. Upon mentioning Midnight, she shared the story of how they'd gotten caught sneaking out several years earlier. Chris laughed loud and long. He confessed he'd had no idea where Midnight's nickname came from. At first Bryn didn't believe him, but his insistence was sincere. She shrugged her shoulders and said, "Yep, it was me."

Chris replied. "Should I be jealous of that?"

"Jealous of what?"

"Of Midnight."

"No. I've known him forever, and anyway, it's really Claire…"

She let the sentence drop and tilted her head back in the water, wrapping her legs around his waist, using his torso as an anchor to float from left to right and back again. She was hoping to distract him, but he said, "Claire what?"

"Nothing. I'm not supposed to say anything."

"Well, sometimes not saying something says it all."

"You must promise to never say anything."

"I don't know what I'd say, since you didn't tell me anything."

Bryn hesitated and let out a sigh before she answered.

"Well, Claire told me a while ago that she has a thing for Midnight."

"No kidding."

"Yeah, no kidding. She's had a crush on him forever, or so it seems."

"She's a pretty girl. He should take advantage of that."

"What do you mean take advantage?"

"Nothing more than he should take her out."

"Well, he doesn't know anything about it."

"Want me to say something to him?"

"No. Claire would kill me."

"I'd think she'd want him to know, so maybe he'd ask her out. Isn't he with someone though? I feel like I see him with the same girl all the time."

"It's Nora Brandt and I never know with the two of them. Please don't do anything about Claire. Claire would know I told you."

"OK, but I think he has the hots for you."

"Yeah right."

"Well I have the hots for you, so why not him?"

"Midnight has been my friend forever—nothing more."

"Yeah, I guess, but I'm not convinced. Listen, I don't really want to go with all those people on the Fourth. Let's go by ourselves."

They swam out to the diving raft and held onto the metal ladder and one another. Chris told her his head was spinning and he wanted to be with her more than anything.

"You're with me right now."

"I think you know what I meant. I meant in a more intimate way."

She did know what he meant and admitted she had thought about it on many occasions, but the time wasn't right. She had searched on-line for information about dating and the *right time,* but the information was close to useless. And she stopped poking around when it occurred to her that Richard could look at her browser history. He'd have a coronary.

As her head was swimming faster than her arms were treading Chris said, "Don't freak out, but is that your neighbor, Gary Jensen behind the boat livery? I swear there's someone behind there."

Bryn turned her head to the side and strained to see. "I don't see anyone."

"There's someone there. I can see his shadow."

"You're scaring me."

"Don't freak. I think it's Jensen."

"I feel terrible for saying it, but he creeps me out. Is he spying on us?"

"I don't know. I guess so. He's an OK guy, though. He's not a perv or anything. He's a little different, kind of eccentric. I think he's gone now, anyway. C'mon let's do it."

"With my father at the bay window and someone hiding in the shadows? Great idea. It could be anyone and they could be doing a slo-mo video for all I know. This is like a B-horror movie that could wind up on YouTube."

"C'mon Bryn, you're looking for excuses. Whoever it was is gone now anyway."

"Believe me, I'm not looking for excuses, but this isn't the right time or place."

"So do you want to go in or do you want to stay out and swim for a while? It's pretty great out here."

"I think I want to go in."

"Because of Jensen or because of me?"

"Neither. I feel perfectly safe with you, but my dad's bound to come out pretty soon and tell me it's time to come in and time for you to go home."

They swam in unison toward the shoreline. He smiled as he climbed out of the water. "I had a really nice night. Thanks Bryn."

"I did too. It'll come out sounding stupid, but no matter what we do together, I have a nice time."

"Didn't sound stupid. I'll call you tomorrow, but I'm walking you to the front. I'm sure that was Jensen, but nonetheless, I'm making sure you get inside. I don't want a dead girlfriend, 'Elm Street' style."

"Thanks. I don't want that either."

"Yeah, I'm a sweet guy."

"What about you walking home, though?"

"It'll be fine, Bryn. You do know that *Nightmare on Elm Street* is pure fiction, right?"

Smiling, Bryn replied, "If you say so, but be careful and text me when you get home."

"Jesus, Bryn, it will be fine."

"Text me anyway."

"OK. See you tomorrow."

Fifteen minutes later Bryn got a text image of Freddie Krueger playing air guitar.

The summer passed with them as a couple. Claire saw very little of Bryn but had few complaints since Wally and Midnight were around to fill the gaps. Claire had been angry about the Fourth of July picnic, more so because Midnight and Wally wound up not going, but her anger didn't last very long. She understood how much Chris meant to Bryn and envied their being together. She still hadn't said a word to Midnight about liking him or suggesting they go out—without Wally—and probably never would, but she seemed happy enough hanging out with him and her brother.

For Bryn, it was heaven. When they walked into a Starbucks or down the street holding hands, kids looked at them, for no other reason than because they were a couple. It was a universal truth, since the ark hit high water, that pairs were more important than singles. They had been girlfriend and boyfriend throughout the summer, which in high school was a milestone—dating time measured in dog years.

Chris would stop by unannounced at the Wilson house and Bryn's father would usually bark, "Does he have to be here 24 hours a day? Every time I turn around, he's here. I don't even think he knocks anymore." Bryn thought about saying Chris could hear him, but sat silent enjoying the idea of Chris's persistence, no matter what her father said.

In a show of solidarity and a level of affection Bryn rarely glimpsed, Charlotte awkwardly put her arm around her and gave it a gentle squeeze and told Bryn she thought Chris was a nice boy from a nice family. In contrast, Richard never encouraged the pair and would ask what they did for hours on end, on the way to the park or after a movie or after a ball game. She would tell her father they talked or listened to music or watched TV at Chris's house. She was not lying. They did listen to music and talk and watch TV or sat at the Rendezvous or went to the movies, but they also petted and necked and awkwardly made love. How could she ever tell her father that? He might kill Chris, and her. He wouldn't understand Chris was the only person who thought she was pretty and smart and funny, including her own mother. He would never understand that she saw Chris as the person she would spend her life with—going to college together, getting married, buying a house, having kids.

Claire said it was way too soon to be having sex, but on this, Bryn completely shrugged Claire off. She and Chris began having sex not long after their late night swim. She could not stand keeping him at bay any longer. She wanted to be with him, rationalized that she was about to turn seventeen and despite the general idea of losing her virginity, the thought of losing it with Chris made her happy. While gushing and blushing with Claire, she also assured her they were taking all the necessary precautions. She had gone to a free clinic in Andover where birth control was dispensed with few questions asked.

Bryn had planned their first time down to the smallest of details. She had searched quaint hotels and B&Bs within a hundred miles of Andover. Something that wasn't so far that the drive would take up too much of their night but wasn't so close that they would run into parents or classmates or anyone else they knew. She decided on La Petite Famille in Cain

Bluff, which was 47 miles from Andover. Bryn made reservations for a Friday night, made sure that Claire would cover for her despite some protest and told Chris about her master plan.

Chris took the night off work, told his father he was spending the night at the Porters', borrowed a car from a friend and they set out at four o'clock and arrived just before five. The desk clerk was a young woman not much older than Bryn. She was welcoming and not at all inquisitive when they paid for the room in cash. Chris opened the door to the room and waited for Bryn to enter. The room smelled musty, but was exactly as Bryn had envisioned. There was a small fireplace. The linen on the queen-size bed was crisp and white. There was a patio that looked out onto a pond, where a family of ducks swam and dunked. The bathroom was small but clean and had fluffy white towels and primrose bath products. Chris held her and kissed her and said, "Thanks for this. It's really nice."

They had dinner at the nearby Weary Traveler, but returned to the room early. Bryn went into the bathroom and changed. When she came out of the bathroom, Chris was in bed waiting for her.

He stared at her for what seemed a long time and then he said, "You look amazing."

"Thanks."

"Don't be nervous."

She stood fidgeting. "I'm not really nervous. I'm more, I don't know… yeah, I guess I am nervous."

He leaned across the bed and pulled back the cover for her to climb in. "Don't be. It's going to be great."

Bryn got into bed. "So you've hooked up a lot?"

"Well, I don't know if it's a lot, but... I'm not sure it's the right time to talk about that. You know?"

"You want to tell me who with?"

He smiled. "Nah. I don't think so."

Bryn smiled too and said, "You're right, it's not the time to talk about it."

They consummated what was on both of their minds. Chris had been gentle and attentive. He whispered "I love you" into her ear.

Making love sealed the deal. They were officially a pair. Forget spending too much time with one another; Bryn didn't think they spent enough time together. She even wanted him to quit one of his three jobs so they could have more time together, but Chris assured her his father wouldn't have any of that. When Chris held her and kissed her and slid his tongue into her mouth, he never failed to solicit a tiny gasp from Bryn's lips—she was living in a dream. A Wild West boy liked her, not Claire or the girls who went to school with him, but her, Bryn Wilson.

In Bryn's euphoria the summer was slipping away. The new school year was a couple of weeks away. She began to worry about him leaving for college the following year. Chris would be gone for weeks and even months at a time. There were 30,000+ undergrads at the University of Wisconsin, which meant around 15,000 girls, and she guessed about 5,000 would be pretty, certainly prettier than she. Secretly, Bryn wanted him to stay home for a year and wait for her to graduate so they could head off to UW together, but knew he'd never go for it.

They had already started arguing about it. He was going

for a long weekend with his father to check out the smaller campus of UW in La Crosse. Bryn was miserable at the idea of being without him and said, "I thought we agreed you'd go to Madison and I'd come there the next fall."

"Bryn, you don't have to follow me to college. You should go where you want to go and I should go where I want to go and besides, I could never play football at UW. Those guys are out of my league. At least at La Crosse I have a chance to make the team even if I don't play much."

"You're telling me you don't want to go where I want to go. We had a plan and all of a sudden you're changing your mind."

"I'm not necessarily changing my mind. All I'm saying is I'm not even close to good enough to play football there. Here's the thing, you're sixteen years old and we can't make plans for the rest of our lives right now. You may change your mind. Jesus, Bryn, we're not married. You can't take everything so seriously!"

"First, I am weeks from being seventeen and I think that you don't take us seriously. I am going where I want to go. You're the one getting all indecisive about UW and us."

"I wasn't saying that either. You get me so worked up. I'm not sure what I'm saying. You know what, Bryn? I don't want to get into this right now. All I'm doing is checking out the campus in La Crosse. I'm not signing any contracts, including with you. You shouldn't get so serious about everything."

She skipped dinner and sat sulking in her room until the cell rang and it was Chris telling her he was sorry. He explained he wouldn't do anything more than look around the campus. The trip was more about appeasing his father who thought La Crosse would be more affordable and Chris's application would be accepted without question. His dad thought it was advisable to have a Plan B. He said Bryn shouldn't worry about it and that he was going to hang up and get some sleep. She whispered, "I love you" as she pressed the end-call button.

Charlotte Wilson sat in her favorite chair at Salon 213 paging through the most recent *Vanity Fair* and *Glamour* magazines. She perused a couple articles and interviews, but was paying more attention to the ads. She stopped on a Louis Vuitton ad that featured their Cruise Collection. She dog-eared the corner, but then asked her manicurist Gwen if she could tear out the page. Gwen shrugged her shoulders and told Charlotte it didn't bother her in the slightest.

Gwen asked, "Out of curiosity, how do you pronounce that name?"

"It's Loo-ee Vwee-ton."

"It sounds expensive coming out of your mouth. Do you speak French?"

"No, but I looked up the name and how to pronounce it and committed it to memory. Their signature bag is a few thousand dollars."

Gwen shook her head back and forth and jiggled Charlotte's hand. "Well that seems crazy to me."

"It may sound crazy, but it's not. They're beautiful and you get what you pay for. The quality and craftsmanship is written all over their products."

"I guess if you say so. I have other priorities."

"Oh, I know. I do too, but that doesn't mean I don't still want one. Maybe that's what I'll ask Richard for as my big birthday gift this year."

Gwen was filing away and didn't look up when she asked, "When's the big day?"

"The 28th. It's depressing."

"Oh, get out! You look amazing! I'm sure Richard will want to get you something special."

"He likes to surprise me with travel, which is nice, but that's always more about what he wants and not what I want."

Her colorist came up to her and asked that they try to finish up the manicure since she was ready to start in on the color. Charlotte continued poring through the magazine as the thick base color was pulled through her hair. She knew Richard could afford to spend the money on a new designer bag and much more. As she sat and waited for the color to set, she continued to page through the magazine, paying close attention to Breitling and Chanel and Chopard, making a mental checklist of all the things she wanted. She pictured the Vuitton bag with an Hermès scarf tied around the leather handles—so very Princess Di.

Her colorist began their conversation. "So, how are Richard and the kids?"

"They're fine."

"I overheard you saying you have a birthday coming up."

"Yes. Forty-eight, but no one knows that. I forget how old I am sometimes, because I tell everyone I'm four years younger than I actually am."

Her colorist put her hands on each knee and leaned into Charlotte. "Good for you. Let me tell you, honey, I have a few years on your real age and you're a billion times more successful and better situated, so don't fret."

"Oh, I'm not fretting, but Richard is the successful one. I quit work ages ago."

"That's my definition of success."

Charlotte smiled up at her and said, "Not mine."

"Oh, honey, you don't have it that bad."

"No, I'm not complaining necessarily, but I feel so out of place and at odds in my own home. I very much want to go out and do something."

"Then why don't you?"

"I wouldn't know where to begin. I don't have any experience or training in anything and I'm not positive what I'm searching for. I do know it's not the place where I am right now. I married Richard right out of college and I've been working at that for a long time, but never seem to get anywhere with it—no promotions, no raises."

"Richard seems like a good enough guy and certainly a good provider."

"He's fine. It's difficult to explain, but I'm not happy. I'm not explaining it very well."

Reaching out and touching Charlotte's hand she asked, "Why aren't you happy?"

"I don't know. I feel like there's nothing exciting around the corner, you know?"

"Not really. I'm too busy paying for what's right here and now. I don't spend much time looking around corners."

"I'm sorry. I realize I don't have a lot of cause to complain. I get that."

"Can I ask you a really personal question? I won't be offended if you say no."

"It's fine. Go ahead."

"Does Richard sleep around?"

"I don't think so, but I wish he would since it would give me license to do the same without an ounce of guilt."

"Wow. I'm not sure what I expected you to say, but that wasn't it. I guess I thought you'd respond with an emphatic no or a yes, and if it were yes, that you're completely torn up about it."

Charlotte paused and then said, "It's just that it's always the same thing day after day. I traded in excitement for comfort."

"But everyone reaches that stage. You have to spice it up a bit."

"It's not our sex life necessarily. It's something deeper. It's like Richard is so serious and, well, old. I think that's it. I still feel young and vibrant and he seems like an angry old man, even though he's actually younger than I am."

"Really? I never knew that. By how much?"

"Without getting too specific, let's just say a few years, but he seems tired of life. He seems like an old man, shuffling around complaining that the music is too loud or someone is driving too fast or someone is making a scene. Worse, he's making me feel old too."

"If that's what you have to say about Richard, I don't want you judging my husband."

They both laughed, but Charlotte asked if she could close her eyes for a bit and rest. She had to close her eyes and take deep breaths to stop from screaming. She didn't want to lose what she had with Richard—the clothes, the car, the travel, but on the other hand, she craved a new life and looked for ways she might meet other men. She was still good-looking. If she set her mind to it, she might meet someone and blow the small town and leave everyone in her dust, her family included. Bryn was no longer a child. She was about to turn seventeen and would be off to college very soon. Charlotte knew in her soul that Bryn would be fine, perhaps better without her. Charlotte craved nothing more than that person who would make her feel young and wanted again.

She had met Richard Wilson in West Lafayette, Indiana at Purdue. He was a sophomore with his eye on the Krannert School of Management. She was a freshman in Purdue's Exploratory Studies program, which meant she didn't know what she wanted to do once she graduated.

There were thousands of undergrads at the university and they probably wouldn't have crossed paths if not for Richard's roommate and best college friend, Wheeler H. Davidson.

Wheeler and Richard made for an unlikely pair, having grown up under dramatically different circumstances. Nonetheless, they struck up a quick friendship. Richard was a privileged son of privileged sons of privileged sons. Wheeler H. Davidson was the son of someone, but he did not know whom. He was from Muncie, Indiana and named after the campground in Wheeler Gorge, California where his mother believed she conceived him through a tryst with a local biker. She'd added the H. Davidson in homage to the motorcycle manufacturer and the likelihood that said conception took place on the biker's motorcycle—the biker having straddled the bike and Wheeler's mother having straddled the biker. She thought long and hard when naming her son and liked the sound. She said it kinda rolled off your tongue. The memory of her encounter with the boy from the Ojai Motorcycle Club, gave her pause to smile and reflect, although for the life of her, she could not remember the boy's name. Billy? Donny? She was sure it ended in a 'y'.

Wheeler grew up poor and grew up fast. His mother sent

him to work after school when he was thirteen at a Muncie paper mill. She had him tell the job supervisor he was sixteen and that his father had died in a car accident and he desperately needed the work. Luckily for Wheeler, the biker must have been a bright guy. Wheeler didn't do well at the mill, but he excelled in school. He made A's without study or conviction, was the editor of the school's yearbook in his junior and senior years, was usually the lead in any school play and led the team's batting average every spring. He was offered a full baseball scholarship from Purdue in November of his senior year. Despite his mother's protests for him to stay home and continue footing some of the household bills, he arrived in East Lafayette a month before the beginning of the term. He arranged for a full-time job at the local self-storage facility as their night shift desk manager so the job wouldn't conflict with his classes or baseball practice.

Wheeler met Charlotte at a lecture that a local historian was giving on the Ohio Indian Wars. She was considering a history major and it was a required lecture for Wheeler's advanced husbandry class. After the lecture, Wheeler bounded toward Charlotte and made a point of asking her about her class schedule. He continued to run into her accidentally on purpose, until he finally asked her out. She said yes. Wheeler was so surprised at her response that when she asked where they'd be going, he didn't have an answer, but added that he wanted to take her to a nice dinner and maybe a club after. As their Friday night date got closer, he suggested they drive to Indianapolis, have dinner at Morey's Steakhouse and then do some dancing at The Roxy.

Wheeler borrowed a car and headed to Charlotte's dorm.

The hour-long drive into Indianapolis was made longer by a Friday traffic jam on the 65, but it gave Wheeler a chance to talk about his classes in the College of Veterinary Medicine. He'd always wanted to be a vet, but the coursework was heavy on math and organic chemistry, which weren't his strong suits. He talked about his mother and his humble background. Upon arriving at the restaurant, he apologized for hogging the entire conversation, but Charlotte reassured him she was glad to hear about his past and wasn't that keen talking about hers, anyway.

It was at The Roxy that Richard ran into his buddy Wheeler and the lovely girl Wheeler introduced as Charlotte Bolandz. He studied her face, which was smiling back at him with perfect white teeth. Her hair was pitch black and her eyes almost as dark, but her skin was pale. On the HTML color palette, she would land dead center. She was utterly and completely memorable. He told Charlotte her name sounded like a character in a Noël Coward play. Seconds after they shook hands, Richard asked her to dance and kept her on the dance floor for most of the night, relegating Wheeler to a corner table where he sipped club sodas. He had spent close to half a week's salary on the evening and it was not turning out as he planned. As he sat brooding, Charlotte and Richard briefly waved from the dance floor, but did not go back to the table.

Richard had worn khakis and a navy blue blazer. Charlotte wore a brown skirt and baby blue cotton top. Her lipstick was scarlet, but there wasn't a hint of any other makeup, not even a brush of mascara. Her nails were cut short and sported the same dark shade that she wore on her lips. They talked about their separate journeys to Purdue, the towns they grew up in, the classes they took, which ones they liked and disliked and their guilt about ignoring Wheeler. Their guilt didn't bring them any closer to rejoining him. They were openly flirtatious and daring. Richard Wilson knew he would at the very least sleep with this girl and he hoped, as he held her very close, that there might be more.

It was painful for Charlotte to recall that exciting night with Richard when years later they were in the middle of yet another argument. It was hard to picture that dance floor. Time and circumstance had somehow become her enemy. She was living with a temperamental, disengaged man who she thought drank too much. She had thought about Wheeler on many occasions through the ensuing years and wondered if she had made a mistake dancing with Richard and ignoring him. She never told Richard she had found Wheeler on LinkedIn. He had asked her once in passing, but she lied and told him she would never bother herself with trying to find him. Truthfully, she had been poking around on both Facebook and LinkedIn. LinkedIn had a page for Wheeler Davidson, DVM in Richmond, Virginia. She pressed the connect icon, but never heard back from him. Charlotte thought it was silly of Wheeler not to respond. So she had hurt him, but how many years had it been? In a stroke of narcissism rivaled only by politicians, she sent him a second invitation with a brief message saying, "You couldn't possibly be holding any resentment or anger toward me after all this time, could you?" Again, Wheeler did not reply. Maybe he had blocked her. She didn't care. His loss.

Bryn and Claire were sprawled on a diving raft twenty yards out in the water in front of the Wilson house. Heavy chains attached to cinder blocks, which rested on the muddy bottom of the lake, anchored it. At that distance, the water was fifteen, maybe twenty feet deep, but still cold from the spring that fed the lake. Bryn wondered about the source and hoped it would never dry up, leaving a soupy concoction of mud, motorboat oil and dead fish.

Claire was sleeping over on Friday and Saturday night while Chris went to La Crosse with his father. The temperature was high, and unbearable humidity was making everything sticky. As the flow of the water gently moved the raft in a small circle, they lay there and talked about the past year and the events of the summer.

Bryn asked, "What do you want to do this coming year? I can't believe we're going to be juniors."

"I want to get a real boyfriend. Can we manage that? Why don't you and Chris find me a boyfriend?"

"Claire, really? I do not get it."

"Get what?"

"You have to be one of the prettiest girls in a fifty-mile radius. You could go out with anyone."

"Stop saying that. It's starting to bug me. I don't want to go out with just anyone. I'd like to date someone who I actually like. Silly me."

"Touchy, touchy—speaking of which, how is Midnight?"

"Oh, I don't know, but I've been thinking about it a lot.

I'm kind of lost."

"What do you mean?"

"He really doesn't see me that way, I can tell. It's time to bring in some heavy artillery to make him jealous. It has to be someone from Wild West, so he'll actually know about it. I'll get to show up at a dance or two with Mr. Fabulous, who will be his classmate."

"All right then, I'll set Chris off on the hunt—has to be a Wild West man and heavy artillery."

Claire laughed, despite not feeling happy at all. She told Bryn the first specification was he had to be over 5'9". He also had to be smart, funny and sexy. And, if he could actually be Midnight, that would avoid all the other nonsense.

Bryn smiled, but didn't know what to say about Midnight. She knew he didn't pay any special attention to Claire. It had to be Wally's fault. If Midnight and Wally were no more than acquaintances, Midnight would be dating Claire. Rather than get into that, all Bryn said was, "We never do this anymore."

"Do what?"

"Just the two of us doing nothing but talking and spending the day together."

"That's because you're always with Chris. Where is he, by the way?"

"He's at UW La Crosse for the weekend."

"Ah, so that's why I got invited for the whole weekend." They sat staring out at the water and then Claire asked, "So, what's up with La Crosse? Is he thinking about going there?"

"I guess."

"And the two of you have talked about that?"

Bryn bent her legs into a sloppy kind of lotus position and

continued to look out onto the water. "We have. I hate the idea he's even considering it. I want him to go to Madison and then I'd follow him there. I'm thinking about trying to graduate in January rather than June to get there faster."

"So you've really given this thought."

"Of course."

Claire sat up to face Bryn. "I haven't given much thought to where I'll go but I'd like to go somewhere on a swimming scholarship. I have to talk to my parents about it. There's UCLA, but that's never going to happen. Maybe I could try Purdue or Michigan or someplace in the south like Vanderbilt or Florida. Or maybe I lower my bar and wind up at Wagner or Fisher or someplace in South Dakota or something. Didn't your parents go to Purdue? Maybe they could help me out with a recommendation."

Bryn gazed past Claire and sat silent for a moment. "Yeah, I can totally see that happening. They haven't taken the time to even talk to me about any college plans, but they'll take the time and effort to write you a long recommendation letter."

"Well, it's a while off. They'll get more interested in your plans next year."

Bryn held her hand over her eyes to shield them from the sun and said, "Right. The timing is why there is a total lack of interest. I'm sure next fall, they'll be all over me, like they were with Jack."

"See?"

Smiling at Claire, but managing to roll her eyes, Bryn said, "You know I am being totally sarcastic, right?"

As Claire began to list other schools with Division 1 scholarships, a group of boys skiing out on the lake came parallel to the raft. They'd circled once before, but the girls hadn't paid much attention. On this lap, the skier tilted his body almost horizontal to the water. His ski sliced the water at an angle and sent up a great arc of water that splashed onto the diving raft. As the cold water hit them, they let out a scream.

"Oh my God," shouted Claire, "that water is cold!"

She got up and dove in, barely leaving a ripple. She surfaced, saying, "Once you're in, it feels kind of good."

Bryn followed Claire's lead and jumped into the cold water. They splashed each other and dove deep into the seaweed, pulling up fistfuls and placing it on each other's heads like layers of green dreadlocks.

Claire treaded water and squinted up into the sky. "I love being at your house. I don't fit in, in many places and no one except you really likes me, so I love it here."

Bryn reached for Claire's hand. "That cannot be true. What about your friends on the swim team?"

"It's a solitary sport. I think they tolerate me because I'm a good swimmer, but we don't hang out, so most of the time I'm going back and forth in my lane with my own voice ringing in my ears. I'm not even on the relay team."

Bryn laughed. "What about your family? You have them and they're wonderful."

"It's not the same as friends." Claire paused. "Oh forget it. I don't want to talk about it anymore. Let's go over to El Caliente tonight. Razor Sharp Morons are playing."

El Caliente was a bar and dance place on the lake. It was nothing more than a big barn blessed with a waterfront location. It had a dance floor the size of a gymnasium and an elevated stage that was about twenty feet wide and fifteen feet deep. More often than not it smelled like a combination of stale beer, potato chips and cedar. The sound system was awful and the bands that played were usually second-rate, but it was a place to go on weekends where locals and weekenders let their hair down, had some fun and got to know one another.

Minors could pay to get in and see the bands play, but an ID was needed to get out onto the beer garden and the bouncer who checked IDs didn't miss a trick. The beer garden's patio hung out over the water and on crowded nights, with the weight of its customers, it sagged terribly in the middle. The whole place creaked like an old rocking chair and looked like a lawsuit waiting to happen.

Bryn thought about the couple of times she had seen RSM play at El Caliente. "They're pretty good to dance to. Let's get inside and have something to eat and start to get ready."

Claire and Bryn getting ready to go out on a Friday was like being backstage at Miss Universe. The longest part of the process was deciding what to wear. Claire finally stopped holding hangers against her chest when Bryn said, "That's enough. The green cardigan with the boyfriend jeans is the best and at the rate we're going, it'll be time to come home when we finally get there." Three hours had passed since they had gotten out of the water.

Heading toward the front door, the pair gave a wave to Charlotte and Richard, telling them they were off to El Caliente.

Charlotte and Richard were watching HBO with their scotch glasses poised, paying no attention to the girls. Richard grunted something unintelligible. They sat staring at the TV—two zombies biding their time until the apocalypse. Bryn yelled back at them before they opened the door to leave,

"Okay then, we're off to rob First Federal, don't wait up."

The girls giggled and shook their heads when Charlotte, without taking her eyes off the screen added, "Okay don't be late."

Bryn entwined her arm with Claire. "You know, they are all over me for the dumbest things—things that have no importance, but more often than not, I feel like they wouldn't notice if I was on fire and wouldn't waste the water to put me out. It's one of the things I love about Chris. He listens to me, pays attention to me."

"And what about me? I listen to you."

"Of course you. My gosh, that goes without saying."

As soon as they arrived, a couple of boys asked them to dance, but they turned them down, opting to dance with each other. One boy worked up the nerve to ask Claire three times and she finally said yes. Bryn took the opportunity to tease her every time she caught Claire's eye as she was spun around the floor. The boy was a good three inches shorter than Claire and as the band began to play a slow song, Bryn could see how uncomfortable Claire was—her partner's forehead perilously close to the bridge of her nose.

Another boy asked Bryn, but she said, "No thanks, I don't feel much like dancing."

When Claire saw the guy walk away from Bryn, she stopped dancing, sidled up to Bryn and asked, "Why don't you dance with him?"

"Oh I don't know. If I'm going to dance with someone, I'd rather it be with Chris. I wouldn't want this guy to get any wrong ideas."

"I think he just wanted to dance, not get married."

"Yeah I know. It would feel weird though."

Retying her ponytail Claire added, "He seemed like a nice guy."

"What makes you think he's a nice guy?"

"What makes you think he isn't? You shouldn't have to stop doing or not doing everything because of Chris."

"I'm not stopping everything. I'm not dancing with someone."

"But he might be really great."

"This is a pretty stupid conversation. For God's sake, Claire, why don't you dance with him if you think he's so fabulous?"

"He didn't ask me, Bryn, he asked you and you should think about doing stuff without Chris."

Bryn pulled at Claire's forearm. "Why? Have you heard something about Chris and me?"

"No. That's not it at all. Oh, never mind."

"No, tell me what you've heard."

Claire threw her arms in the air. "I haven't heard anything. I swear. There's nothing to hear. You're missing the point. Just forget it."

"Just be happy for me, okay?"

"I am happy for you."

"You don't seem to be."

Claire rolled her eyes and said, "Forget it, okay? I don't like this band after all. Let's get out of here."

The argument was tabled as they walked home around the lake's winding perimeter, talking and giggling about Wally and Midnight and even Chris. Conversations about Chris had dwindled over the summer. Claire's eyes would glass over when Bryn began a sentence with "Chris," so Bryn stopped elaborating. Initially Bryn was offended with Claire's lack of interest or enthusiasm, but soon she became comfortable and even welcomed the distance. It was completely irrational, but she never really wanted Claire too close to Chris, so she was fine with this breach they had created. Bryn thought losing her boyfriend to her best friend seemed like the kind of shitty thing that could happen to her.

Claire got home on Sunday to the inevitable crowd. Bryn's house was so nice and quiet and spacious. It had room to move around without running into someone. Despite what Bryn might think, Claire loved Bryn's mother and thought she was fabulous. Her hands-off approach was like a cool breeze coming through a window on a hot day. Charlotte would glide through a room wearing cashmere and smelling of expensive perfume, leaving a hint of the treasured scent in her wake. Claire's house smelled like shortbread, pine needles and firewood. How nice it would be to sit at a dining room table with fewer than a dozen people and live in a home where silence wasn't countered with *what's wrong, did something happen at school today, is everything okay.* What were her parents thinking, having ten kids? Claire figured at best you could give three kids the finer things; ten was a complete impossibility unless you were a Hilton or a Hearst and those people had the good sense not to have ten children. She could spend forever at the Wilsons'. She would shop for clothes with Charlotte and have Saturday night dinners at the country club and she'd be given a car and the chance to be alone, blessedly alone.

She hated that she shared a house with a gaggle of people and she wanted her own room, which she would never get. She wanted Midnight to love her and that seemed more and more remote every day as well. It was torture to see him all the time. He seemed to live at her house. Why didn't Wally hang out at the Wrights'? There was nothing special about the overcrowded Porter place.

And Bryn was bugging her, too. Why did Bryn keep on telling her she was beautiful? It was annoying, along with every detail of every date and her gushing about how wonderful Chris was. She considered telling Wally how she felt about Midnight, but knew he'd make fun of her and go blab to Midnight in completely the wrong way.

Claire's mother was calling to her from the bottom of the stairs, so she trotted down the stairs asking her what was up.

Her mother began, "Hi sweetheart. Before I forget, I wanted to tell you I ran into the St. Agnes swim coach, who said you are her superstar."

With a broad smile on her face, she told her mother it was nice of the coach, but she didn't think she was that special. She sat down on the steps to listen and her mother cozied up beside her.

"But you are. Your coach told me specifically that she does not dole out compliments willy-nilly."

"She said willy-nilly?"

"She did. She thinks you could be in line for a scholarship and we agreed that when school resumes, you should set your sights with that in mind. She said we should create your profile and post it on the NCSA site and go through the available programs, since apparently there are a lot of NCAA 1 level schools with great swim teams. It sounded like a long process, but your dad and I will help you. She mentioned three schools in particular that she thought might be right for you: Lehigh, Pepperdine and Vanderbilt. I'm not crazy about the idea of you being all the way out in California, but we'll keep Pepperdine on the list for now."

Claire was smiling ear to ear. "That's so exciting. She's

never said anything to me."

"Well, don't get too excited. We have a long way to go and you have loads to contribute. Maybe she didn't want to say anything prematurely. You are going to have to get your grades up and probably give up the more frivolous things on your schedule this coming year."

"Like what's frivolous?"

"Well, I'm thinking off the top of my head, but I think jazz dance should probably go and spending every waking minute at Bryn Wilson's house could get cut back."

"But those are my fun things."

"I thought swimming was your fun thing."

"You know what I mean."

"Not sure that I do, but the point is that you have to be deeply involved and not expect your father and me to do all the groundwork."

"Thanks Mom. This is the best news ever!"

"I love you, Claire. Don't forget that you're terrific even if you don't feel like that some days."

"Most days."

She grabbed Claire's hand and held it in hers. "Claire, not every hit can be a home run, not even for the best of players."

"But I don't feel like I get any home runs, ever."

"That's nonsense. You are so fortunate in life. You have beauty, health, athleticism."

"You have to say that because you're my mom."

"No, Claire. If I didn't think it, I could, well… not say anything."

"But you tell all of us we're special and that doesn't make mathematical sense."

She laughed and said, "See? You're funny too."

Claire's mother squeezed her shoulder and Claire took two steps at a time as she ran to her bedroom. She couldn't wait to tell Bryn. She would hunker down. She never missed swim practice or a meet, but she'd be there even earlier and swim better than ever to show her coach that she was a serious athlete. She was sure Midnight would come around too. What was it her mother had said? That she was beautiful, and athletic, and funny.

But she did say that to every one of them.

Fall

Summer came to its inevitable end and Bryn headed back to St. Agnes while Chris headed to Andover West for his senior year. That small, seemingly insignificant event altered Bryn's universe. He no longer came by the Wilsons' house unannounced. He didn't look happy when Bryn made surprise visits to The Rendezvous, where he continued to work after school and on weekends. Something had gone off kilter, and her questions about it were always answered with Chris telling her he was just busy and she was crazy. Then one day when Bryn and Claire were sitting at the bay window struggling with chemistry homework, they saw Chris behind the wheel of his father's SUV with a girl Claire identified as Olivia Ward. They looked pretty cozy. Bryn stared down at her textbook. She couldn't look Claire in the eyes or bring herself to ask anything about Olivia Ward, because as her stomach roiled, she knew the answer. Chris keeping her at arm's length was making nauseating sense. She told Claire she needed to get home. She snapped her book shut and without saying goodbye, she left the Porters' house.

Bryn spent the evening calling him, but it went to voicemail time after time. On the fifth call she left a message, which came out sounding like she was prying and desperate.

"Where are you? I haven't seen you in a couple days and this evening—I'm sure I must be wrong, but I thought I saw you in your dad's car with Olivia Ward. I don't know her at all and didn't know you did. Claire told me who she was. I guess Claire knows her from the recreation center where Claire swims. Ugh, tangent. Call me when you get this."

He did not return her call, and almost a week had gone by when she ran into him in the parking lot outside Mojoe's Coffee Hut. By that time, there had been countless messages and a few side trips along his street on her bike. Her knees knocked as she walked toward him.

Bryn began, her voice shaky and wavering. "Where have you been? Why haven't you called me?"

Chris nervously looked back toward MoJoe's. "I've been super busy with school and work and everything."

"Too busy to call me?"

"Well, I've been meaning to call you and talk to you about stuff, but haven't gotten around to it."

"Well, I'm here now. What stuff?"

No sooner had the question left Bryn's lips than she saw Olivia Ward coming out of Mojoe's. She was obviously headed to Chris—her smirk more pronounced with each step she took toward him. Olivia stood at Chris's side and plucked an errant hair from his shoulder. He took his car keys out of his pocket and handed them to Olivia asking her to go wait in the car for a second. She protested, but he said, "Please Liv, wait for me for a sec."

Then he looked at Bryn. "I don't know if I ever told you but before this past summer, me and Olivia were kind of together, you know, and then when school started we hooked up again." He paused. "So that's what I've been meaning to talk to you about."

Through tears that began to blur her vision, Bryn asked if he was breaking up with her.

He stared down at the gravel of the parking lot and shrugged his shoulders. "You want me to say it? I think it's pretty clear."

She eked out, "None of this seems very clear at all."

Chris continued to stare at the toe of his Nikes.

Bryn added, "And so that's it? You're with her now?"

Chris raised his eyebrow and let out a sigh. "Well, yeah."

"I thought you loved me like I love you."

"Jeez Bryn." He paused and continued to kick at the gravel. "Look, all I'm saying is Olivia and I were together before I ever met you and, well, we're together again."

Bryn stared into the distance, looking at nothing in particular, and for a moment lost her train of thought. The conversation was the worst thing she'd ever had to endure, yet she didn't want it to end. She wanted him to stay there and talk it out and make Olivia wait in the car. "And were you ever going to tell me that this Olivia person existed?"

"I don't know, Bryn. I don't know what I was planning. I swear I wasn't going to lead you on or anything, but I didn't know what to say. I didn't know how to tell you about her."

"And what about us? Is there still hope for us?"

"Christ Bryn, I have to go."

Despite biting the inside of her cheek with her molars to will the tears to stop, they didn't. Bryn stood there outside the coffee house with tears streaking down her face and watched him walk away toward his car and Olivia—no hug, no brief kiss on the cheek, not even a pat on her shoulder. But once the crying did stop, some two hours and three lattes later, Bryn decided to never cry about it again. If she started again, she feared she would never stop. Instead, she resolved right there as she walked toward the empty parking lot to unlock her bike and ride the five miles home, she would somehow get him back. She would forgive him for Olivia, because she knew that girl couldn't mean as much to him. Bryn understood him. Something had been forged on that first trip down the river and in the small room at La Petite Famille. It couldn't be discarded. It had value. No one would transform her resolve, not Claire, not Midnight, not even Chris himself. He hadn't actually said the words *break up*—maybe there was still hope. They needed to talk it out without Olivia waiting 50 feet away—pariah that she was.

Bryn planned to dedicate herself to stellar grades and school activities so she could graduate at midterm the following year. Then she would make Chris see the better choice of Madison over La Crosse. Despite 5,000 pretty freshman co-eds, she could already see him in UW's bright red helmet.

She considered calling Claire and getting her input, but thought better of it. Claire would tell her it was foolish. She would remind Bryn she was a moron to care about someone who cared about someone else. No, Bryn wouldn't ask Claire's opinion. How good a judge was she, anyway? She sat around mooning about Midnight while a handful of perfectly nice guys pursued her. She would wear Chris down, make a nuisance of herself if necessary, even stalk him if need be, and have him back by Valentine's Day.

Bryn's September 3rd birthday came and went without Chris acknowledging it, while she dedicated hours searching for the perfect gift for his birthday on September 22nd. She finally chose Beats Solo and a $100 Apple music credit, hoping he might fondly recall the times they spent sitting in his room, backs against the twin beds, listening to music. Richard would have a cow over the credit card charge, but she didn't care. She'd forgo her allowance for the next month and use money from her savings to pay for it. She had been saving to buy seats at the CIBC Theater in Chicago to see a modern dance ensemble with Claire, but she would give that up to get something special for Chris.

UPS sent her an email saying the gift had been delivered, but two days later Chris still hadn't acknowledged it. She sat in her room staring at her phone and her computer screen and justified calling him to ask if he had gotten it. She wanted to hear his voice.

She opened Word and began typing the things she wanted to say to him. She'd ask if he had a nice birthday and what he did to celebrate and fit in asking if he received her gift, if he didn't mention it first. After dedicating more time to the bullet points on her document than she had her history homework, she opened the contact list on her phone and scrolled down to Chris's name. She stared at the number, trying to muster her nerve. She finally punched the number and it rang twice before it went to voicemail. She recited her list of questions and then hung up. No more than a minute passed before her phone pinged with a text from Chris that said "I got it-TY." He had to be sitting there watching her name come up on his caller ID. The brush-off stung.

There had been one bright spot to September. She had gotten her driver's license and Richard had gotten her a car for her birthday. The gift required she agree to a list of stipulations. She would have to help run errands for her mother and play chauffeur at his or her request. He warned that might mean picking them up after dinner at the club on occasion, and she'd have to be flexible and uncomplaining. She eagerly agreed to the preconditions. If Richard wanted her to become his and Charlotte's full time Uber, she didn't care. The car would bring her the freedom to ride by The Rendezvous and Chris's house and drive to the field adjacent to Wild West, where they held football practice.

She sat in the driver's seat of her new Honda Hybrid like a cop on a stakeout, going through emails and hammering through reading assignments as he practiced with his teammates. Once she saw one of his buddies pointing to her car and smacking the side of Chris's helmet, whispering something into his ear. She pretended to be engrossed in her textbook, but looked up and smiled back at them. She had every right to be there and only once did he come to the car and tell her she was distracting him. Her pulse raced as he came toward the car. He didn't seem angry. Distracting him could be interpreted as a compliment. Sometimes he actually seemed pleased to have such a vigilant admirer and occasionally gave her a crooked smile before running off to join his teammates at the end of practice. And, since his practice gave her at least two hours of quiet, uninterrupted study time, she was making real progress toward the goal of early graduation. She imagined him playing in Madison. Maybe all he needed was a little encouragement about making the team. She wasn't sure of the exact dynamic between him and his father because he had never elaborated about their relationship, but from the conversations she did recall, Mr. Bello seemed short on understanding and inspiration. Apparently that ran short in most families. Charlotte and Richard never encouraged her about classes, although she was an ace student and had even been asked to participate in a substitute-teaching program in her history class—Charlotte said she paid too much tuition to the damn school for the kids to be doing the teaching. They never asked about her sketching although she had won a local art contest in her freshman year. They never asked her much of anything, but Bryn speculated there was something even deeper and darker in the Bello household. The Bello children would have naturally assigned some blame for their mother's death. Did they despise his younger wife? Had Cathie and his father known one another while Mrs. Bello was still alive? Throughout the summer Chris never said much, and Bryn was content to let it go. It never seemed that important, but now, she wondered. He wasn't a big talker and like everyone she knew, he had things to hide. She considered how he had kept Olivia a secret during the entire summer. Yes, everyone had something they wanted to hide.

One evening while driving home after a particularly long vigil, Claire called asking what had happened to Bryn that afternoon. It had been the relays for the county swim meet and Bryn hadn't shown up. With a gasp, she remembered she was supposed to attend to cheer her on.

"What happened to you? You were supposed to be there at four."

Bryn let out a long sigh. "I completely forgot."

"Well that's super nice. Where have you been?"

"I've just been hanging out."

Claire's voice was raised when she said, "You mean hanging out stalking Chris."

Bryn paused for a moment, but then said, "I'm not stalking him."

"Right. I think it's getting creepy that you hang out across the street from West. I don't want you to make a fool of yourself. You're lucky someone like Olivia doesn't start tweeting about it."

"It's not so creepy and I get a lot of studying done. Yesterday I finished the best sociology paper I've ever written. And, I think he's actually flattered by my attention."

"I think you're actually deluded."

"Yuck, yuck. You're so funny."

"I'm not trying to be funny."

"Give me a break, okay? I like to see him. It's not a crime and I don't want to give up on him, us."

"But you're so obvious about it."

"What would you prefer? I hide behind a tree? Now that's creepy."

"It might do you good for him to think you have something better to do with your time."

"I guess you're right and the last thing I want is to have Olivia Ward circulate a Snap or Tweet."

"It certainly is the last thing you want and do me a favor and don't miss the next swim meet. They're important to me.

You might not give a shit, but they're important to me."

"I know it's important. I didn't purposefully miss it. Besides, your little sisters are always there."

"It's not the same as having a friend there. I don't want to go on and on about it, but I'm not someone you should be forgetting about."

"Of course not. I understand and agree with you for heaven's sake."

Bryn felt scolded and it burned because Claire was right. Their disagreements were rare, but the ones they did have, stuck with Bryn for a long time. She wanted to take Claire's advice and drive away from Wild West on her way home as opposed to gravitating toward it. What Claire said made sense and she would stop hanging out there—at least for the time being. Maybe her absence would trigger something, but wouldn't Chris tell her to go away altogether if he really didn't want to see her? She wasn't crazy. There was something there that could be salvaged. She was convinced. She knew Claire had her best interest at heart, but sometimes thought she couldn't possibly understand. Family, classmates and admirers surrounded Claire. Siblings were always around. Her parents were home every night for dinner. Bryn would walk through the front hallway of the Porters' and into their kitchen and feel like she wrapped herself in a plush, warm Snuggie. Her own home felt more like a Brillo pad. The Porter home was a spectacular three-story brick Victorian that mister and missus had painstakingly restored to its late nineteenth-century origins, but there was always more work that needed to be done. The house had six bedrooms and four baths with a huge wraparound porch on the lakefront side. The house was large, but with so many Porter kids still living at home, it was like bread rising, squeezing over the tin. That rising usually snapped something—a pipe here, a hinge there, a squeaky floorboard or an overused appliance. Mr. Porter complained "it's always something with this place," but he loved their home.

Zach Porter had been a successful attorney and was now a justice on the district appeals court. He was known around town for his big brood, serious dedication to the law, equal dedication to environmental causes, the Victorian remodel, and his shoulder-length gray hair. He kept it harnessed in a topknot, much like Claire, as he rode his bicycle to and from the courthouse. In Wisconsin, commuting by bike in the dead of winter was not considered environmentally responsible or even avant-garde. It was considered borderline crazy.

And Mrs. Porter, Mary, was deemed a bit of an eccentric herself, mostly for marrying Zach Porter and then proceeding to have ten kids with him. Mary was tall, blond, quick to laugh, completely non-judgmental and fun to be around. She didn't actually seem like the parenting type, but there she was, a mother ten times over. She was an open book. You could ask her any question about anything—periods, boys, sex—no topic was off-limits and she always seemed to have time for the topics. She had started having babies with Zach Porter at twenty, which brought authenticity to her answers.

Snarky comments abounded about the Porters. Bryn assumed they were based on jealousy. Mary and Zach were both pretty sweet to look at, and be around. She overheard one conversation Charlotte had via speakerphone with some lady from the country club. It was presumptuous, since her mother didn't know the Porters at all.

"That Zach Porter is so odd. Do you see him on that bike of his? A grown man pedaling off to the courthouse every morning is bizarre, don't you think? I swear, it was 20 degrees yesterday and I saw him around nine o'clock pedaling through the frost. And it's not even a sensible 10-speed. It has a basket on it, for God's sake."

"Yes, he is a strange fellow."

"And what about that crazy hair tied in a topknot? Who knows what he's on?"

"I can't believe he's a judge. He looks like he should own a dispensary in Southern California."

Maybe he was a bit odd, but Bryn adored him, as did Claire. He was a serious person, but he was generous in his praise and affection for his wife and children. He'd walk through the front door of his house looking content, asking Mary, "How many are in attendance this evening?" With seven of the 10 children still living at home, there were evenings with 14 people around their huge dining room table. Bryn recalled many nights when she was not the only guest. Midnight was a regular, as well as their grandmother Josie and friends of Claire's younger siblings.

Bryn felt terrible about disappointing Claire. And Claire was right about the horror of a Snap or Tweet or Instagram photo—she'd be ridiculed mercilessly. Claire was a wonderful friend and would do anything for her and she had let her down. Bryn longed for a day when she could feel good about herself again—one day when everything went really well. She wanted the summer back. The summer had been happy.

Her parents didn't notice that Chris no longer came around. Or neither thought about it enough to ask. She got up in the morning, made her bed, did her usual chores, ate the usual meals and did her homework. As far as they were concerned, all was right in Bryn's world and they were too caught up in their most recent argument to notice much of anything. It had erupted midweek and by Saturday Charlotte still hadn't spoken to Richard. He came home after 9 p.m. having gone out with his employees after work without making a phone call, sending a quick text, or shooting Charlotte an email. Bryn could hear every word of their argument from her bedroom, which was almost the length of the house away and, her door was closed. She guessed her mother had rolled her eyes or sneered at her father because it began with Richard yelling, "Don't give me that look, okay?"

"You mean that look which calls you out for drinking and driving?"

"I am perfectly capable of getting home safely on a couple drinks and we had dinner, might I add."

"Oh, so you ate? That makes all the difference in the world. Do you understand the jeopardy you put other people and this family in if you got a DUI or worse?"

"Don't get me started on how much you care about this family."

"Don't go there Richard."

"If you gave a shit about this family maybe you'd spend more time worrying about it. Shit, Jack can't even stand to look at you."

"That's an awful thing to say."

"Well, the truth hurts."

"And you think you're so goddamned special. What time do you spend with our kids? You're either going to the office, at the office or thinking about the office."

"That office keeps a roof and plenty more over your head sweetheart. I don't need to remind you where you came from. Your old man was a goddamn garbage man. You don't want to go back to that lifestyle, do you?"

"That's what you have to say with a handful of scotches under your belt? You bring that up?"

They continued to argue, but their voices were lower and Bryn had to strain to hear. Then there was dead silence for a moment followed by the sound of a glass breaking. Suddenly Charlotte screamed she was not going to stay in the same house with Richard. Bryn heard the front door slam and moments later the roar of the engine on her mother's SUV.

As Charlotte sped down the street and headed toward the highway, she understood more than ever that they had built on a foundation of quicksand. From the beginning it was how it all looked that seemed great—they never really stopped to ask if it would work. She admitted Richard's money had turned her head, but he was to blame too. At the start, it was superficial. He liked the way they looked together: physical opposites, Charlotte with dark hair, dark eyes and pale skin, he blond, blue-eyed, perpetually suntanned and healthy-looking.

Charlotte recalled the day she told Richard she didn't want children. He had said, "We'll figure it out after we're married" and joked that he wouldn't want it to look like he was gay. She let it go at the time, not wanting to begin an argument with her new fiancé, but regardless of the ensuing arguments, Richard insisted upon having a family. Scarcely a year and some months after their honeymoon, Jack came along and then seven years later there was Bryn. Too many years separating them to even consider a reprieve down the road. She loved them, but below the surface of what nice people admit to, she thought about what her life would look like without them. She wanted to wander through museums, dance in the Rainbow Room, attend galas, but she was stuck at home. She employed a nanny, but they were always there, demanding her time, and despite Richard's grandiose talk about being a caring, dedicated parent, he was rarely around. He spent the better part of his time at his office or the damn country club. When he was at home he seemed to want everyone to be quiet, which was completely unrealistic. God, she resented him. His list of violations made her cringe and his pettiness was recorded and catalogued by Charlotte into a seemingly endless Dropbox that was ready to burst. There was the time a few months after Bryn was born. Richard looked at her as she changed for dinner and said, "You still haven't taken off some of the baby weight." Charlotte had told him she was struggling with the last few pounds and sensitive about it, but she let that go too. Then one day, she stopped editing what she said and didn't say and the arguments came and never seemed to stop. They had become as predictable as Halley's Comet and as regular as tornados in Kansas. And then there was the drinking. It was sad to see him stagger to their bedroom at the end of the day—a young man who began to look old before his time. The sadness hung around him like a thick fog rolling across the Grand Banks. The years passed, her closet and cases filled with endless stacks of hand-knitted Halsbrook, La Prairie crèmes and La Perla panties. Her Cayenne Turbo S was nestled in their three-car garage. Her wine fridge was bursting. She loved her things—she wouldn't give them up easily, so she never bothered telling Richard how dismal she thought their marriage was. Instead she disengaged from him and from Jack and Bryn. She was so wrapped up with all the things she never had, and making up for that deprivation, that she avoided coming face-to-face with the wisdom of their getting married in the first place. They all suffered for it, but she guessed Jack and Bryn did the most. There were those couple years not long after they moved to Crane Lake she thought she'd been rescued, but that wound up disappointing her too.

Bryn had poked her head into her brother's room the next morning to ask if he had been home to hear them arguing. Jack told Bryn he heard every word and thought they might have heard it the next town over. He said for first time in memory he actually felt sorry for their mother. He thought Richard had been mean-spirited and wished he'd leave him out of their arguments. He also thought she was right about the drinking and driving.

Bryn whispered, "Can you believe it? Our grandfather was a garbage man in Tappanook. God knows she never talks about her family, but I never pictured that."

"It's not such a bad thing to be—good pay, plenty of benefits, good hours if you're okay with being up early."

Bryn leaned against the doorframe, but then walked in and moved clothes off a bedroom chair to sit down. "I don't think it's bad at all, but I would have thought the head of snootiness at someplace fits our mother more."

"It actually makes me kind of proud of her, that she wasn't

born with a silver spoon like Richard. I'll never understand what the big secrets are about though."

"She obviously put a lot of effort into becoming the person she is—Dolce, cashmere, Porsche, you know. And if you avoid any talk about your past, it can in a way, be different than what it actually is. You know what I mean?"

"Well, yeah. Of course I know what you mean, but it's such bullshit."

"I wonder what else there is to know?"

"I sure would like to ask her. I could tell her I overheard her and Richard and want to know more."

Bryn laughed and said, "You could add that they're wondering in the next town over too."

Jack told Bryn he had to get ready for work and she needed to scoot, but he didn't head straight to the shower. Instead, he continued his search for rentals near the town village, which he had been doing when Bryn came in. He disliked the biting arguments between his parents and they seemed to be getting more frequent. He couldn't stand living there much longer. He'd never figure out his mother, but then he didn't understand Richard that well anymore either. He seemed worried about some phantom misfortune ready to happen, but Jack figured he'd do much better if he left Charlotte. Poof. Trouble gone. He could kill her sometimes for the way she acted around his friends. It was embarrassing. Whenever he confronted her to tell her to stop flirting, she'd feign surprise and insist it was all his imagination. Yet another reason to get the hell out and into his own place. He figured a few more months of working and saving. It couldn't go fast enough. Then he wouldn't have to deal with either one of them.

It was the shortest of phone calls. Charlotte's sister had called from DC to ask her to come to town. She jumped at the chance. The plan was to have a full-blown girls' weekend, which they hadn't done in a long time—play tourist, overeat, binge watch.

Leaving no room for discussion or argument, she made the plane reservations and then informed Richard of her plans. Charlotte was sure Richard would welcome her absence as much as she'd enjoy being gone.

She pre-boarded along with the other first class passengers and took her time taking out her tablet and headphones before stowing her carryon. She plugged her headphones into the tablet, leaned against the window and closed her eyes for a few moments of rest. A young girl, no older than Bryn, sat next to her. She nodded hello to her, which the girl barely acknowledged. This was a blessing—the teen didn't look like she'd want to make conversation with a middle-aged woman. Charlotte could enjoy her book and her music and not have to engage with anyone except the flight attendant who, once airborne, would bring her a nice cold martini.

Despite the commotion of passengers in the aisle heading for their assigned seats, Charlotte felt a calm wash over her, a sweet dreaminess that was almost sleep, while still aware of her surroundings.

She heard muffled voices and opened her eyes. The flight attendant was telling the girl that the gentleman seated next to her father was offering to change seats. The girl was explaining she didn't want to change seats, but the attendant persisted and the girl got up. She checked her back pocket for her phone, shrugged her shoulders and gave a half-hearted wave to Charlotte. Charlotte looked out the window and watched the baggage handlers and maintenance crew. She looked back into the cabin to scan the faces of her fellow passengers. There was a man standing in the aisle. Like Charlotte had, he was going through his things deciding what he'd keep with him during take off. He was on the short side, probably late fifties, wearing a Seattle Mariners baseball cap and had one of the warmest smiles Charlotte had ever seen.

Despite herself, Charlotte smiled back and said hello.

He began, "I think you're stuck with me."

"It was nice of you to change seats. I'm guessing she'd rather have stayed here, but I'm sure the father foresaw some kind of trouble. I have to warn you I am the worst seat companion. I'm a bad flyer and my airplane conversation leans toward the banal."

"I spend half my life on airplanes and can talk any nervous flyer through bumps, shakes, even jolts. And, I can guarantee you a great conversation; heavy on the substance, light on the banter. While I'm still standing, let me grab the flight attendant. Would you like something to drink?"

"I guess a glass of orange juice."

"Sounds good, I'll join you."

He held out his hand and introduced himself as Mike Accosi and asked her name.

"I'm Charlotte Wilson."

The captain came out of the cockpit smiling at Mike. Apparently he was telling the truth about spending half his life on airplanes, since the pilot seemed to know him well and was genuinely pleased to see him. They shook hands, talked about the Mariners' standing in the AL West, the previous night's match-up between the Cubs and Cincinnati and other baseball business. Apparently the pilot was a big fan. Mike interrupted the sports conversation to introduce Charlotte.

Charlotte smiled at Mike as the captain walked back to the cockpit. "You weren't kidding about spending your life on airplanes."

He grinned back looking sheepish and said, "He's a nice fellow. I can assure you we're in good hands. Now, tell me why are you on your way to Washington, DC?"

"I'm headed to see my sister. And you?"

"I have meetings with the league."

"The league?"

"Yes, I work with the Seattle Mariners in the front office."

"That sounds like a fun job. Now I get all the baseball talk."

Mike let out a laugh. "Yes it is fun. I love baseball and I've been lucky enough to spend my life around it. It's been a big part of me since, well...Jesus, probably little league. I kid you not. But, like any job or career there are stale moments and bumps in the road, but let's not focus on that. It makes me seem more interesting if people think my job is extra special."

"I have to admit I don't know much about baseball, but I've always liked sports and there's something exciting about someone spending a career in it. Oh sorry, something extra special."

"At the risk of incriminating people, I'll entertain you with a couple of rather scathing baseball stories. Well, I hope they'll entertain you. I won't disguise names or protect the innocent. I promise it will make the flight go much faster."

"Any gossip on Jennifer Lopez and Alex Rodriguez?"

"Who's Jennifer Lopez?"

"You're kidding, right?"

"Yes, of course I'm kidding, but I go further back than even David Justice and Halle Berry."

"Monroe and DiMaggio?"

"Very funny."

Their pilot made a quick announcement there would be a slight delay as they had the maintenance crew take a look at a cabin light, but as the announcements continued, Mike told Charlotte he thought they were going to be grounded. As the rest of the passengers moaned at every update from the pilot about a delay that could not be estimated, Charlotte and Mike didn't seem to hear the public address at all. They got off baseball and began to talk about their lives on a level reserved for best friends. As the minutes turned into hours, Charlotte knew Mike was right. There wasn't going to be a flight. The pilot finally signed off and canceled the flight when the time had come to change crews. Rather than try and find another flight right away, the pair opted for the Hilton O'Hare. The hotel was an easy walk through the corridors of the airport and sported all the necessities for weary travelers: dependable Wi-Fi, a sports bar and a few restaurants. Mike asked if she might like to grab a steak and listen to some jazz at the Gaslight Club. She enthusiastically agreed and told him she was starving, but added, "So after dinner we should think about speaking with the concierge to find flights out of here."

"Charlotte, after a long, relaxing dinner, I intend on leaving a message with my office that I am getting a room here at the hotel. Then I'm going to instruct that same office to work on finding me a flight around 10 a.m. You should do the same. Stay with me. C'mon, it'll be fun. It's kind of like playing hooky."

"It does seem silly to rush around trying to find another flight tonight that will put me into DC at an ungodly hour. Easier to start fresh tomorrow, right?"

"You don't have to convince me. It was my idea. I'm camping here tonight, but I really would love the company and I'd love to get to know you better. You are a very interesting lady and you have the most beautiful eyes. I could look at you forever."

"Flatterer."

"I wouldn't say it if it weren't true."

They sat talking over dinner for hours. They were a couple with a clean slate. They hadn't heard one another's same old stories, jokes or viewpoints and they began to flirt—laughing, leaning into one another. How much more engaging the stories and viewpoints seemed as they landed on fresh ears.

Charlotte's cell vibrated on the table. She glanced at it and let Richard go to voicemail. Mike looked at her knowingly and said, "Do you know it's after 9. I'm going to ask for the check, unless you want something else. I'm going to head to the gents as well and give you some privacy if you have to return that phone call."

Charlotte sat alone and thought about what she'd say to Richard and opted for a top-line version of the truth. She got him on the second ring and explained her flight had been cancelled and she was sitting down for the first time with a minute on her hands to get in touch with him and her sister. She saw Mike heading back to the table and told Richard she had to run—she still needed to call her sister and find a flight out first thing in the morning.

They headed toward the hotel's front desk, but Mike touched her at the elbow and asked if they could hold back for a moment. And then he asked her to share his room. He explained that he probably wasn't very good at asking or debonair for asking, but he didn't want their time with one another to end. He swore they didn't even have to share the same bed, but he didn't want to let her go. They walked to the desk clerk holding hands and when the young woman asked if they'd like two queens or one king, it was Charlotte who quickly said, "One king, please."

They were alone in the elevator when Mike turned and kissed her.

Charlotte pulled back slightly. "I don't want to scare you off, but there's so much about me that I'm not sure I'd like to admit. I'm a terrible wife and mother and maybe a terrible person."

He held on to her tight and kissed her forehead and then he said, "We've all done bad things, that doesn't necessarily make you a bad person."

"You know I'm married?"

"Yes, I kind of figured that out. I don't know what to say about it Charlotte. I want to be with you more than anything, but I'm no home wrecker either. I'll take my signals from you."

"Not sure there's much of a home to wreck, but I don't want the full burden of responsibility here."

"I didn't mean it that way. Look, you get to a certain age and there's bound to be some skeletons. If it helps, I have a twenty-five year old son who doesn't speak to me, but let's save all the bad stuff for some other night. For right now, let's forget about everyone but us and play it by ear."

He kissed her deeply with an open mouth and held her tight enough to squeeze the air from her lungs. For the first time in as long as she could remember, she felt completely comfortable in her own skin. She wasn't self-conscious or guarded about how she looked, what she was saying or what she was doing. It was completely liberating. She had feelings the likes of which she hadn't experienced since she was twenty and as Mike kissed every inch of her and made love to her for the second time, she decided no matter how it turned out, on her return, she would talk to Richard about a divorce.

The sun poked a sliver of light through the drawn curtains. Mike rolled over toward her, kissed her on the cheek and said, "Now, that was my idea of an overnight."

"Yes, I think Chicago has become my favorite layover."

"And mine. And who would have guessed the Hilton has become my favorite hotel. Screw the Four Seasons, screw the Mandarin."

Charlotte laughed heartily. "Well, let's not get crazy."

He stared into her eyes and softly said, "I don't want this to be the last time I see you."

She said nothing, but leaned into him and reached for his hand. She enclosed her fingers with his and held on tight.

Mike smiled that warm, wonderful smile. "Okay, so we agree we shouldn't let this fade away into a sweet memory."

"So how would we make this work? Forget about the nuances. There's a basic challenge of geography. I'm in Wisconsin and you're in Seattle?"

"Remember, I'm Mr. Airplane, so that's not difficult for me. But first things first, I'm in DC for the weekend and through the week for meetings with the league. If you can and I'm hoping very much that you can, stretch your trip by a couple days."

"I'll call my husband when I get to my sister's place and tell him I am staying through Wednesday."

"I have to say that I feel so great about you, but I also feel a thousand pangs of guilt when I hear the word husband."

"I'm sorry."

"No, you don't have to apologize. Do I?"

"No. Let's drop it. You want to tell me where I'll be staying from Sunday on?"

"Believe it or not, despite my earlier conviction to the nice folks here at Hilton, I'm at the Mandarin."

"I can stand it if you can."

"Funny, I thought this had the chance of being terribly awkward. You know, we'd be wondering if we did the right thing, kind of poking around the room and avoiding eye contact. But man, I haven't felt this good in ten years. I feel as young as one of my players."

"Well for goodness sake, you can't be that old. God knows, last night …"

"Before you go any further, when I was a kid, there was still a car called a Pontiac and going to the moon was something completely awe inspiring."

"There can't be that many years separating us. I just turned forty-eight and you know what?"

"What?"

"Right now, for the first time in a long time, I'm actually feeling pretty damn good about it."

"Christ, you weren't even born before Woodstock. I'm feeling ancient."

"You mean the Peanuts character?"

"You're joking, right?"

"Yes Mike, I'm kidding."

He hugged her tight and rubbed his hand along her back. They stayed like that for a full minute before he told her they should hurry up and get in the shower or they wouldn't have time for breakfast. He still had to call his office and wanted to take a look at the morning sports news, so she'd have to be quick. The water flowing through her hair and down her back was draining all the tension she had ever known out of her entire body. She hoped it would be as easy to wash away the past twenty years.

Bryn was home studying for a Spanish test. The doorbell rang and her mother yelled, "Bryn, Chris Bello is here to see you."

Bryn opened her bedroom door a crack and was frozen there—nauseous with excitement. Charlotte was busy making conversation with him and Bryn was straining to hear. She had to resist the impulse to run to him like a sprinter at the gun. She held her position and continued to listen intently. She didn't know what to do. Her heart raced, standing there like a robot, but one that was beginning to sweat.

She heard her mother say, "So, why haven't we seen you around?"

"Well, I'm always working and um, y'know Bryn and I really haven't been seeing one another anymore."

"Aren't seeing one another? Bryn didn't say anything."

Chris didn't acknowledge the remark, saying only, "So, I left my friend Pete in the car. Do you think you could call Bryn again?"

Her voice echoed down the hall and Bryn made her way closer to the living room. She decided to go for a devil-may-care nonchalance, despite knowing she couldn't pull that off for two reasons: 1) she was not carefree and nonchalant and 2) she had been in her bathroom picking at a stubborn pimple. Despite a quick dab of concealer, a red circle formed around the area like the corona of the sun.

Tentatively, Bryn moved into the living room and said, "Hey, what's up?"

"Can we sit for a sec? I have something to ask you about."

Bryn's head was spinning. Did he want to get back together or ask her out? She might faint there on the spot. "Sure, anything."

As Charlotte turned to leave the room, she asked if she could provide soft drinks, but Chris shook his head and she left, shaking her rump like a Hollywood ingénue—still the same old Charlotte.

"Your mom always looks nice. My dad asked how she was doing. I guess he figured we still hung out."

Paying no attention to his second remark, Bryn said, "Yes, she always keeps herself together."

There was a long pause as Chris fidgeted with a loose thread on the buttonhole of his shirt and Bryn sat there shielding her unsightly pimple. Finally she said, "So, what did you want to ask me?

"You know Bryn, I am really pissed off."

"What are you pissed off about?"

Chris sat staring into his hands.

Bryn urged, "What? What's the matter?"

"Someone spray-painted the word *'tramp'* on Olivia Ward's driveway and I figured it was you or you had something to do with it."

It didn't matter that Bryn considered Olivia Ward on par with a sea slug. She was shocked someone would do that to anyone. It would be all over both their schools and Bryn was sure it would take days before Olivia's parents would be able to get it removed. She sat staring at Chris and finally said, "Chris, I promise you I would never do anything like that. It's a terrible thing for someone to do and whoever did it better hope they don't have a camera outside or a smart home."

"No, the Wards don't have any idea who it was."

"I swear it wasn't me."

"I see you outside my house and at the practice field all the time and figured you hate her."

"I couldn't even tell you where she lives."

"I guess in my gut, I knew you weren't the type, but I had to ask. I'd sure know if you were lying, so I guess we're good."

"I think we are. Yeah, we're good."

"You know Olivia is really cool, if you'd get to know her."

"Chris, do you hear what you're saying? That's going to happen somewhere in between maybe and never."

"Well, she is a really nice girl and I've known her a long time, so I know."

"Yes, I think I remember you telling me that."

"I've got to go."

"You sure you don't want to stay? We could hang out and listen to some music or watch some TV in my room."

"Nah, I really have to get going. Pete's in the car."

"Pete Wright? Midnight's brother?"

"Yeah."

"Oh, say hi from me."

Bryn didn't see him to the door. She went back to her bedroom and sat in her vanity chair. All she felt was hopelessness. Resignation had taken over where some semblance of confidence had been. It would be easier to avoid him, to never see him again, rather than see him with Olivia Ward. She looked in the mirror. The red mark on her forehead overshadowed any application of concealer and she understood why he didn't love her. She was unattractive and Olivia was pretty. She picked at zits, while she was sure Olivia never had any. Bryn was boring and Olivia was some combination of Jennifer Lawrence, Zoe Saldana and Brie Larson. But no matter how wonderful Olivia might be, how could he come there and think, even consider, she would do something like that. It was a terrible thing to do, even to Olivia. Did he think she was that kind of terrible person? He said he felt she wasn't the type, but he had to ask her anyway—he had to make sure. The idea made her hurt all over like she had a bad flu coming on. He didn't really know her at all.

As Bryn sat staring at herself in her dresser mirror, she wondered who the graffiti artist might be. Who would have the nerve to go to Olivia's house with a can of spray paint and paint *tramp* for everyone to see? Her first thought was Claire, because she knew how much Bryn disliked Olivia—no one else knew the degree of animosity Bryn held for her, and Claire could be a devil. There was the time she took Father McIntyre's Vespa for an unauthorized spin around the block. It had been her idea to sneak out of the house on a cold January night, too. And she was always hiding under the bed or in a closet waiting to scare her little sisters. But this was not quite something Bryn could picture Claire doing. Besides, she would never do anything so incredibly ballsy without telling Bryn.

The following day she sat at her desk and stared at the blackboard as her Spanish teacher handed out the exam. Her Spanish was mediocre at best, and with her mind in other places and not in *¡Avance! Intermediate Spanish,* she nearly failed the midterm test. Damn Olivia Ward. Her eyes were close together and her hair was dyed an awful color. She was not Zoe Saldana, for God's sake. She was awful and she most certainly got zits, just like everyone else. It was a new day and Olivia didn't seem all that fabulous anymore. The class bell rang and Bryn pulled Claire aside just outside the classroom door.

"I tried to call you like fifty times last night."

"Someone gave my dad an article that said Smartphones are adding to student anxiety and that was enough for him. He took everyone's cell phone for two days. He thinks it's a good experiment. Wally thinks he's lost his mind."

Bryn went on to tell Claire about the graffiti on Olivia's driveway. Claire didn't think it was quite as awful as Bryn had, but she agreed whoever did it was lucky there wasn't a small camera on a gutter spout recording everything. Bryn was puzzled that Claire wasn't more flustered. Bryn had been completely shocked when Chris told her. Her reaction, or lack of it, made Bryn wonder whether Claire had moved from devil to delinquent.

Bryn was tired. Tired of school and Chris and her parents and the metronome of her life—up, dress, school, home, home-work, bed, up, dress, school, home... Chris didn't care about her. She was spinning her wheels in quicksand. She had to get on with her life and it was Wally who gave her the idea about how she might do that. She ran into him after school and asked if he'd like a ride home. In transit, he said the school play was going to be *The Crucible* and he was going to go for the lead of John Proctor. He thought Bryn should tryout for the role of Abigail Williams, which was the lead, or Elizabeth Proctor. Wally pointed out they could spend some fun time together and it would occupy her time and get her mind off any other dumb stuff. He had been in *Almost, Maine* the year before and assured Bryn she'd have a really good time, make friends and add to her college resume.

She dropped Wally off telling him to say hi to everyone and spent the better part of her evening reading about the play, the players, Arthur Miller and some sexy French guy who played the role of John Proctor in the 1950s. She agreed with Wally. It would be good for her. She decided to add her name to the list of potential players the next day.

There was an old school signup sheet outside the auditorium with a large note that read: You Must Have Your Name On This List by Friday, 3PM If You Hope To Tryout For The Play. The subtext said that each student should be prepared to read something from the material, preferably the role they were auditioning for. Auditions would be held on Tuesday.

Bryn was nervous when she got up to read her lines in front of the drama teacher. He asked her which part she hoped to play and she told him Elizabeth Proctor. She began to read a small, but pivotal scene staged in the courtroom of John Proctor's witchcraft trial, Act IV.

Two other girls read for the part of Elizabeth as well, but thank goodness didn't choose the same passage. Bryn thought they were both very good and was convinced she didn't stand a chance. Three hours had passed since they began and finally everyone had auditioned. Their teacher insisted they all stay for one another's auditions since it gave the feeling of being in front of a live audience. He thanked them all and told them the parts would be posted by that Friday and rehearsals would begin the following Monday evening.

Bryn texted Wally at the end of the week to ask if he had gotten the part of John Proctor. He said he had no idea, but they should meet at the auditorium to console one another.

Bryn wasn't surprised Wally got the part. He had been very good at the auditions. Bryn hadn't a clue who Arthur Miller had in mind when he wrote the play, but somehow she figured it was someone who looked like Wally. As they scanned through the list of other players, Bryn felt Wally's arm tighten around her shoulder.

"You got it. Holy shit Bryn, you got the part of Elizabeth."

"I can't believe it."

"I knew your reading was good. I didn't want to get your hopes up, but it was. It was really good."

"Oh my God, we start rehearsal this Monday."

They hugged and jumped up and down and Wally tousled Bryn's hair. He said he had to run. He wanted to get home fast and let his mom know he had gotten the part—she would be so excited. As he walked down the hall and fist-pumped the air he told Bryn he'd see her after school on Monday to start rehearsing. He yelled congratulations again as he walked away and she did the same.

Bryn looked forward to the three weeks of practice that would, along with homework, consume all of her time. She worked hard and memorized her lines. She took their drama teacher's direction to heart and rehearsed the part over and over on stage and in her head. Despite all the preparation, she was a wreck the day of the performance. She was consumed with stage fright and told Wally she wasn't going to do it. They could get some other girl to make a fool of herself. Wally finally convinced her it would be fine and reminded her that he was on stage with her most of the time. All she had to do was look his way and he'd help her through the performance, even feed her a line if she needed it.

Bryn scanned the audience from behind the stage curtain. Her parents were out of town and unable to attend the performance, but all the Porters were there and Midnight was there too. He sat next to Claire in the second row. Bryn was so happy for Claire. She looked comfortable and contented sitting beside Midnight and hoped it would stay that way.

The curtain went up and as she spoke her first lines, an odd calm came over her and she didn't need to look toward Wally for confidence. Her shoulders were back and her voice was clear as she delivered her lines.

They got three curtain calls and the audience cheered loudly as she took her bow. Not like they did for Wally or their classmate who played the role of Abigail Williams, but enthusiastically and earnestly.

The cast high-fived and hugged backstage and thanked their drama teacher. Wally stood next to his leading lady. There wasn't an inch of space between the two of them and Bryn realized it had been that way since rehearsals began weeks before. You could ignite wet wood with their electricity and when Bryn looked at them, she felt delighted. Wally said he had to rush since his parents were hosting the cast party. He first kissed his leading lady's hand and made sure she was coming to his house then he looked at Bryn and asked if she would be heading over.

"Of course, but don't wait for me. I have to change and I brought my car, so I'll meet you at your house."

As she was headed for the auditorium door, she spotted Chris in the very last row, sitting by himself. She hesitated, but she'd have to pass him to leave the building. Chris stood up as she approached.

"Hi. I've been sitting and waiting for you. I wanted to tell you how good you were."

"I can't believe you came."

"Sure I came. Looks like the whole town showed up."

"I was so nervous when I first saw all the people. I didn't think I'd remember one line."

"Well, I don't know much about the play, but you did great. Next stop Academy Awards."

"Yeah, right."

"No really. I wouldn't have said anything if it wasn't true."

"Well thanks."

He reached out and took her hand and squeezed it. "I have to head out. Just wanted a quick 'hey'."

"I do too. Midnight is waiting for me. I'm driving with him over to the Porters."

"You going out with Midnight?"

"Well, no. I'm just his ride to the Porters."

"I thought those parties were for cast members only."

"They are. I'm dropping him there and then he's going out with Mr. and Mrs. Porter and Claire. She will be so thrilled."

"Yeah, I remember you telling me she liked him. Look, I have to go. I just wanted to tell you I thought you were really good."

"Thanks."

Midnight was waiting by Bryn's car and he saw Chris come out of the auditorium shortly before Bryn. They gave a slight nod to one another, but nothing more.

As Bryn neared the car, Midnight said, "Hey helpless. What did he want?"

"He waited to tell me he thought I was good in the play." Bryn couldn't hide her wide smile.

"You know you're a great girl. Chris Bello is an ass, but you're a great girl."

"Thanks, Midnight, but Chris is not an ass. We just...I don't know, but I know he's not a jerk."

"Can't believe you're defending him, but that's your prerogative."

"Why wouldn't I defend him? He's not a bad person. Look how nice it was for him to come to the play."

"Oh my God, you're right. That's such a huge deal."

"Now who's being the jerk?"

"I think the dude used you."

"What do you mean?"

"I mean he and Olivia had split up and he wanted a summer girlfriend and there you were."

"That's a shitty thing to say."

"Look, I'm sorry. I don't want to get into it. I'm tired of feeling the way I feel about it."

"I don't even know what that means."

"Never mind. Let's get going to the Porters before they leave without me."

Claire was standing at the front door when they walked in. Midnight went straight for the kitchen. She assumed he went to look for Mr. and Mrs. Porter so they could get to dinner. Claire held Bryn back and asked her what they talked about on the ride over. Claire had wanted to ride with them, but her parents made her ride with them and their star, Wally. Bryn explained about Chris being at the theater and that they talked about very little on the drive over.

Claire began, "Maybe I'm wrong about Chris. Maybe we're all wrong."

"About what?"

"I don't know. No matter how much time you spend rooted next to West's practice field, he doesn't tell you to buzz off. And him coming to your house to ask you about Olivia's driveway was stupid. Anyone would know you would never do anything like that. It's almost like he wanted to see you and nothing more and then tonight, he clearly did want to see you."

"You really think so?"

"Yeah, I guess I do."

"What do you think I should do?"

"I think you should do nothing, absolutely nothing. Let him continue doing something."

"Advice taken, stored and put in my cloud."

"On a completely different topic, do you notice how weird my parents have been acting?"

"I just walked in Claire. I haven't even seen them. Weird about what?"

"I don't know, weird."

"At least they showed up. Did you happen to notice my parents didn't bother coming?"

"I wasn't going to say anything. Where were they?"

"I don't know. I think my mother is on some shopping trip and my father is on some business trip, but that's nothing more than a guess based on constancy."

Claire said she was sorry, but she couldn't help laughing.

"I can't make them interested in what I do. They're so much more interested in what they do."

Midnight came up to them and asked Claire what was so funny. Bryn explained that it was her parents who were the regular laugh-riot. He told Claire her parents were getting their coats and making the last round of phone calls to assure the smaller kids were settled in with friends and neighbors. He opened the door for Claire and she gave a small pinch to Bryn's upper arm, a timid smile and an okay sign behind Midnight's back. Bryn gave her a thumb's up in return as the pair walked to Mr. Porter's car in the driveway.

Midnight was the first person Bryn ran into on her way to school on Monday. He smiled wide and asked Bryn if she wanted a ride as she wheeled her bike out of the driveway. Saint Agnes was only a few miles from Wild West and would be on his way. He had his mom's Prius and his advanced science project was sprawled across the back seat. Bryn declined, telling Midnight she was actually going to ride her bike and get some exercise rather than drive.

"Suit yourself, but before you pedal off, how long did you stay Friday night?"

"I left about an hour after you guys did."

"Have you seen Wally or Claire at all?"

"I talked to Claire a bunch over the weekend and she sounded kind of weird after her swim practice. I must have asked her ten times if anything was the matter, but she said nothing was wrong. I haven't actually seen her since after the play, though. She was at a family thing at her grandmother's on Saturday, so maybe something happened there."

Midnight paused and shook his head slightly. "Well something's up."

"Like what?"

"I don't know. Just something. Wally is acting, well... not like himself. I saw him for a couple minutes last night at El Caliente."

"I'll definitely see her at school, so I suppose I'll find out."

Bryn got to school and set off to find Claire. She quickly did. She was sitting on the cold linoleum in front of her locker.

She looked kind of gray and shaky, like she might be sick.

Bryn knelt beside Claire and said, "Are you okay?"

"Can we not talk about anything until the end of the day?"

"But Claire, you don't look well."

"I'm fine, okay? I don't want to talk right now."

"Okay, okay, but if you need a ride home or anything, let me know. Shit, I didn't drive today, but I could go home and get my car."

"No, forget it. We'll talk later."

For Claire, the day progressed like lava into the sea. At one point during science, she thought she might be having a heart attack or at least an anxiety attack. She had pins and needles in her left hand and her breathing seemed shallow. She considered she might have been holding a beaker too tightly and possibly even holding her breath. Maybe it was carpal tunnel. She wasn't sure of anything, but at 3:30, the final bell rang and she left in a rush, grabbing for her back-pack and blazer.

She and Bryn agreed to meet at Badger's for sodas and something to eat. Badger's was a drive-in/diner and not pop-ular among most students. The food was bad and overpriced and the service was nonexistent, which made it a perfect place to talk. They sat at the counter and swiveled the stools to face one another, knees just touching. There was a counter-top jukebox and Claire deposited all their change, a few dollars' worth, which played ten songs.

She started the conversation by telling Bryn she went home the prior afternoon after a Sunday swim at the Y. When she opened her front door, everyone was sitting in the liv-ing room, except her sister Lili. She asked what was going on and her dad said, "We have something to tell all of you, but we'll wait until your sister gets home. It should be just a little while." They sat staring at one another, but began peppering their parents with questions. The older kids were asking if everything was okay with their grandmother while the younger ones were focused on whether they might be going on vacation. Q&A from the Porter children was like a small press conference. To quiet things down, Claire's mom asked about their day. No one responded in any detail. A few moments passed before Lili walked through the door. Her mom said, "There, now we have you all together."

According to Claire, her dad began. "There's no good way to tell you this, but your mother and I agree it's best to tell you all together and to be as candid as possible with you. You're not babies anymore. You're all old enough to hear what I have to say. So, your mother and I have decided to separate." There was a painfully long pause before he said, "I am moving out."

They stared at one another, not knowing what to say. It was Wally who finally spoke up. "You've got to be kidding me. What's all this about? Like, how long have you been married? Forever?"

Her father said, "We've been married 28 years, but that's not the point and God knows I want to stay on point or I may never get through this. As we've told you kids, all of you together, we've decided we're going to live separately. That's the bigger issue."

Wally cut their father off and said, "Ya think? No shit, Sherlock, but it has everything to do with it! You've been married for 28 years, but now you decide to separate?" Wally ran his hands through his hair and said, "This doesn't make any sense."

"What's the story here, Mom?" asked Lili.

Her mother had tears welling up at that point. She looked at her children and said, "Your father and I have grown apart. He and I agree there is no reason to drag you all into the details. That's not healthy for anyone, including your dad and me. You shouldn't worry about this changing your life. We aren't going to move. You'll be staying in the same school. Everything will be exactly the same except your dad won't be living here." She paused several times to regain her composure and even managed to give them a half-hearted smile.

Wally spoke up as their mother's voice trailed off. "You can spare me the happy speech, okay? If everything is so fine and dandy, then why are you about to start balling?"

Zach stared into Wally's eyes and said, "I've met someone. Your mom and I didn't want to say anything, because you all have nothing to do with our problems. You're all terrific and we love you."

Wally interrupted his father saying, "Yeah, you can spare me the pep talk too." Then he scaled the stairs and headed to his bedroom. The slamming of his door almost shook the house.

Bryn asked Claire what else they said after Wally left the conversation, but Claire couldn't remember many of the details. The words "met someone" were all Claire could recall verbatim. She said after Wally went to his room, her father had looked at the floor more than at them and didn't seem to say a whole lot.

Claire began to cry as she was telling the story. Her entire body was caving in. She was suddenly a whisper of a thing, all five feet, eight inches of her.

She told Bryn they had to physically restrain Wally when

their father retrieved his suitcase from the hallway closet and started to walk out the front door. Wally was yelling at their father, "You're so full of it. You act so honorable, but it's all about some young babe, isn't it? Right? Don't be such a liar." Claire said her father didn't respond. He walked toward his car without acknowledging what Wally had said, but that didn't stop Wally from ranting. He continued yelling out the open front door. "How old is she? Is this your midlife crisis? What is she like, 25 to your 55? Ten kids aren't enough for you? You want to get started on another batch with a younger model? You're a joke. You're a hypocrite—all your heart-to-hearts about treating women with respect and this is how you treat my mother!"

Mrs. Porter finally tugged at him to come back into the house and only then did he comply. Claire was proud of Wally. She figured he had said what everyone else wanted to, but they lacked his nerve. They all moped about the house after that. Claire's mom tried to engage them and reassure them once again, but they had all heard enough. Claire didn't want to talk. All she wanted was to shut down.

Bryn told Claire they would get back together and she shouldn't worry, but Claire rolled her eyes. She knew that wasn't true—Bryn hadn't been in the living room to see the look on her parent's faces.

Claire's father had morphed into a thief in the night—in his big black bag he dragged off their security and camaraderie and even how wonderful Claire had felt about a possible swim scholarship. Alone, her mother would never have the time to complete the necessary paperwork. Claire felt lost. Little bits and pieces of her world were escaping into the ether.

The father she loved so much wouldn't be at the supper table. He wouldn't be around to help with her NCSA profile or her scholarship applications and she wouldn't see him grab his bike in the morning and pedal off to the courthouse. The family life she had always depended on was blowing away, caught on the air like dust in the desert.

Claire thought about her odd, loving, anti-establishment dad who turned out to be no different than any other middle-aged creep. She told Bryn she hated this other woman and knew it was all her fault. She figured she'd thrown herself at her dad and wanted her to pay for it—she wished something dark and sinister would happen to her. Claire suggested she might be murdered in her sleep.

Bryn interjected. "Oh no, maybe stranded somewhere without food or water. Which is worse, dying of starvation or dehydration?"

"Oh, what about decompression? I read about it in science class. I don't know how we'd lure her into a decompression chamber or a space ship, but it would be worth a try."

Claire actually laughed at her own macabre joke and Bryn joined her. They sat quietly for a second, listening to the music as Bryn gently rubbed Claire's hand.

Against all reason, Claire was furious with her mother too. She didn't understand her not fighting for her husband and her marriage. "Twenty-eight years. That's how long they've been married and she just watches him go out the door. Are you kidding me? If he were into child pornography, wouldn't she do something to stop him? She can be such a wimp. Wally is almost as angry with her as he is with our father and I agree with him. How could she be so calm? They didn't meet yesterday and immediately decide to go off and live with one another. That's a major commitment. There had to be signs. Right? What a shit show!"

Bryn responded without conviction. "Gosh, Claire, I don't know. Your mom is pretty great."

"Well, not in this instance! I bet your mother would never stand for something like this. Sometimes I think my mother seems terrific because she's so nice to everyone and never really gets angry. My God, I think she'd open the door to this chick, give her a hug, ask her if she wanted something to drink and whether she'd eaten yet. *Hi honey, it's so nice to finally meet you. Have you eaten yet? I bet you're starving after screwing my husband all day and I've got some lovely oven-roasted chicken with winter vegetables.* UGH!"

Despite herself, Bryn laughed at Claire making fun of her mother, but said, "That's not so."

"Oh yeah? Name me one thing she's ever gotten angry about."

"Well, off the top of my head, I can't. I don't know. I'm not around her all the time."

"I'll give you a day to think about it and still dare you."

"Oh, Claire."

"I didn't mean to be funny. Never mind, it's all screwed up."

"I'm sure she's angry about your dad."

"That's just it. She doesn't seem angry. I'd like to think I'd be crazy, but she seems more...I don't know, withdrawn or even compliant. I'm sure she's in her room right now in a lotus position, telling herself that everything is the way it's supposed to be. I don't know. I don't know anything. I wonder if the girlfriend is pregnant? I wonder if that's why my mother is so docile."

Bryn's muscles began to feel stiff and sore and her bones ached, like they might break under the pressure of Claire's pain. Bryn had seen Judge Porter walk through the front door of the Porters' house a hundred times and he always smiled and greeted whoever was there. He looked a lot happier at home than the majority of people Bryn knew. He looked much happier than her parents ever did, except when they were on their way out of town. Bryn's father mostly looked exhausted. Bryn thought the Porters were happy. Everyone thought they were happy.

So maybe it was this other woman that made Zach Porter smile at everyone. Wally was right. Judge Porter didn't seem so honorable anymore. At best, he had cheated on his wife. At worst, he had abandoned her and their children, ten of them, four of them still in grade school. Bryn continued to console Claire. They managed to change the subject a couple of times, but after hours of sitting at Badger's, they parted with the agreement they would talk again first thing in the morning and Claire should call any time during the evening if she felt like venting.

Bryn's mother opened dinner that night with the news about the Porters. Apparently all the town criers knew and they were all so smart because they'd seen it coming. They gossiped at the speed of light through a prism.

Charlotte turned to Bryn and asked, "How is Claire doing with all of this?"

"About exactly like you think she'd be doing."

"Well I'm not familiar with the dynamic at the Porters', so I really don't know how she'd be doing, which is why I asked."

Bryn frowned and let her forehead rest on the kitchen table. She spoke into her placemat, "She's doing horribly. This came out of nowhere for her."

"From what I've heard, he has a girlfriend."

Bryn put her fingers in her mouth and faked a gag. "Really? You've heard that?"

"What? He doesn't have a girlfriend stashed away somewhere?"

Bryn clinched her fists and moaned.

"Don't be so melodramatic, Bryn. This did not happen to you. It happened to a different family."

"Yes, I know that, but they're like family. Claire is my family."

Charlotte slammed her fork on the table. "Oh really, Bryn? You have a wonderful life and a wonderful family. How many classmates have a car and a closet full of clothes and anything they want?"

"Yes, I have plenty of stuff. That's not what I'm talking about."

Richard chimed in saying that if Bryn wasn't happy with the stuff, he could take it away as fast as he had given it.

All Bryn could muster was, "Oh, never mind."

Claire cried herself to sleep for two weeks straight. She confided that she would sit in her room after finishing her homework and catch herself staring at her phone, waiting for it to ring. Hoping it would be her dad on the other end. When more often than not it turned out to be Bryn, she couldn't mask her disappointment. This other woman may not have taken her father's love for his children, but she took away his being there—the warm, physical presence. Claire wouldn't hear his groan from the den if the Packers were losing or see him at the kitchen table struggling to finish the New York Times crossword puzzle or watch him get frustrated trying to load the dishwasher after a full house was home for dinner. None of that was ever coming back.

Months later, Bryn noticed Claire replaced a family photo on the inside of her locker door with a picture of Bradley Cooper. When Bryn asked about it, Claire replied, "Can't bear to look at all of us together like that, looking happy, now that I know it was all a lie."

"Maybe it wasn't then. Things change."

"No, I think it was a lie then. The more I think about it, the more I think this thing he's got going on with some woman isn't all that new."

Charlotte told Richard she was headed to Chicago to see an old friend for a few days before the holidays began and everyone got too busy doing other things. Richard thought it was completely out of character for Charlotte to want to see anyone from her youth, but figured it was more about an opportunity to do some shopping in Chicago. She would be gone from the 9th through the 12th, which would give him a few days to get Christmas cards out to clients and hone his Christmas party speech for the rank and file. He was delighted.

Charlotte wheeled her overnight bag along the Hilton's entrance corridor, eyes fixed on a bank of house phones. "Mr. Accosi's room, please."

He picked up on the second ring. "I thought you'd never get here. I'm in 713."

The elevator couldn't move fast enough and when she finally got off, she could not make sense of the directional arrows off to the side. Had she ever been this flustered in all her life? She knocked softly on the door and Mike answered. He was smiling, wearing a bathrobe and reaching his hand out to guide her into the room.

"I hit terrible traffic about an hour outside the city."

"As long as you're here, it's fine."

They kissed and he led her to the bed, which was strewn with newspapers and other paper. He apologized for the mess and hurriedly made a stack that he moved to a table by the window. He undressed her slowly, taking her in inch-by-inch and kissing her softly, first on her mouth and then her chin and then her neck, making his way down her belly. He whispered that it gave him great pleasure to please her. She nibbled his earlobe and told him he had learned a great deal in his years and thanked his many ex-wives. Charlotte knew she wanted Mike in her life and more than anything she wanted change. The want was palpable, but she would not behave like a schoolgirl. She had made that mistake once before and she wouldn't make it again. She would put herself first, despite all the coaxing from Mike, and she explained that as gently as possible, without hurting his feelings. They agreed to meet at least once a month over the next six months and see where they stood. Mike assured her he wouldn't change his mind no matter how much time passed, but she reminded him of their first meeting, when he had told her he wasn't much of a success at relationships.

"Okay, we'll take it at your pace. For now, you hungry?"

"I'm starving."

They dressed quickly in the hope of getting into town in time to snag a table at The Palm and some jazz at M.

Winter

"Claire, do you think you could get us invited to Wally's Christmas party?"

"He really doesn't want anyone except classmates and people his age, and I have a hard time talking to him these days. He's so angry all the time. Well, I guess we're all angry all the time. He wanted to call it off, but my mom said no way. Too much prep and money spent on food."

"It sucks that we're not invited. We hang out all the time together and then it comes to something fun and he doesn't want us around."

"That's not exactly true. I think he feels he has to cut it off somewhere. If he lets us come, then what's to keep the rest of the hoards from coming? My little sister will wind up with a handful of sixth graders getting in the way. Why do you care about Wally's stupid party anyway?"

"Chris will be there."

"What ever happened to taking my advice, storing it and putting it in a cloud file? Besides, he'll be there with Olivia. Are you trying to punish yourself?"

"No, I've been doing some intel and she's gone for the holidays. Apparently there are close relations in Terre Haute. Very cosmopolitan of her to have relatives in the pork processing center of America."

"Let's not be snooty about cosmopolitan upbringing, shall we?"

"Good point. I just want to see him before Christmas."
"Why?"

"I don't want to sit idly by. After the play... I don't know. I've wanted to talk to him. You're the one who said things may have changed."

Claire grabbed Bryn by the upper arms and shook her a little. "I'm also the one who said to play it cool. Ugh! Okay, I'll ask, but don't count on anything and don't blame me if it doesn't turn out well."

"I will have no one to blame but myself."

When Claire came back to Bryn with a solid "no," she called Wally and when she got the same answer, she appealed to Midnight to ask and finally got an "OK." Wally wasn't happy, and Bryn felt bad about that, but she was pleased that her nagging finally got her an invite. Wally wouldn't stay mad for long.

Bryn hopped in her car and headed for the Porters' house. It was 7:20. She planned on being there at 7:30. Thirty fashionable minutes late. She was preoccupied by how she envisioned the night going, some combination of a real-life variation on a Jane Austin novel and romcom. She was nervous and combined with her preoccupation, she nearly ran into the back of a BMW SUV stopped at a red light. The driver looked into his rearview mirror and glared at Bryn. She didn't blame him. She'd have to pull herself together.

She found a parking spot four houses down from the Porters'. Over the course of the short walk, her nerves began to rattle again, and despite a December temperature hovering around 35 degrees, she was sweating a little.

Seconds through the Porters' front door and she saw Chris a few yards away, leaning against a dining room breakfront. She couldn't hesitate or she might lose her nerve, so she walked directly to him and said, "Hey, how are you? Can I talk to you for a sec?"

"I guess."

"Not very enthusiastic."

"I feel kind of talked out."

"Certainly not because of me. We haven't talked since the school play. Let's go up to Claire's room. She won't mind. It's nice and quiet up there compared to down here."

"Okay."

Bryn took his hand, leading him to Claire's attic room. They sat on the floor and talked about school and of course football. She asked him every mundane thing she could think of while she mustered the nerve to ask him what happened. Why had he dumped her, running back to Olivia? She told him how humiliated she was the day she ran into them at MoJoe's. He responded by telling Bryn he thought she was great, but was too serious about him—that feeling started back when he was looking at schools. She shook her head and rolled her eyes.

"What did you think was going to happen when we started sleeping together? Was I not supposed to take that seriously?"

He touched her knee and told her that of course she should take that seriously, but she pushed his hand away. He leaned in to kiss her and she didn't push him away. She knew he still cared about her. She and Claire were right about everything— showing up at the play and coming to her house. Breaking from their kiss she said, "See, this is what kind of confuses me. You show up at the play and you continue to flirt with me—a smile, a touch, a kiss. You hold on, then you push back, but you never really exit my life. It's all hard to read."

Chris got up off the floor and walked toward the bedroom door. He looked like he was blushing. "I was just trying to console you. I have to get going."

"Console me about what?"

"I have to get home. I have some stuff to do."

"Right now? It can't even be eight o'clock."

"Yeah I know, but I have some stuff to do for my dad and you know how he can be. I'll call you."

"See that's what I mean. You haven't called me in months. Why would you start now?"

"Look, I like you. I don't want to stop being your friend."

Bryn looked Chris in the eye and said "Chris we were never friends."

"Well then stop following me around and showing up everywhere uninvited."

"Fine, but so you know, this was typical of what I mean. And PS, no one invited you to the play."

Chris left and Bryn sat there for a couple minutes. When she decided to leave, she didn't pay much attention to how she looked as she descended from the attic bedroom. She saw Midnight. He looked at her like she was missing a piece of clothing.

He came toward her and gently touched her sleeve. "What the hell happened to you?"

"What do you mean?"

"You look like you're playing left tackle. You've got black makeup streaks under your eyes."

Bryn ran her index fingers along her lower eyelids. "Oh, I was rubbing my eyes, allergies."

"In December?"

"Yeah, I guess."

"Hold up. What happened?"

Bryn leaned against the stairwell wall. "Nothing, I had yet another thing with Chris. Ask a direct question and you get some ridiculous answer."

"Bryn, will you stay away from that guy? He's not good for you. He's a two-faced jerk."

"What would you know about it?"

"I've known him a long time and I'm just saying he can be a real jerk."

"Really? You think so?"

"You don't have to be sarcastic."

Bryn looked at her cell. "I have to get home."

"Do you want me to take you?"

"No, I've got my car."

"Well, someday I'll tell you the full scoop on Bello."

She flew through the front door of her house and into her bedroom, pulled off her clothes and put on a pair of warm flannel pajamas. She shook all over from the cold. She stared at the ceiling and thought about Chris. He drove her so crazy, but she still missed him. Nothing changed that and she thought hard about what she actually did miss. There were so many things: that he truly loved his mother, that his feelings got hurt easily, that he had the slightest cowlick over his right ear, that he sang off key, but more than anything it was the way he held her. There was nothing half-hearted. It felt like he held on for dear life—like he was hugging her for the last time. Exactly the way she held on to him.

Her cell rang and the caller ID displayed Midnight's

name. She was going to push him to voicemail, but decided to answer.

"Hey, what's up?"

"So what happened with you and Bello?"

With a sigh, Bryn said, "I don't really want to talk about it. It's not worth it."

"All right. I'm concerned, that's all."

"That's nice, but I'm okay. What ever happened between the two of you anyway? Why do you dislike him so much?"

"You mean besides treating you like crap."

"Yes, Mid, besides that, which you know zero about."

"It's going to sound stupid coming out, but Wally and I were pretty tight with Chris. When we went to high school and Wally went to St. Agnes and Chris and I went to West, he completely ignored me. He wrote me off as nerdy while he tried out and made the junior varsity football team. Once that happened he acted like I had Ebola."

"That doesn't sound like him."

"Well, it is. That's what happened. I always cut him some slack because of his mom, but he didn't want to hang out if it was just me. No big shit for me. Then one day I overheard him and some football Neanderthals talking about me behind my back. They were sitting in the cafeteria and I guess they didn't see me in line, or maybe they did. It doesn't matter, but it was Bello telling this guy how he thought I was weird and a geek and probably didn't like girls and all sorts of 'jock boy' crap. Whatever, that was it for me. I really never talked to him again as a friend."

"Him thinking you were gay upset you that much?"

"No, I could give a shit about what he said. It was about

him talking behind my back in the first place."

"Well, I guess everybody can't like everybody."

"That's true, but it pissed me off and I figured I wouldn't spend any more time trying to be his friend."

Bryn paused and thought for a moment. "Fair enough."

"Moving on, do you want to come by Wednesday and have supper with us? I'm going to ask Wally and Claire too."

The thought of dinner seemed kind of boring, but Midnight had said "us," which would imply Mr. Wright might be home, which would cheer her up. Mr. Wright was funny and interesting and looked like he and some handsome mega-star were separated at birth. She was also longing to ask Midnight more about Chris. She responded with a relatively enthusiastic "yes," which caught Midnight by surprise. He hesitated before he said, "Great, see you Wednesday around six."

Bryn called Claire to recap the evening and before Bryn could say very much, Claire asked, "Did you have sex with him?"

"No, we didn't, but he did kiss me."

"Did he kiss you or did you kiss him?"

"Are you angry with me for some reason?"

"You completely invented this reason to see him, despite my, and I think everyone's advice to ease off the pedal. Typically, he responds enough to give you hope that there's some connection and you go through all the motions again. I think it's all going to lead to you getting your heart broken, yet again. Let's drop it for now. See you at the Wrights'."

Bryn took a deep breath taking in what Claire had said. "But you were the one who said he probably still liked me."

"And you were the one who said you were going to play it cool."

"Let's drop it, all right? Don't be mad."

Claire leaned against her bed and took a long pause. "I'm not mad, but I think you're shamefully stupid."

"And that's a rotten thing to say. I am not stupid—far from it."

"I'm sorry. I know you're not stupid. I'm just angry with you for still liking him."

"But why? Why does it bother you so much?"

"I guess because I don't think you're dim and this infatuation with him makes you look it."

Bryn was getting upset. "And what about Midnight, Claire? Just because I'm the only one who knows about how you feel, doesn't mean you're moving on with your life at any rapid pace. If you ask me, my approach is more sincere."

"Sincere and stupid."

Claire hung up the phone without saying goodbye or goodnight. Bryn set her phone on her bed in front of her and with the speaker button still on said, "I love you anyway, Claire."

Bryn was sorely disappointed when it was the four of them at dinner, no Mr. Wright. She wished immediately she hadn't said yes. They talked over plates of roast beef from Christmas, chicken from the night before and a variety of vegetables, but the conversation was strained. They talked about the remainder of the Christmas holiday, things to do when school resumed, unwanted gifts from aunts and grandparents—all pedestrian. Midnight's kooky presents always topped everyone else's. He had three aging aunts, sisters to his mother who lived in Bend, Oregon, Pittsburgh and Joshua Tree, California. There was always a bounty of hand-knitted socks, edible arrangements, pounds of peanut brittle, 6-foot scarves and other useless gifts.

Wally was laughing to the point of tears, but Bryn couldn't get into the spirit of it and got up to use the powder room. When she returned, they were all talking about her and Chris. Claire didn't sound like herself. Her tone was nasty and mean spirited and Wally and Midnight seemed to be lapping it up.

Bryn stood there with her hands on her hips and said, "If you want to talk about me, I'd prefer you do it to my face."

She had never been really angry with any of them until that moment. Bryn sat through the rest of their supper with nothing to say despite Midnight trying to start a number of conversations. Telling him she wasn't feeling very well, she begged off some NFL recap, which began to depress her for a number of reasons. She didn't say goodbye or goodnight and vowed to stay away from the three of them until they apologized for talking so nastily behind her back. Midnight in particular had a lot of nerve, given his reason for not liking Chris. Hypocrite.

School had been back in session for a week and Midnight did a good job of avoiding Chris, but he couldn't take it anymore when he did see him in the locker room after gym class. Chris was laughing and joking with some guy. Midnight came within an inch of his face. Chris took a poke at Midnight's chest and said, "What's your problem, man? Get out of my face."

Midnight stood his ground. "What is my problem? You have got to be kidding me."

"Whatever the problem is about, I'm sure it's none of your business."

"Then you know what it's about."

Chris rolled his eyes and threw his hands in the air. "Well, let's see. I'm guessing it's about Bryn. What happens between Bryn and me is between Bryn and me."

"You need to be truthful with her."

"Screw you, Midnight. You don't know anything about it."

"I know you have a girlfriend."

"And?"

"And I think you need to have a conversation with your ex-girlfriend about that."

"Mind your own business, Midnight."

"Bryn is my business."

Chris smirked. "Since when? I asked her point blank after her play if she was dating you and she said no. Does it bother you so much that she likes me and not you?"

"Screw you. I'm just into being decent with people. You should try it."

The basketball coach walked in and said, "Is there a problem in here, gentlemen?"

Chris quickly responded, "No, there's no problem. We're just talking."

The coach stood tall and in a firm voice said, "Things look a little tense for 'just talking.' Why don't you get your stuff together and get to class or wherever you're supposed to be."

Midnight walked into his English lit class texting Bryn *411, CB decided 2go2 La Crosse.* As he pressed the send button he regretted it, but he wanted to hurt her. He knew the message would do that, not because she didn't suspect Chris had cooled on the idea of Madison, but because the news about his choosing La Crosse wasn't coming from Chris himself.

The argument in the locker room hung heavy in Midnight's mind. He was proud he confronted Chris. It took nerve calling him to the mat—Chris owed Bryn a conversation. Bello actually looked a little nervous, which was particularly gratifying for Midnight, but why was he so angry with him in the first place? In part he was angry with himself. He and Claire and Wally got caught talking behind Bryn's back and the talk was not nice. He knew Bryn was still angry with them. He also knew that Chris did nothing to dissuade Bryn—showing up at her play was lame and then there was the kiss at the Christmas party. Claire told him all about it. No wonder Bryn held out hope they'd get back together. But at the heart of it, Chris was right. Midnight was jealous of the idea of her wanting Chris and not him. He thought about that kiss again. It was taking on epic proportions in his imaginings and it made him nauseous. Bryn wasn't so crazy to see Chris still cared for her, but he didn't want to hear about it anymore. He didn't want to overhear her discussions with Claire or even think about her being with him. And that's why he was angry. All he ever wanted to hear was "it's over," and that never came from her. Time and again she worked her way in to being around Chris, and time and time again it left her confused and hopeful. Midnight couldn't understand what she saw in the guy. For that matter, what did Olivia see in him? She seemed like a sensible girl. Bello wasn't bad looking, but he certainly wasn't great looking, and he played football but he was no star athlete and he certainly wasn't that clever.

His English teacher's voice made him jump. "Mr. Wright? I'll ask you again. What does the green light at the end of the pier symbolize to Gatsby?"

"What? Sorry, Mr. Klein, I wasn't listening."

"Anyone else want to take a stab at it? I don't seem to have Mr. Wright's attention today."

Midnight didn't respond. All he could manage was writing down the reading assignment for that night. He rolled his eyes to the heavens when the bell rang. God, he was Jay Gatsby, pining after a Daisy who never materialized. "...So we beat on, boats against the current, borne back ceaselessly into the past...."

Mr. Klein called out to him to wait a moment as he headed for the door.

"So, what's up with you? I thought you enjoyed this class."

"It's great, Mr. Klein. It's one of my best classes and I really like the reading assignments, but I've got something else on my mind."

"Anything I or anyone else should know about?"

"No, I'm good. Just girl trouble."

"Ah, I'm sure you'll be able to work it out."

"Yeah, I'm sure I will. See you tomorrow. I'll come better prepared."

Chris disliked Midnight. He thought he was conceited for no good reason. Ever since they went to West. Midnight had never been happy about Chris's achievements, like the football team, but was expected to sing Midnight's praises about boring stuff like being the only freshman on the debate team and making great grades. But what Midnight said about Bryn in the locker room made him feel bad and he was determined to call her to apologize for abruptly leaving the party. It was lame. He should have been candid with her right then. He liked Bryn, but he shouldn't be leading her on because he really liked Olivia too. They had been making plans together, including toying with the idea of going to La Crosse together. He was royally pissed off at Midnight for sticking his nose in, but Midnight had been right. It was time to clear up a lot with Bryn.

He thought she'd be pleased for the phone call, but her first words were, "I can't believe you've decided on La Crosse over Madison."

"I decided a while back."

"I still thought we both might go there."

"Doesn't look like it. Who told you, anyway?"

"You and Midnight do go to the same school, you know."

"Man, that guy can't stay out of my business."

"I guess."

"Look, I don't want to get into a long talk about college. It's not why I called. I want to talk about the night at Porter's house and some other stuff I want to be clear about. I thought maybe we could meet up for coffee—just coffee though. I don't want you to read anything into it."

"When?"

"How about this Saturday? Maybe Nostalgia? I like that place."

Without a moment of hesitation or a quick check of her calendar, she said, "Okay, I'll see you Saturday."

As she sat on her bedroom floor thinking about seeing Chris, her phone buzzed. It was Claire. She considered sending her right back to the wireless ether. She was still stung by Claire's nasty gossiping with Midnight and Wally, but she couldn't resist telling Claire the news that she and Chris were meeting for coffee that coming Saturday.

Claire began, "I'm glad you picked up. I take it you're not mad anymore."

"Well I'm still kind of mad."

"But not as much?"

"No, I guess not, and guess what?"

"What?"

"Chris invited me to meet him for coffee this coming Saturday."

"That's interesting. What do you think brought that on?"

"Well, he called saying he thought we should talk about the night at your house and some other stuff that's on his mind."

"An apology would be a good start for leaving you hanging and then from there, who knows."

"Maybe that's what he intends to do."

"Maybe."

"What if he wants to get back together?"

"I don't know, let's not get too crazy. I don't want you to

get your hopes up. One thing for sure, I'd try to stop giving Olivia the weapons she needs to hold on to him. Your clinging makes her look very good. The crazier you look, the sweeter she becomes. Try to be cool, well cooler."

"Thanks a lot."

"You know what I mean. I know it is super hard, but try to be a little distant. Oh my God, I have to go. I've got about three hours of reading in front of me. Bryn, I didn't mean to hurt your feelings at Midnight's house. I'm sorry. You know how much I care about you. I really called to say I was sorry, again."

"Thanks. All I can say is I still miss him. I know it's been months, but I can't help the way I feel and I'm not going to minimize my feelings. I've never believed we should give up on each other. I felt, no we felt, like we made a difference in one another's lives. At least that's what we told one another. Does that sound really corny?"

"No, I think it's kind of sweet, and for what it's worth, I'd never minimize how you feel about anything. It's terrible that things didn't or aren't going well with Chris and you. I wish more than anything you didn't have to deal with this, that you were never hurt. All I want is for you to be happy, and happy with Chris if that's really what you want. I swear. I hope things go beyond terrific on Saturday."

Bryn sat and stared at the front of her phone. She swiped through her apps and thought about meeting Chris on Saturday. She'd have to think about what she was going to say. She knew she wanted to get back together. That was the easy part, but how could she justify that after all that had happened? One thing was clear. Before she met Chris she was apprehensive and uneasy—she waited for something bad to happen. Chris made her feel good about what might be around the corner. Was it wrong to want to feel that way and rely on someone else to make you feel good about the day ahead? It didn't seem like such a crime when you couldn't muster the confidence on your own. How many articles had she read about being self-assured? The articles usually quoted rock stars and super models. She could Google her way through a million references and not come up with quotable teenagers who were completely inconsequential and unattractive.

Saturday came and Bryn headed to Nostalgia where she and Chris decided to meet. She sat in her car outside the restaurant willing it to go well. She intended to be candid. His signals were confusing, but she still wanted nothing more than the two of them to get back together. She could overlook some of his miscues and duplicity. She had wanted this small coffee date to be their reconciliation. She checked her lipstick in her rearview mirror one last time and then headed into the coffee shop. She barely had a chance to say hello before Chris started to talk about Olivia and on the slippery slope of bad days, Bryn was in Navy SEAL gear, repelling downhill face-first. He gave her a litany of the wonderful qualities Olivia possessed, how unfair Bryn's perception was, how they probably shouldn't have gotten so serious so quickly over the summer, but that he still wanted her to be his friend. Finally, he got around to asking Bryn how she was doing and then promptly asked for the check. Bryn hadn't said very much—didn't even finish her coffee. What was she suppose to say? She took him at his word that Olivia was fabulous and had little to add to the conversation. He walked her to her car and hugged her goodbye.

Two minutes after walking through the front door, Claire was calling her.

"So, how did it go?"

"Did you know that Olivia has an Olympic medal and she's a Ford model and is related to Gisele on her mother's side?"

"What? What are you talking about? You're kidding, right?"

"Of course I'm kidding."

"Where is all this coming from?"

"Oh, nothing. It's just that we spent the majority of the time not talking about us, but talking about Olivia. From Chris's lips, it sounds like she's nothing short of miraculous."

"You're the superstar. He should be with you."

"Yeah, well. That doesn't seem to be happening."

"She really isn't that great. I know her a little from the Y and she's kind of a jerk. We should think up some way to get you and Chris together and in front of her. Maybe she'll break up with him."

"You are so wonderful and smart. I am open to all your suggestions."

"I'll put my thinking cap on."

"Hey, on a totally different topic, have you seen Midnight at all? I feel like I haven't seen him since we all had supper at his house. I hope he knows I wouldn't stay mad at him or Wally."

"Of course I've seen him. It's like he lives here, which on one hand is fabulous, but on the other hand, drives me crazy. Why do you ask?"

"No particular reason. I was wondering, that's all. Hey, how's that coming along, by the way?"

"I can't imagine he's oblivious to me liking him, but I don't know. Maybe he is. I feel like I've shown a million different signs. I'm always asking him if he wants anything else when he's here for supper or when we're watching television and he comes in I always move over and tell him I saved him a seat. Now I think I'm going to sit back and kind of admire him and hope that he will see it."

"The suffer-in-silence plan?"

"Better than the in-your-face, nothing-could-be-more-obvious plan."

"Yeah, yeah. I'll see you tomorrow."

"Hey, Bryn?"

"Yeah."

"I really do wish things were different for you, more than you know or I let on sometimes. I know I can sound insensitive or sarcastic, but I completely understand how you feel about Chris. I guess I just don't want to see you hurt anymore."

Bryn's voice was barely a whisper. "I don't want to see that either. I don't like to see anyone hurt. I wouldn't want to see Olivia in pain, but I know she's not right for him."

"It's too bad they don't have some kind of midterm exam that tests characteristics like sincerity and loyalty and the things that really matter."

"The challenge with that, is the people who are the most insincere would probably lie on the test."

Midnight was up at seven lying in his bed thinking about the afternoon to come. He'd take his chances she'd be free to go to the art festival with him. First, he would ask his dad if he could borrow his car. His father drove a brand-new Mercedes-Benz. It was gunmetal grey with a black interior. There was so much interior leather it smelled like a horse's saddle. The car was a million times nicer than his mom's and it was certainly more befitting of a date. He wanted the day to be special. He'd have to position borrowing the car just right. After all, if he owned that car, he wouldn't let anyone borrow it, especially a teenage son who spent a quarter of his life being grounded. He weighed his options and decided on the direct approach. He would tell him he was planning to take Bryn out—on an actual date. He'd had enough of sitting around and watching her chase Chris. His dad was a softie. He'd understand the need to make a good impression, and if Bryn wasn't free, his dad would welcome the car staying in the garage—no harm, no foul.

He would call Bryn and ask her if she was interested in going to the winter art festival. It always sounded pretty lame even though it was a cool event, highlighting the work of local painters, sculptors and artisans, and she loved art. She carried her sketchbook around a lot and he remembered she had won a school contest a couple years back that she was particularly proud of. As always, she would ask if Wally and Claire were joining them. He would tell her "no" saying they had other plans for the day and he'd pick her up at noon. They would drive to the university auditorium, where the event was held, and even though it was pretty cold outside, he'd suggest they go for a walk around the campus to catch up. He would hold her hand as they made their way around the perimeter. Then they'd head inside and critique some of the work and go to Lila's to get something to eat. The upscale restaurant was directly across the street from the main entrance of the university. He'd make sure they were seated at a secluded booth and while they were enjoying their lunch he would kiss her and damn it she would kiss him back. He would exude confidence—bold as Beckham and cool as Clooney.

It seemed like a solid plan until he realized Bryn wouldn't consider it a date, whether he did or not. He would sound like a complete jerk if he actually told her it was a date and not just hanging out for the day—and they had hung out for the day together a hundred different times. He was agonizing over a day she wouldn't give a second thought to.

He lay there musing to the walls—*damn, damn, damn Chris Bello. Why did he ever have to come into Bryn's life? He's like a tumor growing on her. He keeps getting bigger and bigger. He's becoming a damn urban legend.*

He threw back the covers and decided to have breakfast and get outside and play some hoops. There was always a group of guys ready to pick up a game at the school's outdoor court. He'd get out some frustration on the court for a few hours, then come home, take a shower, call Bryn and pick her up by noon.

Hoops sucked. He couldn't relax enough to have any fun and decided to come home after less than an hour on the court.

As he showered, he felt better. The day was going to be fun. He convinced himself all Bryn needed was a little push in the right direction. First thing out of the shower, he'd get the car from his dad, but getting the Mercedes outside of an emergency was going to be tough. But in a way, this was an emergency. It was time he started making an impression.

Midnight approached his father. "Hey, Dad, can I ask you a big favor?"

"Sure. What is it?'

"Can I borrow your car for the afternoon. I want to take Bryn Wilson to the art festival."

With no response, Midnight continued, "We're going to maybe walk around campus a little and look at the exhibits and probably get something to eat. You know, hang around and stuff."

"I don't know, Jon, why don't you take your mother's car?"

"Because it's junkie and I want to kind of take her out in style."

"I don't think so, Jon."

"Come on, Dad. Please. I'd like to make a good impression."

Smiling at him, his father said, "Jon, just this once you can borrow my car, but I don't think it's going to make a great deal of difference with Bryn. I don't see her thinking a car is that big a deal."

"Thanks, Dad. She may not see it as impressive, but it'll help me."

"You know son, you are a terrific young man. You're smart and funny and considerate, and you're a good-looking guy. I'm not sure if this girl is capable of seeing any of those things about you."

"I have to give it a shot."

Gently patting the back of Midnight's head, his father

said, "And I applaud that in you. I hope the car can help."

"Thanks, Dad. I mean it, really, thanks."

"By the way, no eating or beverages in the car."

"No worries, we won't eat in the car. I think I'm going to spring for Lila's."

"Wow. Can I come along?"

"Very funny."

He took two steps at a time as he bounded toward his bedroom to call Bryn. She answered on the second ring and without hesitation said she'd like to get out for a while. The art festival seemed just the ticket. She had thought about going by herself earlier in the week, so this was a pleasant surprise.

Once he hung up the phone, he shouted to the same walls which hours earlier, he had been swearing at. "She actually said yes. This is going to be great. She actually said yes!"

Midnight knocked on the Wilsons' front door for some time before Bryn's mother answered.

"Hi Jon. Why didn't you ring? I barely heard you."

"I have no idea. I guess I'm a little nervous."

"What in the world do you have to be nervous about?"

"Nothing. I guess I was lost in thought. Is Bryn here? I mean, is she ready?"

She smiled flirtatiously. "You do sound nervous." Her look made him blush.

Bryn coming down the stairs put a smile back on his face. She looked so pretty. She had on washed-out jeans and running shoes with a green comic-style Wolverine T-shirt and yellow sweater that matched Wolverine's chest patch. He wasn't sure what he liked about the outfit, but she looked sporty and pretty at the same time.

"Hey, Midnight."

"Hey. You ready to go?"

"Yeah. Let me grab my coat." Looking at Midnight, she asked, "What time do you think we'll be back?"

"I don't know. Late afternoon or early evening?"

Charlotte replied, "Have fun, but not too much fun, if you know what I mean."

Midnight replied, "We will. Thanks."

He opened the passenger side of the car for Bryn to get in and she said, "God I hate when she says stuff like that."

"Parents always think they're funnier than they are. My dad is the greatest, but there are some things he thinks are funny and they're not even on the same planet as funny."

"You're acting weird. Why are you so formal, opening my door and everything?"

"I'm not acting weird. I'm opening the car door for you. I'm being polite."

Bryn shrugged her shoulders. "All right. No big deal. Thank you."

"You're welcome. So, let's go."

"We're taking your dad's car instead of your mom's? I feel very special."

"Yeah, my mom needed hers today and Dad said it was okay."

"We could have taken my car or even walked."

"No. I wanted to drive and it's too cold out."

As they drove to the university Bryn breathed in the pleasant scent in the car. It smelled like oranges or lemons and some kind of spice. It was Midnight. He was wearing aftershave lotion. She smiled to herself picturing Midnight splashing on a dab of aftershave. She couldn't imagine him shaving. His skin was smooth and clear and there wasn't a hint of stubble.

They got out of the car and decided to stroll around campus before doing anything else.

The sidewalk surrounding the commons was broken and cracked. The roots of hundred-year-old oak trees had won the battle with the concrete long before. Bryn stumbled on a deep crack as they walked along the perimeter and Midnight grabbed for her hand to keep her from falling. He was relieved she hadn't jerked her hand away, but a few seconds later she said, "It's making my hand sweaty. Sorry." She released her grip, suggesting they go see some of the exhibit before it got too late.

They entered the auditorium. There were paintings and crafts everywhere. There wasn't an open piece of wall space. It was overwhelming, but Midnight commented on how great it was to have so many local artists and Bryn agreed as she drifted along one particular section. Then one painting caught her eye. It was a café or trattoria on a small street. There were no customers at the outdoor tables and a soft moon hovered above, but the colors of the trattoria were not the colors of night. The painting was fat with reds and yellows and greens—the restaurant's awning, seat cushions, empty wine bottles. She read the placard adjacent to the piece and stared at the artist's signature. Bryn grabbed for Midnight's hand and said, "God, it's beautiful, isn't it?"

"Yes, it really is. I wonder how long something like that takes? It has to be six square feet. I could never spend that much time on any one thing. I don't have the attention span."

"That's not true. You're totally focused on whatever you do."

"Thanks, I think."

Bryn continued to stare at the painting, but said, "Hey, I'm hungry. Want to get something to eat?"

"I was thinking about going across the street to Lila's."

"Fancy. You sure?"

"Yeah, completely my treat. It's a great place and close by, so if we decide to go back in, we can."

Bryn looked down for a moment and then said, "I think I'd like to see more. I feel like I spent a lot of time in this one place."

"But that's cool."

"Oh, it's totally cool. We weren't meant to follow a map, right?"

Midnight entwined his arm in Bryn's. "No, I completely gave in to this one section too. There was so much to look at and I didn't want to miss anything, so I kind of went frame by frame. You know what I mean?"

Smiling wide at him, she said, "And you think you lack focus?"

They walked arm in arm out of the auditorium and across the street to the restaurant. Seated at the window, they talked about many things. There was never a time Bryn hadn't asked how his dad was, so they got that off the list quickly and moved on to other topics. Midnight mentioned they hadn't seen one another in a while. He smiled on the inside when she confessed she had noticed that as well and had asked Claire if she had seen him around. They talked about the day and the tremendous extent of the show. He thought about bringing up the night of the dinner at his house, but since Bryn hadn't, he thought it might be better to just let it die. Instead he told her he received his acceptance letter from UW, along with a small scholarship provision from the Department of English. Bryn was openly excited for him and they talked through lunch about his going to Madison in the fall, all the exciting things to do and classes to take. He fell in love with her all over again. He had been so angry with her about Chris, but it melted as she genuinely, excitedly shared in his happy news.

Bryn was smiling wide and looking out toward the university's tree-lined entryway.

"Isn't that Claire?"

Midnight was about to be caught in a lie and his brain raced to figure a way to spin it. Please, God, don't let this day get ruined. "I don't think that's her."

"Yes, it is." Bryn began to wave and knock on the glass. Midnight had about fifteen yards of space and a solid DON'T WALK sign to think of what to say.

As Claire got closer she waved and then stood next to Lila's front window, mouthing, "What are you two doing here?"

Bryn replied, "Come in, come in."

As Claire headed toward the booth, Bryn instinctively scooted over to make room.

She asked, "Why aren't you at your grandmother's?"

Claire squinted her eyes and shook her head quickly from side to side. "What? Should I be?"

Bryn looked at Midnight and he said, "Wally told me you guys were going to be at your grandma's today."

"That's a weird thing for him to say, especially since he's working all day."

Midnight eyed the vaulted ceiling saying, "Huh, that is weird. Maybe he got the time mixed up."

Claire looked up trying to figure out what Midnight was looking at. "He's pretty tuned in about his schedule."

"Weird. I'll remember to ask him about it later. For now, why don't you join us? I'll go grab you a menu."

Claire looked around the room. "No, it's way too expensive and it looks like you two are finished."

Midnight felt a little wobbly and excused himself to the men's room.

Claire began immediately, "So what are the two of you doing here?"

"We came for the art festival."

Claire moved in her seat to face Bryn. "Just the two of you?"

"Well, now the three of us."

"I'm sure the two of you don't want me around."

"Don't be crazy. You are totally invited along. You heard Midnight. He wants you to get something to eat. He thought you were at your grandmother's."

"That sounded completely made up."

"Why would Midnight ever make that up?"

"To be alone with you."

Bryn rolled her eyes. "That's crazy."

"Not so crazy."

"Shh, he's coming and if you don't stay then I'm not staying either. Actually, this is a great opportunity for you to spend time alone with him. Midnight wants dessert, so we'll let him order, but when it comes I'll look at my phone and say 'oh my God, I have to go' and then he can drive you home."

"Not sure it's a great idea."

"It's a fabulous idea."

Claire squeezed Bryn's knee. "Okay, that's the plan then?"

"Yes, that's the plan."

As their waitress headed toward the table bearing Midnight's pumpkin cheesecake, Bryn said she had to get going. Midnight offered to wrap up the cheesecake to go and drive them both home, but Bryn insisted he and Claire should stay. After all, Claire hadn't seen any of the art show and he should go back in with her. With some protest about Bryn leaving, Midnight finally agreed. Bryn thanked him for lunch, congratulated him again on the news from UW and walked off. She smiled as she strolled along University Avenue, thinking about her plot and how happy it would make Claire to spend some time alone with Midnight. He was right, it was cold and she pulled her coat tight around her, but she would have frozen to death to give Claire the time with him.

As Claire and Midnight walked inside the auditorium together, Claire began to ask Midnight questions about school and his family and then suddenly asked, "So, you really thought Wally and I were at our grandma's house?"

There was a long pause before Midnight began, "I thought Wally said something like that. I guess I should have made sure, but sometimes it's nice to do things without the group, you know?"

"So Wally and I are a group now?"

"No, I didn't mean it like that. You know that."

"Hey, Mid, there's something I want to say to you."

"Shoot."

The pause was long, but Claire finally said it, "I really like you."

"I like you too, Claire. I always have."

"I mean I really like you."

Smiling, Midnight said, "Aw, I'm flattered. You're like the kid sister I never had and I really like you too."

Midnight's head was swimming. Could he be hearing this? He felt nothing for Claire and Wally would smack the shit out of him if he did feel something. He needed Claire to stop talking, even thinking about liking him. He quickly said, "You guys are all like family to me."

Claire paused and looked down at the terrazzo floor. "Yeah, you're like family to us too. Hey, do you mind if we go home now?"

Midnight was surprised, but grateful. "You're absolutely sure you don't want to see more?"

"Not really. I kind of feel like going home."

"Let's go out the east side exit. I want one more look at this painting Bryn and I admired so much. You know, every year I think this is going to be shabby, but then it winds up being pretty great."

"Yeah, I guess so. Let's go look at Bryn's painting."

Midnight talked about how beautiful the play of light was and how the colors were so breathtaking, but Claire didn't think it was that hot and reminded Midnight they were going to head home. They got in Mr. Wright's car and talked very little. The silence between them was uncomfortable, so Midnight tried to make conversation. "So, what are you doing the rest of the weekend?"

"Not really sure. I may go to the Y and get some laps in."

"Sounds good."

"Yeah, I'm trying to get a swim scholarship. I have to get in all the pool time I can."

"You're really trying for a scholarship?"

Claire had been staring out the window, but shifted to her left and stared at Midnight. "What, you think I couldn't qualify?"

"I didn't mean it that way."

"It sounded that way."

"You're being overly sensitive."

They drove the remaining blocks in complete silence. As they pulled into the Porter driveway, she said, "I'm sorry I'm being weird. Seeing you with Bryn in the restaurant threw me. She tells me everything and she didn't tell me you two were going out."

"Well, we're not going out in the way I think you mean. We went to the festival together and that's pretty much it." Even he heard the strain in his voice and he suddenly felt spent.

"Oh never mind. It's all good. Do you want to have supper with us later? We're eating around seven. I'm sure it would be okay with Mom. We're having chicken pasta."

"Thanks, but I don't think so. Have a good night."

"You sure?"

"Yeah, I have to get the car home and I had that huge lunch."

Midnight pulled the car out of her driveway, shaking his head about the day. What a disaster! He'd have to tell Wally to cover for him about the grandma thing if Bryn or Claire ever asked. He slammed the front door of his own house and headed upstairs toward his room, but stopped as his father said, "You're home awfully early. Is everything all right? There's nothing wrong with the car, is there?"

"No, Dad, your precious car is fine!"

"Jon, you could have just said no."

"Dad, can I say thanks for letting me borrow your car and leave it at that?"

"Yes, that's fine. I don't like the tone though. I guess there's no need to ask you about your date."

"No there's no need."

"Okay, I get the message. Dinner's at 6:30."

"Yeah, I had roasted chicken with some turnip thing and a huge side salad along with pumpkin cheesecake for dessert. I don't think I'm going to be hungry."

"You're a lucky man. Your mother told me we're having her special barbecue meatloaf."

"I did luck out. Score maybe a half point for the day. Sorry I snapped at you, Dad."

At the same time Midnight closed his bedroom door Claire was calling Bryn. It had gone horribly, despite her and Bryn's high hopes. She had felt awkward and fumbled for the few idiotic words she said. He knew she was fishing about his feelings for Bryn and she sounded pathetic telling him she "really liked" him. She prayed Midnight wouldn't say anything to Wally or she would be teased for the rest of her life. More than anything, she regretted all the times she had berated Bryn about Chris. Here she was in the same boat, caring deeply for someone who did not reciprocate. Midnight would continue to see her as Wally's little sister. There was no alternate universe where Midnight didn't adore Bryn and Claire knew that was absolutely the truth despite Bryn acting like there was no basis for it.

Bryn walked through the front door of the Porters' house. She felt sick about it being Valentine's Day and here she was going to Wally's party alone. She had sworn she'd have Chris back in her life by this very date, but they hadn't seen one another in over a month. Now she saw him across the room standing next to Olivia, his arm resting on her shoulder. Bryn's stomach lurched. Claire was tugging at her sleeve, saying it was Wally's fault for telling just about everyone in town about the party. Wally posted it as a place for the dated and dateless to spend the evening. Mrs. Porter acquiesced, since she didn't know what to do with her night and this would preoccupy an otherwise depressing evening. She warned Wally about alcohol and pot, but her heart wasn't into keeping too keen an eye. Most of Wally's friends were 18 and he had never been anything but responsible. She loved all her children and would never admit to it, but Wally was her joy. He seemed to need less attention than the others, yet he gave more than anyone. He was charming, talented, slightly bohemian and genuinely friendly—begrudgingly, she admitted he not only looked like his father, but was very much like him as well. Claire was pulling Bryn into the kitchen toward the center island while Bryn was still struggling to get her coat off. They sat down and put on happy faces and talked about their troubles with boys. Mrs. Porter told them her heart still raced when Mr. Porter walked through the door on some errand or to pick up the children for their weekly Wednesday dinner. It would slow in equal measure as he drove away. Claire asked why she didn't fight to get him back, but Mrs. Porter seemed to think it was past the point of ever happening. Apparently Mr. Porter was serious about the girlfriend, and as tears welled up in her eyes she said, "I've said too much already and I've only had one glass of chardonnay. I don't want to burden you kids with discussions about your father. It's not fair to him or me and Wally made me promise no tears tonight. I can get banished to my room if I start to cry."

It was depressing all around and Bryn was about to take a very early departure when it occurred to her that she belonged there a lot more than Chris. As she headed to Claire's room to toss her coat on the bed, she caught his eye, but looked away quickly. She still couldn't bear to look at him with Olivia. They stood comfortably together, making it all the more painful.

She opened Claire's bedroom door and a waft of nostalgia swept through her. Two months earlier was the last time she had seen Chris alone. Her outlook had been better then. Maybe it was Valentine's Day. It sucked being alone and doubly sucked having to see the guy she adored with the girl he adored and the girl wasn't her. She might have sat and reminisced, but there were some kids in the room smoking pot and laughing at something that wasn't slightly funny—so much for Mrs. Porter's warning about pot. She quickly deposited her coat and decided she wasn't in the mood for reminiscing anyway.

She ran into Midnight on her way downstairs. He was headed up to Claire's room to drop his coat and asked Bryn to wait for him. She stood waiting on the steps for a few minutes and then they headed downstairs together. Midnight asked if she knew Chris was there and she said yes, she had seen him when she came in.

"What is Wally thinking?"

"I don't think he thinks much about my life, ever." She actually smiled and added, "And I don't blame him. It's a train wreck."

"Apparently he doesn't think about mine either. He knows I can't stand the guy. They went back into the kitchen and sat around the table and talked—Bryn, Claire, Midnight and Mrs. Porter. The conversation at first didn't deviate from how much Valentine's Day sucked and they were all quite above celebrating it, even if they had someone to celebrate it with. Bryn saw how happy Mrs. Porter was to talk, no matter how indiscreetly, among younger people. In equal measure she saw how happy Claire was to sit with Midnight without Wally around.

"I never thought I'd have to worry about Zach. I guess after a certain number of years, you'd think you wouldn't have to worry, especially over a 30-year-old public defender."

Bryn asked her what happened. She wasn't sure whether Claire had ever heard her mother talk this candidly and wasn't sure whether she wanted to hear, but Bryn knew Claire well enough to know she would tell them to stop if she didn't want to be a part of the conversation. Bryn wanted to know exactly what happened with Mr. Porter, and Mrs. Porter was on her second glass of chardonnay.

"That's how old she is?"

"Yep. Thirty."

"That's a big age difference."

"Yes it is."

"So what happened?"

"Well, I can't say what happened exactly, because I never saw it coming. Funny, it was just over a year ago this past

New Year's Eve. We toasted and kissed and Zach said to me, 'Well, I guess it's you and me for the long haul.' It's not lost on me that I now know he was already seeing this girl."

Bryn said that it sounded like Mr. Porter was messed up, but Claire cut her off, saying she didn't think her dad was messed up. She was sure it was the other woman's fault.

"Oh, honey," her Mom said. "I don't think your father is messed up either, but I do think he was looking for approval on my part. After as long as we were married, I guess I let that slip through the cracks. In hindsight it was a huge mistake, because there was someone else around telling him how fabulous he is."

Claire reached for her mother's hand. "Mom, I am so sorry."

"It will be all right, my sweet girl."

And Claire replied, "I don't feel like that's true at all. It doesn't feel like anything will be all right."

The conversation had become dreary and it was Midnight who interrupted Mrs. Porter, saying, "I guess I'm going to leave you ladies to it."

Mrs. Porter was relieved he had interrupted. "No, Midnight. That's enough indiscreet talk. Let's change the subject. I'm up to date on celebrity gossip, breaking news and even sports. Any subject you choose."

A short time into laughing about a long string of people, including professional athletes, musicians and actors, Bryn excused herself to the bathroom, saying "Hold any good gossip until I get back."

She turned out of the kitchen and toward the powder room. The last person in line was Olivia. Bryn would not retreat. She rolled her eyes slightly and sidled toward the line, keeping a safe distance. Olivia looked Bryn up and down and then said, "You know, you're a joke, hanging around West, pining over him. You know he told me he went for coffee with you." Bryn stared down at her shoes and said, "I'm sure he did." She knew she was a joke, but the last person she could take hearing it from was Olivia Ward. It felt like splinters of glass in her insides. She fought back the tears and walked back into the kitchen. She announced she was going to head home. Mrs. Porter said, "What, so soon? Why the change of heart?"

"Yeah, I think it's about that time."

Claire walked her to the door and Bryn's watering eyes made their way to the bathroom line, where only Olivia stood now.

Claire nodded toward Olivia. "Bryn let's go outside."

"You don't even have your coat."

"It's fine, let's go out on the porch for a second."

They walked onto the porch and Claire gave a quick shudder. "What happened in there?"

"Nothing, I just feel like going."

Claire grabbed at Bryn's arm and said, "Come on, tell me."

"I know I am a huge downer, but I don't want to be here with the two of them here, together. I sing this chorus over and over, but it's a little hard to take."

"I get it. It sucks, but maybe it will be all right. You never know, maybe Olivia won't be a part of his future—a lot can happen, especially once he goes to college."

"I love you for saying that and you're right, a lot can happen." Bryn walked toward her car, but turned to give a small wave to Claire as she was headed back inside.

She thought her bladder would explode on the way home, but she made it to her bathroom. As she was settling in for the evening, it occurred to her that if Olivia thought she was a joke, then so was her boyfriend. He was the one who wanted to go out in the first place. Olivia hadn't been out of town or away for the summer when Chris struck up their romance. Whoever spray-painted Olivia's driveway should win the Nobel. Bryn laughed to herself—she had moved from the denial phase into the anger phase and she was pretty happy about it.

It was Officer Dan Meyer who spotted an old black SUV, license plate PACKMAN, swerving over the middle yellow line. He was in pursuit within seconds. It matched the license plate of the car radioed in not long before—a plate so easy to remember he hadn't needed to jot it down on his dashboard pad. According to dispatch, the call had come from an unidentified woman who said, "The kid driving might kill someone."

Officer Meyer pulled Chris Bello over and asked him for his license and registration. He could smell beer on his breath and asked him to get out of the car.

"I want you to walk a straight line from your car to the squad car."

"I swear, I had one beer."

Meyer looked at the name on the license again and said, "Mr. Bello, I don't want any trouble from you. If you will, please walk a straight line."

Chris stumbled and the officer asked him to lean up against the SUV and proceeded to search him.

He reached into his pocket and found two small bumps in the lining below the right pocket. It could have been sugar packets, but he asked Chris.

"What's this?"

"I don't know what you're talking about."

"Take off your jacket for me."

Chris's voice was shaking from nerves and the cold, but he tried to sound like nothing was wrong. "Sure, but if I catch pneumonia, I'll blame the Andover PD."

"I'm not laughing, Mr. Bello. Take off the jacket."

Chris took off his jacket and handed it to Officer Meyer. Meyer fumbled with the small hole in the lining, but finally retrieved two small plastic packets filled with white powder, which he recognized immediately as crystal meth.

Despite Chris's protests to the officer, swearing he did not know what was going on or why he was pulled over, he was taken into custody and booked for possession and driving under the influence.

The jail cell was a terrifying place to be. It was cold and dark and smelled awful, but Chris was relieved he was alone—must be a slow Saturday night. He would have to call his father. The idea of that, the cold slab he was sitting on and the cold beers he had drunk combined to make him shake so badly his teeth were chattering violently and he could not will them to stop. He almost didn't make it the few feet to the corner commode before vomiting. His father might kill him for getting into this kind of trouble. Over and over in his mind, he kept repeating what he had said to the police officer when he saw what was in the palm of his hand—"Those drugs aren't mine—I swear they are not mine!" He would have to piece it together, but for the time being he had to get out of there.

The phone call woke Samuel Bello from a deep sleep. Oddly, he had been dreaming of his late wife. It was a sweet dream filled with lovely colors and sweet smiles. He was with her in a green forest, walking side by side along a long path that was bordered with purple wildflowers. She was singing softly and caressing the top of his hand, which she held tightly. Along with her singing, he heard a distant bell tolling from the top of a small village church. His eyes squinted open. The ringing was his cell phone. It was on the bedside table and Cathie was gently stirring him to answer it.

"Dad, it's Chris."

"What in the world? Where are you? What's wrong?"

The pause was long, but Chris finally answered, "Dad, I'm in jail."

"What?"

"I'm in jail, Dad."

"What have you done?"

"I'm not actually sure of anything. I'm really confused, but they've booked me on DUI and drug possession."

"Jesus, I'm leaving the house in the next five minutes to get you."

He took his time driving there, not because he wanted Chris to stew, but because he needed the time to process what Chris told him. Chris had always been a good kid, brooding and distant sometimes, cocky others, but basically a good kid, never in this kind of trouble. At least thirty minutes had passed, but he was finally there, laboring down the hallway feeling like he should be hauling an oxygen tank.

"What have you done?"

"Dad, I'm so scared."

"Chris, what happened?"

"I got pulled over after being at the Porters' and the cop found packets of crystal meth in my jacket pocket."

"Meth? You're doing that shit?"

"No, of course not. I had a couple beers, but that was it."

"So what was it doing in your pocket?"

"I don't know."

"Well, let's try to get you out of here and let's get Bill

Caruso on the phone first thing tomorrow morning."

"Who's that?"

"He's an attorney."

"How am I going to get out of here tonight, though?"

"Well, I'm going to see if they've set bail and will let you go in my custody."

"It sounds like you've done this before."

"You're not the first person I've known to get into trouble."

"Who else ever gets into trouble?"

"How about I save the stories for some other time?"

Chris actually smiled at his father. He had surprised him. He was being pretty nice and he was definitely being helpful. Chris had thought he'd make him spend at least one night in jail, but they were headed home instead.

"So how much was my bail?"

"Too much, but what else are we going to do? The court has agreed to a 10% cash deal and you are certainly going to make your court date, so I should get most of it back minus some fees."

"So tell me how you know so much about all this."

"I worked my way through college at Universal Bail Bonding in Racine."

"No kidding?"

"No kidding. I met an interesting group of characters. I worked Saturday nights most weeks, so I saw the cream of the crop."

Chris held his hands directly in front of the car's dash vent. They were still shaking and the heat helped—the warmth comforted him. "It's hard to picture you doing that."

"Why?"

"I don't know, it just is."

"Well I worked there for four years. The guy that ran the place actually thought I should go to law school. Said I would have been a natural. I was too stupid to listen to him and instead came right back here and started working at your grandfather's restaurant. You can't turn back the pages."

"Yeah, I know."

"Then I met your mom and fell in love with her and didn't want to be anywhere else but here."

Chris rubbed at his eyes to hold back tears. "I don't remember that much about her anymore."

"She was quite a gal. Look, I know I can be hard with you Chris, and for good reason. Look at this mess we're facing right now, but I'd rather you respect me and if that means disliking me, then so be it. I have buddies. I don't need my kids to be my friends. I notice this all the time around this town, a bunch of parents aiming to be young again with their children as BFFs."

"What does that have to do with Mom?"

"Well, she was a softie, so I'm reminded of her and maybe our differences too. But she was a great gal."

"In what way?"

"I think we should be focusing on other things we need to talk about."

Chris looked at his dad. Tears were still welling in his eyes. "No come on dad, tell me."

Samuel let out a sigh. "Oh my God, so many."

"Name some."

"Well, she was funny. God, could that woman make me laugh, but she had a dark side too. I guess that's obvious.

You're a lot like her in many ways."

"Yeah."

"I didn't mean that to come out sounding bad."

"I didn't take it that way."

"She was terrific and so are you. Anyway, at first meeting her, that dark side made her kind of mysterious and sexy. I don't know, a million different little things."

"So come on. Tell me."

"Well, okay. It sounds like a cliché, but she was a good person. She kind of always cheered for the underdog, which was sweet. She was generous to a fault with her money and more importantly, with her time. I don't know if you know it because you were pretty young when she passed away, but your mom was a statewide director for the St. Elizabeth women's charities. They help women and kids who are abused. I think that's part of what made her such a pushover with you kids."

"Wow."

"Yeah, it was a big thing for her and it really was a big deal. She was also a great tennis player and poker player, for that matter."

"I remember her playing tennis, but mom liked to play poker? I don't think I ever knew that."

"She was a natural. I once saw her outplay a table of pretty sophisticated men with a pair of fours. The jackpot was over $300. God was she pleased with herself."

"I used to think of her every day, but I don't anymore. It's hard to remember what she was like."

"I know."

They had arrived at home. The porch light was still on, which meant Chris's stepmother would still be awake. Chris stopped his dad from turning off the ignition to ask him one more question.

"Don't get mad, but it seems like you married Cathie pretty quick after Mom died. Did you know her while you were still married to Mom?"

"It may seem it, but it really wasn't that quick. It was over two years."

"I guess, but you know what I mean, right?"

"I'd known Cathie socially, but not in the way I think you mean. I loved your mom, Chris."

"Thanks, Dad. I guess I just needed to know."

"I'm not at all happy with the circumstance, Chris, but glad for the chance to talk."

"Yeah, I guess I am too and thanks for believing me about the drugs and for not getting crazy mad at me."

"I think I'm mellowing with age."

"You sure are. I thought you'd slug me."

"What? I've never hit you in my life."

"Yeah, I know, it's only that sometimes it seems like you're going to."

"I think your mom would have kicked me out of the house. You remember your grandfather, right? Now that guy was a disciplinarian. My God, I remember one time—oh, never mind. It's probably not the time for that story."

Chris didn't know what to say about that, but on more than one occasion, he'd heard his grandfather referred to as the Latin lunatic. The talk with his dad had been good and Chris needed more than anything to hear his dad hadn't been seeing Cathie while he and his mom were still married. And he believed his dad. Chris wasn't two feet in the door and

Cathie hugged him and said, "Honey, you should try and get some sleep. I've changed the linen on your bed, so it will feel nice and clean and I've put a bottle of water on your nightstand. Try to get some sleep."

"Thanks. And Dad, thanks again for getting me out of there and well, for everything."

"You're welcome, son. We'll see you in the morning and we'll talk about what we're going to do over the next couple days. I am going to want to know where you were and what went on for you to get into this kind of trouble."

Every hallway, from high school down to primary, was alive with the gossip.

"Did you hear what happened Friday night after Wally's party?" "Did you hear Chris Bello was arrested with drugs?" "Did you hear who got picked up by the cops Friday night holding, maybe even dealing?"

Bryn was completely muddled. After every bell, classmates approached her for details, but she didn't have any. She needed to get to Chris in order to get them. The whole thing, of course, was ridiculous. It had to be a big mistake. Chris did not do drugs and the idea of him dealing them was unimaginable. Football was his addiction and he'd jeopardize playing if he even thought about doing drugs. It didn't make any sense. She would drive to his house and see if he was home and maybe get a chance to talk to him and he'd clear everything up. The stupid story was probably that, a stupid story.

She had never skipped school, but that day she grabbed her uniform blazer, her car keys and her backpack and headed to the parking lot to drive to Chris's house.

On her second ring, Mr. Bello opened the door and welcomed her. The warmth of his smile reminded her of Chris. Standing in the foyer, she was struck by the familiarity of the house. She hadn't been there in a long time. Nothing physically had changed—the smell of pumpkin air freshener, the plaid wallpaper in the vestibule, the Audubon prints above the fireplace, yet the circumstances had changed considerably. The sound of Olivia Ward's voice coming from the kitchen broke her trance. Bryn was glued to the spot, her mouth hanging open. Mr. Bello said, "How are you, Bryn?"

"I'm fine. How's Chris?"

"I think as well as can be expected."

"What happened?"

Chris's stepmother interrupted by announcing that Samuel better get his coat and car keys. It had been a very long couple of days. She explained to Bryn that Chris was going to be arraigned within the hour and they had to hurry to the courthouse to spend a few minutes with their attorney and Chris together. The attorney, a Mr. Caruso, had picked Chris up a few hours before so they could talk more before Chris faced the judge.

Bryn interrupted to ask again. "But what happened?"

Cathie very quickly said that Chris had been arrested for driving under the influence and possession of narcotics. She asked Bryn if she was planning on being at the courthouse but she said no, since she thought Chris would be embarrassed to see a lot of people. Samuel smiled at Bryn and said, "I think you're right, but we'll make sure to tell him hello."

"I can't believe this is happening."

"No one really can, but we know he isn't guilty of these drug charges and we'll get it sorted out."

Olivia brushed against Bryn on her way out the front door. Her nose was in the air and she pretended not to notice Bryn at all. They piled into Mr. Bello's SUV leaving Bryn standing in the driveway tugging at her blazer for warmth.

For the Bellos, it was a short, silent drive to the courthouse. They parked quickly and Cathie was opening her car door before Samuel had a chance to put the car in park. He held her elbow and told her to slow down. They had all the time in the world and she was making him nervous. He held the courtroom door for Cathie and Olivia and then walked slowly and softly along the aisle. He studied the back of Chris's head, his beautiful dark, wavy hair. He looked young and small. His boy seemed so vulnerable, sitting on display, and at that moment he wanted to hit something or someone and not stop until they felt the kind of pain he was feeling. He was angry at being there, at Chris having to be there. He wanted nothing more than for all of it to simply go away.

"Mr. Bello," said the judge, "your bail was set at $10,000."

"Your honor," said Chris's attorney, "Mr. Bello has made all bail arrangements and lives in his parents' home."

The judge looked up from the court brief and replied. "I understand that, Mr. Caruso, I'm looking at the court notes and reading aloud. Bailiff, please take this young man to do the necessary paperwork. Mr. Bello, a trial date will be set to give counsel ample time to prepare background, exhibits, motions, testimony and arguments. It looks like a full docket in the months ahead, but we'll do our best to avoid too long a wait. You will be released on your bond and in your father's custody and will wait for further instructions and notice from the court."

The next day, Chris sat with Nick Caruso in the dining room of his parents' house. Chris thought Caruso was all right but wasn't sure he was up to the task. Apparently he was an associate of Samuel Bello's business attorney.

Nick began. "So, Chris. Let's go through it all again, but this time in more detail. I want you to tell me every second of what happened between the time you got to the Porter's house and the time you were picked up by Officer Meyer. I have all the time in the world, so be thorough. There has to be a clue some-where to help us figure out how those drugs got in your pocket."

"Well, first, the drugs were not mine."

"Yes, I understand that. Now let's start from the beginning."

"Okay. So I got to the Porters' around seven o'clock or maybe a couple minutes after. I know I left my house at 6:30 and the Porters live down the post road, where I got picked up. It rarely takes longer than twenty minutes door to door, but it was icy and the street is super-curvy, so I was driving pretty slowly. Anyway, I got there and I was looking around for my girlfriend and didn't see her anywhere. I went onto the back porch to grab a beer and I saw Wally on my way out there. I asked him if he wanted a beer and he told me 'sure,' so I grabbed us both a Bud and we walked into the living room and stood there talking for a while."

"And Wally is the guy having the party?"

"Yeah, you know, Judge Porter's house."

"Was there adult supervision?"

"Well, the Judge doesn't live there anymore, but I think Mrs. Porter was there."

"We'll get back to that. Go ahead."

"Anyway, we were having some beers and other guys were joining us. I guess we were probably talking for about ten minutes when I spotted Olivia."

"And Olivia is?"

"That's my girlfriend."

Caruso was scribbling names like designated hitters on a scorecard. He noticed Chris had been nervously picking at his cuticle and it had drawn blood. He reached out and gently pat-ted that hand and said, "Got it. You're doing great. Go ahead."

"Then, Midnight Wright comes in with some girl, but they separated and he went to the can, I think. And then she bee-lined it toward Wally and me and the other guys."

Caruso interrupted, "Hold it. Did you talk about anything important in that 10-minute conversation, before you saw Olivia come in? Anything that might be related to those drugs?"

"No. We talked about sports and school. That was about it."

"So Midnight comes in with some girl and who is Midnight?"

"Jon Wright."

"I actually know Jon's dad. Go ahead."

"So anyway, this girl kind of grabbed Wally aside while Midnight disappeared up the steps and then into the kitchen with Bryn Wilson. Midnight's a Class A jerk. We got into it a while back. I dated Bryn and he never seemed to be happy about that arrangement."

"Anything to that?"

"To what?"

Caruso stopped writing. "To him not being happy about that arrangement?"

"I don't think so. He was super angry with me, but it's all water under the bridge now."

"It could be related to those drugs in your pocket."

"No. I don't believe that. We haven't been friends in a while, but it's a stretch he'd do anything this crazy."

"Okay, so you absolutely do not suspect him?"

"No, I don't."

Caruso was back to his notes, but looked up to say, "We'll come back to that too."

"So anyway, he went upstairs and then into the kitchen and

I walked away, since Wally was still in pretty deep conversation with the girl. I think her name is Nora or Cora or something like that, but I'm not sure. She goes to St. Agnes and not Wild West."

"You didn't join that conversation?"

"Nah. I kind of felt like I'd be interrupting and I don't know the girl at all. Obviously, I don't even know her name for sure."

"Why's that? Why would you be interrupting?"

"No particular reason, but they seemed pretty tight. Like I said, it seemed deep. That's all. I went and joined Olivia and a group of her friends."

"So, on to Bryn Wilson, who you made reference to along with Jon Wright. What's the relationship there?"

"We used to hang out, last summer."

"But not anymore?"

"We see each other now and again, which is what Midnight and I fought about."

"Would Bryn harbor any ill will against you?"

"No way. I think she still loves me."

Caruso shook his head and smiled. "Love has been at the core of some pretty messed-up motivation. Regardless, I'm going to add her to my list of people to follow up with."

"Would it be possible to leave her out of this? I don't really want her deep in my business and you'd be opening the door pretty wide. I think I finally got her to realize there's nothing serious between the two of us and she'd be all in my face again."

"I think you shouldn't concern yourself with who I need to talk to. Concern yourself with thinking about every detail of that night. Here's the deal. I need to talk to these people no matter how unpleasant it may seem. If you're innocent, and I believe you are, then someone else isn't so innocent."

"I understand, but keep her at arm's length from me if you can, OK?"

"She may know something about those drugs and if she doesn't, no harm done."

"I doubt if she knows anything about the drugs, but you can ask."

"Well, thanks for your permission. I'll keep you posted."

"I didn't mean it like that. I just don't want her to feel like she can help and then her helping me becomes a thing."

"I get it. We'll keep her at arm's length. Let's continue."

"So, let me think what happened next. I talked to a few other people, mostly teammates and then I got pretty bored. I went upstairs to grab my coat and waved to Olivia that we were going. She said she was grabbing a ride with one of her friends, which I was kind of glad about since she was being a pain. I was too tired to argue with her again, so I left."

"What do you mean, 'again'? Did the two of you have a fight?"

"She was moaning about Bryn and had said something nasty to her. I thought it was stupid and I told her that. She should learn to be quiet sometimes."

"Well, again Bryn comes up in the conversation."

"Had nothing to do with me. There's some bad blood between the two of them. Well, I guess that is because of me, but the argument was nothing too serious. We've argued about Bryn in the past. She still likes to hang around me and Olivia thinks I never made it crystal clear to Bryn that she shouldn't be hanging around at all."

"You sure it wasn't serious from Olivia's point of view?"

"I'm pretty sure. I'd bet she didn't give it a thought after I left. Hey, speaking of leaving, I just remembered something else. Bryn left before almost anyone else. She was out the door early."

"A hasty departure?"

"I don't know about hasty, but I think it was around eight and she didn't show up until 7:30 or so. It's doubtful she would have had time to see much of anything."

"The drugs could have been put there five minutes after you got there or five minutes before you left."

"I guess you're right, but Bryn doesn't seem like the type to keep something important to herself. Well, at least not something important to me."

"Well, it takes all types. I'm presuming everyone had access to this room where your coat was."

"Yeah. Everyone had thrown their coats in the same room. Everyone was in and out of there. I remember actually having a hard time finding my coat. It was buried deep. Anyway, I got into my car around ten, maybe ten-thirty. As I said, I thought the party was boring and didn't want to stay all night. I was maybe five miles from the Porters', heading home along the post road, and saw the sirens behind me. I pulled over right away and when the cop asked for my license and registration I gave it to him. Then he asked me to step out of the car and I did. I never even hesitated, because I didn't think I had anything to worry about. Then I saw what was in his hand and it freaked me out. I wouldn't be the first Latin guy to have something pinned on him that he didn't do."

"Are you saying you think the officer may have planted the drugs?"

"Nah, I guess not. He'd have to be a magician."

"How many beers did you have?"

"I don't really know."

"Take a guess for me."

"I'm guessing five, maybe six."

"You had six beers in less than three hours."

"It sounds like a lot when you say it like that, but I can handle a few beers."

"It's not just one or two and I want to make sure we get the facts straight. Believe me when I tell you, the DA is going to ask you and he'll probably already have the answer from talking with your buddies. He's going to seem horrified by one beer every half-hour. He is not going to care whether you think you can handle a few beers. He's going to have facts and figures about alcohol consumption. He may enact a damn demonstration of someone with your blood alcohol level, which is a matter of public record. He'll show how their senses are dulled and their reaction time is impaired."

"But I didn't get arrested for the beers."

"Well you did in part. There is the DUI, but more than anything the DA will reason that it 'goes to character'."

"What do you mean by that?"

"That you were irresponsible and over-indulgent."

"I'm not those things."

"I'm telling you what the DA will try to make you look like."

"Am I going to go to jail? I can't go to jail. I'm so goddamned scared."

"I am going to try and prevent that from happening, but let me be clear with you. You were caught red-handed with illegal drugs. Don't get me wrong. I'm going to try my damnedest to keep you from going to jail, but you may be convicted of a crime, since it's basically your word against an arresting officer's. But, on the positive side, you are a first-time offender and you did not harm anyone during the course of events. And, you've been very cooperative. We'll suggest probation and community service." Caruso looked down and scribbled more notes. "You can see how great it would be to find whoever did put the stuff in your pocket though, right? Whether malice was aforethought or whether he or she thought it was some kind of funny-ass prank it would be good to prove without any doubt, it wasn't yours. All we'd have to worry about is the DUI which would be easily expunged."

"Some prank! I can't believe this is even happening."

Caruso left Chris's house considering Bryn Wilson. He'd obviously have to talk with her despite Chris's concerns. He had a gut feeling. He couldn't quite put his finger on it, but Bryn Wilson might be able to shed some light on who would do something like this. He didn't give a damn whether she clung to Chris, loved the kid or hated him. He wasn't there to defend or exonerate anyone from anything, with the exception of his client. All he cared about was whether she knew any-thing about the drugs in Chris's pocket. He was completely convinced that someone planted them there. It would be close to impossible to prove without a collaborating witness and he didn't have one, but maybe she had seen something—all the talk about her hanging around him gave Caruso hope that she might have been hanging around at exactly the right time. The cop, Officer Meyer, was squeaky clean and had abso-lutely no reason to lie. Bello being a local kid with fair grades and a solid running game wouldn't hurt, but this battle was going to be uphill. He prayed it would never see the inside of a courtroom or the chance of Meyer's testimony. He also prayed whoever got assigned from the DA's office was a responsible litigator with far too heavy a caseload to worry about Chris Bello. Chris had no record of prior arrests. Maybe he could bargain for regular drug testing and lots of community service. In the meantime, he'd start with Bryn Wilson and her parents. He thought he knew her father from the country club. Sort of a stuck-up type, but he was sure the conversation was necessary and he had to start somewhere. He'd at least check the box and then move on to Jon Wright and Wally Porter and Olivia Ward and whomever that would lead to. Someone had to know something that they weren't saying.

Spring

Bryn was nervous about Chris's attorney coming over. Her mother nonchalantly informed her that Mr. Caruso was coming over at eight to talk about Chris's arrest, charges and "blah blah blah." Bryn wasn't keen on dismissing criminal charges as "blah blah blah," but understood what her mother meant and would let it go. Why would he want to talk to her? Maybe they were talking to everyone who was at the Porters' that night. She stared at her closet for the third time in the past hour, considering what to wear. She wanted to look nice. In her fantasy world, he would go back to Chris and recap the conversation and tell Chris how nice she looked.

Her mother answered the door on the first ring and greeted Mr. Caruso in her usual fashion—wide white smile, hand extended like she was going to hold court. She called to Bryn that Chris's attorney was there to see her.

She almost sprinted down the hallway to hasten the entire conversation, but Mr. Caruso told Bryn to hang back because he needed to speak with her parents privately. Bryn pretended to head to her bedroom, but tiptoed to the den door to eavesdrop on their conversation.

Her father greeted Mr. Caruso, asking him if he knew him from the club. Mr. Caruso said that yes, he was a member of Chase Hill, but didn't get there as often as he'd like and that his golf game was going to pot. Bryn's father asked Caruso if he'd like a drink and he declined, saying he was really working, so he should hold off. Richard said that never stopped him, which did not get the desired laugh he expected.

Mr. Caruso began. "First, I want you to know that I need you to sit with me while I ask Bryn some questions—one of you or both, whichever you'd prefer. Because she's a minor, she should have an adult present. Frankly it's her prerogative to refuse talking to me altogether, but I don't see why she would want to do that. If there is something you find objectionable though, you can cut me off. Believe me, there's no hidden agenda here. I want to get all the facts I possibly can. Get to the bottom of this mess."

Bryn's mother volunteered to sit with Mr. Caruso, but her father intervened and said they'd both sit in on the interview and that he saw no harm in Bryn answering a few questions.

"In talking with Chris about the night he was arrested, several names came up. Your daughter's was one of them."

Bryn's heart pounded.

Richard told Mr. Caruso that she and Chris used to date in a tone that was lukewarm at best.

"Yes, I gathered they used to go out and since Bryn continues to hang around him, I thought she may have seen something that evening and was just afraid to say anything."

Richard interrupted, "What do you mean, hang around him?"

"Well, according to a couple people I've talked to, Bryn follows or followed him around quite a bit."

"What? Let's get Bryn in here."

Her father called out to Bryn to come into the den and join them. Seconds later, she was sitting in a side chair, crossing and uncrossing her legs.

"Mr. Caruso tells me you've been following Chris Bello around?"

Her voice gave away her anxiety. "Well, not exactly following him, but I guess I tried to see him as often as possible." She looked at Caruso when she said, "You see, we went out over the summer but we never really lost touch with one another. I guess I always thought he and I might start seeing one another again."

Bryn's father looked right into her eyes. "And did you?"

"No, not really. He had never really stopped seeing Olivia Ward."

"Who in the hell is Olivia Ward?"

"Dad, it doesn't matter who Olivia Ward is. The point is that we're not seeing one another anymore."

Mr. Caruso interrupted and told everyone that it probably wasn't relevant and he didn't want to get off topic. All he really cared about was whether Bryn had seen anything or anyone around Chris that might explain the drugs found in his jacket.

Richard added that he thought Chris was guilty as charged, but Caruso spoke up saying he completely disagreed. As if to try and spotlight Richard's rush to judgment, Bryn's mother asked if anyone would like anything to drink. Almost on cue, Richard rattled ice cubes in his empty glass, giving Bryn's mother the opportunity to look Mr. Caruso's way. She smiled while rolling her eyes. Mr. Caruso declined for the second time in thirty minutes.

Mr. Caruso asked over and over again if Bryn knew who would or did plant drugs on Chris. Did she see anyone with Chris's coat? Did she see anyone follow him around the party? She worried more than ever about Chris's arrest. Bryn thought this would be a slam-dunk, not guilty kind of thing, but that was looking less likely.

And then he asked again, "Are you sure you can't think of anyone?"

"No, I really can't."

"There must be someone he dislikes or who dislikes him."

"Well, I know he and Midnight don't get along, but Midnight would just never do anything like that."

"Did you go upstairs in the bedroom where the coats were?"

"Sure, I put my coat on the bed not long after I got there."

"When did you retrieve it?"

"I didn't stay long. Probably around 8:00."

"And why did you leave so early?"

"Chris's girlfriend said something kind of nasty to me and, well, I left."

Caruso wondered if this girl's parents were aware of how deeply their daughter felt about Chris Bello. They didn't seem clued in. Given what Chris had told him, her affection was misguided. He looked at Bryn and frowned. "I see. Well, I think we're done here." He stood and took his coat off the back of the chair he sat in, nodded to Bryn's father and said goodnight. Bryn's mother walked him to the front door. She thanked him for coming and assured him that if he needed any more help from anyone, all he needed to do was call.

"Thanks so much. I have a couple of other people to talk with and then we'll wrap it up before our trial date. Some are friends of your daughter, I think—Wally Porter and Jon Wright and a handful of other guys who hang out with Chris. It's a small town and most of these kids know one another. Apparently they all went to the Porters' back at Valentine's Day."

"For what it's worth, I don't know the Bello boy well, but

I can't imagine Samuel's son involved in anything like this. I do know Wally and Jon. They are both very nice young men and I'm sure they didn't have anything to do with it. In fact, you can be sure they'll help you and Chris, if they can."

"I'm sure they are and will. Well, good night, Mrs. Wilson."

She squeezed his hand enough to make him uncomfortable and said, "Good night and drive safe."

Caruso's conversations with Wally and Midnight were equally unproductive. Apparently no one knew anything about the crystal meth and couldn't think of one person who would do such a thing or ever want to hurt Chris. He didn't know who else to go to. The Wright kid was clearly not a good friend of Chris, but seemed sincere in his doubt about anyone doing anything this conspiratorial. It was the same from Wally Porter, who seemed genuinely dismayed at Chris's predicament, but someone was lying. Someone had to know something. He guessed there was the possibility that Chris was guilty, but his gut was telling him "no."

So, his next interview would be with reliable Officer Meyer. He made the discovery appointment through the sheriff's office, which was scheduled for the following day.

Caruso was escorted to an interview room just off the sheriff's reception area. The sheriff's offices were in a drab, industrial-looking building that could have been a self-storage facility. The place was depressing. It smelled oddly like wet cardboard and Lysol.

Caruso stood and held out his hand as Dan Meyer walked into the room. "Officer Meyer, I'm Nick Caruso. I am representing Chris Bello in his upcoming trial."

"Nice to meet you."

Caruso pulled out one of the plastic folding chairs offering it to Officer Meyer. It scraped the floor and made a noise that resonated in the small room. Caruso apologized for the racket and began, "Good to meet you too. I don't want to take up a lot of your time. I know you're busy and I only have a few questions."

"I'd be glad to answer anything you'd like."

Caruso folded a sheet of his yellow legal pad to expose a blank page. He wrote the date and Meyers name at the top of it and began. "Well, thanks. All I really want is to get a better handle on your first impressions of Chris and match up details my client gave of the arrest."

"Not much to tell on details. From what I remember and what's written in my report, I got a phone call from dispatch that ID'd a car as a possible DUI. The plate was memorable— PACKMAN. I was in pursuit maybe five minutes later. I saw the car veer over the yellow line a couple of times and flashed him over."

"He complied quickly?"

"Yeah, almost immediately."

"And?"

"Well, all by the book except finding the meth. I didn't expect this to turn into anything more than a DUI. Not that a DUI isn't bad, but you know what I mean, right? They're sadly, pretty common."

"Completely. So take me through what happened after Chris pulled over."

"Again, by the book. I asked for license and registration. I smelled beer on the kid's breath. I asked him to step out and follow a straight line and he couldn't do that for shit, so I frisked on cause."

Caruso hesitated and put his pen down. "That's the part I'm getting stuck on. Where did you see cause?"

"I thought he might have a weapon."

"And that's a leap for me. Did he give you that impression?"

"Impression?"

"Yeah, impression. Did he seem defiant? Did he act like a cocky gangbanger?"

"No, but I get this all the time with these kids. They're disrespectful and arrogant..."

Caruso cut Meyer off. "Again, it's a leap for me from arrogant to concealed weapon. Chris was disrespectful and arrogant?"

"Well, not exactly. I think it sunk in that he was in trouble by then and he was probably scared as shit."

"Sorry, but it seems like a pretty big chasm between smelling beer on his breath and patting him down for a handgun rather than doing a simple Breathalyzer. Officer Meyer, do you have anything against young Latino men?"

"Nothing at all, but I'm out on the streets all day and I see a good deal that our citizens don't get to see at country clubs and garden parties. It's a mess. These kids skip school and hang out with other bad, and I mean bad kids and ultimately get into trouble. This time, for this Bello kid, it's real trouble that is probably going to be attached to real time and stick to him for a lifetime."

"Well, we'll let the judge decide that and I think it's important for you to know that one, I believe 100% in this young man's innocence and two, this trouble-maker holds down after-school and weekend jobs while he manages to play varsity football and maintain a good grade point average and three, I'm hoping you didn't profile young Mr. Bello."

"Look, Mr. Caruso, you can think anything you want about me, but I'm out there in the trenches. I am telling you that these kids from Mexico and Central America are making our streets unsafe."

"Likewise, Officer Meyer, you can think anything you want about me, but I'm here to tell you that Chris Bello's family has been in the United States for three generations. And, they are from Cuba, not Uruguay or Nicaragua or any other country that you wrap into one non-descript lump sum, which frankly makes me a little sick to my stomach."

"I don't know what else to tell you."

"You said it yourself. This could follow Chris for the rest of his life. Look, I don't want to get myself crazy, but I believe Chris and it's my responsibility to find out more about the drugs. One more question."

"Yeah, sure."

"Who called the DUI in?"

"I have no idea. I got the call on the radio from dispatch."

"Can we check before I leave?"

"Sure. Hold on and I'll have them run the log. It'll take a minute."

Meyer came back into the room shaking his head. He said, "Female, but it's odd, the call came from a pay phone."

"What? They're still around?"

"Probably count them on one hand, but there are a few. Looks like the conversation was short. Woman says she sees a car with the license plate PACKMAN and it looks like the kid is going to kill someone and then she hangs up."

Caruso instinctively reached out for the transcript. "Do you think there are many in the Crane Lake area?"

"You'd have to check with the phone company, but I can't imagine there'd be more than one or two."

Caruso opened the front door, cursing under his breath. He couldn't do anything about Meyer—it might even hurt Chris to try and associate him with any kind of prejudice— but he didn't have to like Meyer. Disliking him felt good and it made him feel even surer about Chris's innocence. Caruso thought it was weird that this one phone call should come from a pay phone. He said it had been an unidentified female. Was it common for nosy ladies peering out their windows looking to bust adolescent males to walk to a pay phone— seemed odd.

One month later, Chris was sitting in the courtroom as his trial for possession and DUI began. Bryn sat there wondering how Mr. Caruso ever let Chris go to trial. It didn't even seem like you needed a law degree to get him off on some kind of deal. Did he ever watch *Law & Order?*

It was Judge Merck who would preside over his trial. Merck was known for being a scratch golfer, a dandy dresser and fair in his jurisprudence, but not lenient—especially toward younger defendants, since he had two teenage children and held himself up to set a good example. Landing him was not a great break for Chris. Drugs were high on the list of the judge's concerns for the youth of Andover and the surrounding townships.

After that first day, Bryn sat outside his house and waited for Olivia to leave. She waited in the park across the street, going through emails and scrolling through free apps. Only forty-five minutes went by and Olivia was rolling out of the Bellos' driveway toward the high school. It wasn't dinnertime yet, so she seized the opportunity and drove slowly through the park and across the street. She parked in their driveway, blocking in Mr. Bello's ancient SUV. She was nervous as she stepped onto the front stoop and thought for a second of turning around, but she took a big deep breath and rang the bell. Mr. Bello opened the door, smiling, and stepped aside to usher her in.

The house was a modest Craftsman-style two-story with three bedrooms and two small, outdated baths. She followed Chris's dad up the steps, breathing in the not-so-fresh smell of pumpkin, and stood next to him as he tapped lightly on Chris's door.

"Chris, Bryn is here."

She wasn't sure, but thought she heard a sigh. Mr. Bello smiled reassuringly and added, "are you decent?"

The door opened and he stood there in a pair of long basketball shorts and a white T-shirt. It took him a second before saying, "Yeah, come on in, Bryn."

Mr. Bello asked, "Bryn, you staying for dinner?"

She looked for some encouragement from Chris, but got none, so she said, "No, I'm expected home in a bit."

"So you want to come in or what?"

"Sure. I came to see how you're doing and I guess ask if there's anything I can do."

Chris plopped onto his bed. "What can anyone do? I'm screwed here, Bryn."

Bryn walked around the bedroom, stopping at his desk, opening and closing his schoolbooks and finally stood at the foot of the bed he was lying on. She held onto one of the bed-posts. "But they must know you're not guilty."

Chris stared at the ceiling. "Who is 'they'?"

"I don't know, everyone."

"The police found meth in my pocket, Bryn."

"But was it yours?"

"No!"

"Then how can you be screwed?"

Chris punched at his pillow. "You can be so naïve. Why would the police know, or care for that matter?"

"I don't know. I just feel terrible."

"You feel terrible. How about me?"

"I didn't mean it that way. I meant I feel terrible for you."

"This is going to mess with my plans in a big way. Forget college in the fall. I've had to put everything on hold. The only good thing is that my dad is being really nice to me and super helpful and positive. When it first happened, I figured he was going to guilt the shit out of me, but he's been pretty great."

"I guess sometimes it takes something bad to show another side to a person—their real side."

"I guess."

"Chris, what can I do? How can I help?"

"I don't know. It's nice of you to come by, though."

"Well, I've missed you."

"I haven't had much time to think about any of that."

"Oh, I know, I was just saying."

"You look pretty."

She wanted to move toward him and kiss him, but he got up right away. All she could say was "I'm sorry."

"No, it's not that. I can't have any more drama in my life

than I already have. You know?"

"Yeah I do. All I want is for you to know I'm here for you. You know that, right?"

"I do. I should probably head downstairs."

I should get going too."

"Yeah, I'll call you."

"OK." She thought about the last time he had said he'd phone and she was angry with him knowing he never would. She couldn't be angry with him anymore about anything. She missed him. She missed the little things. People said that all the time, but it was true. She missed the way his glasses slid down his small nose and he'd have to keep pushing them back up again. She missed his jazz hands when he was excited and his crooked grin when he wasn't quite buying something, even his encyclopedic knowledge of the Green Bay Packers. She missed everything about him.

He walked her to the front door and his parents yelled from the kitchen that they hoped they would see her soon. Chris rolled his eyes, but smiled and hugged her at the door. His body was warm and he smelled of Dial soap. She got in her car and waved goodbye. He still cared about her—there was the smallest spark. As she drove, Bryn considered the past few months. She knew dogging Chris looked foolish to her friends. Had he used her? It was certainly possible. No one had ever given her any information about loving someone, so it wasn't a stretch to think she may have misinterpreted or exaggerated his feelings toward her. So what? Who cared if she loved him more than he loved her? Weren't you supposed to put up a fight for someone you loved—stand steadfast when they rejected you, let go of anger even if it meant losing a little bit of yourself in the process? Was everyone meant to be empowered and independent? No one talked about compromise and when they did, it was like a dirty word.

The case wasn't complicated, but it dragged—continuances, reexamination of evidence, questions of fact, questions of procedure. Apparently the DA's office had nothing but time on its hands. It was already past Memorial Day and Chris's fate continued to hang in the musty courtroom.

Bryn stopped by the Bello house almost every other day. Chris seemed to be pleased and she didn't have to wait across the street, making sure Olivia was gone. Bryn's frequency met with Olivia's lack of it. Just as Bryn thought, as his popularity waned, so did Olivia.

Bryn's time spent in his bedroom increased as he'd share the details of his day and she'd wrap her mind around every word looking for some clue or tidbit that might lead to his exoneration. He'd become so much warmer, needing her in some small measure since he could say things that he wouldn't to his father or his stepmother.

Chris had finished his senior year, but everything else, as he predicted, was put on hold. He wouldn't be going to La Crosse in the fall. He didn't want to continue his application or get his hopes up about anything. He waited for his trial to end with an ever-growing anxiety.

As expected, Olivia stopped all visits. In short order, she found a new boyfriend in the form of a 6'2" basketball forward. Bryn wondered if Chris still loved Olivia. She would never ask him because she was afraid of the answer. She exercised rare caution, because in the final analysis, Chris had to know Olivia's shortcomings. They played out in her favor.

There was no need to talk about it.

At first Chris had seemed hurt when he found out about Olivia's new boyfriend, but he didn't talk about it much, so Bryn figured he had moved on. Well, actually, back—back to her. They didn't just sit and talk in his bedroom anymore. They made out and they went out—to the movies and dinner and the park for walks—anything to help him forget about the trial for an hour or two. Bryn didn't care what they did or why. They were a couple again. They had sex every chance they could, either in the car or at Bryn's house when her parents were out of town, which was more often than ever. They no longer fumbled with zippers and buttons. They were a pair, forming habits, signals and silent languages. His parents would thank Bryn as she'd leave their house and Chris would thank her for being such a great girl and she grew to feel comfortable in his world again.

Bryn's father didn't make a secret of his disapproval and would tell her she was spending too much time at Chris's house, calling him a jailbird, but Bryn didn't care. Then one night when she was pulling into her own driveway, preparing for the inevitable lecture, she saw Midnight sitting on the front porch.

As she walked toward him she said, "Did you ring? Isn't anyone home?"

"I wouldn't know. I didn't ring the bell. I've been sitting here waiting for you."

Bryn sat next to Midnight on the steps. "Sorry. I was over at Chris's. What's up?"

"Yeah, I understand you two are nice and cozy these days."

Bryn looked into her lap, but was smiling ear to ear. "Yeah, we're back together."

"Did it ever occur to you that the meth might have been his?"

"No way. He's not into that kind of stuff. Maybe a couple of beers here and there, but nothing serious."

"Could you look at me when I'm talking to you? He confronted me yesterday and accused me of planting the drugs on him."

"What? That's crazy."

"Yeah, I thought it was pretty crazy too, but I guess I get his trying to blame anyone but himself."

"What did he say to you?"

"Well, he said that he saw me at the party that night and that when he saw me I was headed upstairs to where his coat was and that I could have put the shit in his pocket. I reminded him that about fifty people went up those same stairs to throw their coats on the bed. Any number of people could have done it."

"It's silly. He's just upset with the trial and everything. He's scared. We're all scared."

"Yeah. Believe me, it's no secret that I'm not the guy's biggest fan, but I'd never do anything to screw him over like that. But it's odd—when I thought about the coats and what he said, something very different occurred to me."

"What occurred to you?"

"That's where I saw you that night."

"Well, like you said, me and fifty other people."

"But fifty other people weren't as interested in Chris."

"I get where you're headed, Mid, but I'd never want to see

Chris in any trouble."

"I guess, but it's been awfully nice seeing him all the time and seeing him say goodbye to old Olivia and have nothing but spare time on his hands for you. I'm right, aren't I? He's not going away to school anymore, is he? No La Crosse this year, at least. That keeps him around like a lapdog while you finish up school."

"What are you saying?"

"I think you know what I'm saying. You are so duplicitous that it's scary. I think you'd actually do this to have him around. He's beginning to rely on you, isn't he?"

Bryn stood up, but continued to look at Midnight. "People actually think that? It's ridiculous, Midnight. I have to go in."

"I don't know what other people think. I only know what I think."

"What you think is completely crazy. It is completely off base and you should be the last person to accuse me of being disingenuous. I've always been unequivocal about my feelings for Chris and I would never do anything to hurt him, but what about you? Maybe his accusing you isn't so far off base."

"Oh shut up, Bryn. Think about it. Why would I even waste my time on someone I write off as nothing more than a toad?"

"You think you're so smart. Well, figure it out, because if it's not me, and it isn't, and it's not you and it's not Chris himself, then who is it?"

Her hands shook as she closed the door behind her. She couldn't even hold her backpack and it fell at her feet. She and Chris had gotten so close again. She would not let Midnight ruin this through his nasty speculation. She got into bed running through their conversation. What exactly had Midnight said? He had said it occurred to him that he saw her in the bedroom where the coats were. No, he had said the staircase leading to where the coats were, but he also said about fifty people probably went up those stairs and through that room before joining the party. If Midnight thought for one second he was going to ruin her plans he had another thing coming. She would call him in the morning and tell him not to repeat such an accusation. She pushed and pounded her pillow but couldn't get comfortable. The streetlight seemed to shine exactly where her head lay—it shone like a bright overhead bulb, illuminating the smallest of thoughts.

Summer

She and Chris spent more time in secluded places. Chris didn't want to see a lot of people and had put off seeing Bryn as well, telling her he wanted to be alone with his thoughts. But, here they were in the place they first became acquainted. She was thrilled he wanted to take a day trip down the Argent. He stopped the canoe and told Bryn he needed to talk to her about something. She swiveled in her seat to face him. His eyes were fixed on the hull of the canoe. Without looking up he asked if there was any truth to the rumors he was hearing about Bryn putting the drugs in his pocket. He calmly told her if they were substantiated he would never speak to her again and he might drown her before they got to the end of the river.

"Darn Midnight. He had to talk about his theories to someone, like he's Hercule Poirot. My God, I hope you know I would never do anything to hurt you."

"That's not answering my question. I asked you a very specific question and I want a very specific yes or no answer. Did you plant that meth on me? Is there any truth to what I've been hearing? Because in all likelihood, I'm going to go to jail for something that I'm not guilty of and I don't really care if it's jail for a week or jail for a year." His hands were visibly shaking. "No matter how the trial turns out, this is going to follow me forever and I am going to be screwed. Are your ambitions about going to college together and hanging out all the time so twisted that you would actually do this to me?"

"Can I ask who you've been hearing it from? Was it from Midnight?"

"No, you can't ask. Now answer my question."

"No, I had nothing to do with planting drugs on you."

"Nothing at all?"

"Nothing."

"Honestly?"

Bryn put her head in her hands for a moment, but then looked directly into Chris' eyes. "I swear."

"It's just that a couple guys I know had some pretty strong arguments for that scenario."

"And one of those guys was Midnight?"

"No, Midnight was not one of them."

"Well he's the first person to have said something to me. I think he's the one spreading the ridiculous theory."

"Hey, he's your friend, not mine."

"Chris, do you think he could have done it?"

"No, I don't. It's not his style. I wish it were. I lashed out at him a while back but it was lame. Shit, I guess I wished it were you. Wished I could prove it was anyone." Chris paused and let out a sigh. "The lawyer keeps telling me everything is going to be okay, but it's not going well. He thought the whole phone booth thing was a great lead and it went nowhere, and the testimony from the cop was strong. I can see that. Anyone can see that. He wasn't nervous or fidgety on the stand and I was. He's got this solid record and I'm some Latin kid who could be trouble. Shit, I am trouble. Look at what this is doing to my dad."

"I don't think that's what the judge or the jury see. You did a terrific job. You sounded sincere and confident and you're not some random guy, you're a great guy."

"Thanks for trying to make me feel better, but that's not

true. You know, my dad said something the other day that made sense. If this happened in a big city I wouldn't stand out so much and this would have never gone to trial. These guys at the courthouse have too much time on their hands."

They embraced and kissed and made love in that canoe. As they lay in each other's arms, they talked about the past year. Since their meeting the summer before, chaos had ruled their lives. They drifted for a long time with no need to talk, holding onto one another until Chris finally asked, "Bryn, what do you want in life?"

"Can I stay in this canoe forever?"

"I'm flattered. Not sure all your affection isn't misplaced, but I'm flattered."

"What do you mean, 'misplaced'?"

"Not sure I'm worthy of all that love."

"I think you are. I guess that's what I really want. I want us to love one another. What about you? What do you want?"

"There's only one thing I want and that's not going to jail."

"Well, of course you want that."

She had to wipe her eye and pretend to squint from the sun for fear the tears would travel down her face and betray her, but in that instant, he saw it. He saw how selfish her answer was. It had never occurred to her to have her wish be the same as his. The horror of a possible jail sentence for him never crossed her mind. The crack in the eggshell was barely noticeable at that moment, but it was there. She couldn't take back her answer and amending her initial response seemed dishonest. She lay in bed that night and made her mind push it away, but nothing seemed to help her sleep. When she finally dozed off, she bolted upright in a cold sweat thinking what a complete disappointment she must be to him. Didn't his head shake ever so slightly when she said of course you want that? She swore he said, "nice answer" under his breath. But when she asked what he had said he replied, "nothing, never mind" and then he stared out onto the water, detaching from her.

Those were the last words he spoke to her. "Nothing, never mind." He had killed himself early in the morning in that soupy, gray time before the sun comes up. Cathie Bello called her in the late morning to tell her. He had taken pills just like his mother had eight years before. Her cell phone fell from her hand onto her bedroom floor. She watched the spider cracks grow across the screen. Why hadn't she seen he was troubled to the point of taking his own life? He talked about the future. They talked about college—postponed, but still happening—about Mr. Bello and Chris's growing relationship, his suspicions that his stepmother might be pregnant. He was even thinking of going back to work at The Rendezvous. Where were those signs she was supposed to see? Had he been on meds? She didn't think so, but had never asked him. She hadn't asked him anything. She would never be with him. She would never be able to call him her lover, husband or even friend and on that bright sunny summer day, complete darkness surrounded her.

She asked her mother about skipping the memorial service. She couldn't bear seeing the casket, but Charlotte said it was a ridiculous thing to even think about; the entire town would be there and she had known Chris since the Wilsons moved to Andover—had dated him, for goodness' sake. Her mother said this with a clipped authoritative voice like it was news, something right off the presses. Bryn wanted to insist on not going, but instead she shrank back to her room and looked for something black to wear. She thought about going back to the Argent. She wanted nothing more than to get in a canoe and go down the river and drift into oblivion, to lie down in the hull and be swept out to sea. She wanted to be alone and think about Chris and try to feel him holding her, smell him on her clothes and skin, but instead she would have to bear the drive to the funeral home for the prayer service the Bellos were holding. She crumpled onto the floor and curled up into a ball, holding her kneecaps tightly. It was the only way to make the room stop spinning. As she pulled on the simplest of black shirtdresses, she wondered if Mr. Bello might slap her. Surely he had heard the rumors. She was sure he must hate her, but he couldn't possibly hate her any more than she hated herself. The wallop would feel good. It would serve as some kind of punishment and she wanted to be punished for being completely ineffective at keeping Chris alive.

Miraculously, as she walked through the door with her mother and father, Mr. Bello hugged her tight. He backed a foot from her, but then hugged her again. She was relieved and disappointed at the same time. If he had slapped her, she would have a reason to run out and not look back. Now she would have to stay. All she could whisper without completely breaking down was "I'm so sorry."

He said he knew her heart was breaking—his was breaking too and there was no way to describe his pain, but they would have to focus on the warm memories now. The past five months had irrevocably changed Samuel Bello. She didn't say anything, but she hoped very much that Chris had been right and his stepmother was pregnant. They could try and look forward to something that would bring them joy. As Richard and Charlotte came along beside them, Richard hesitated at first, but then shook Samuel's hand.

The casket loomed at the front of the large room. She considered for the briefest of moments whether Chris's body was inside, but wiped away the image. She didn't want to think of him locked inside that box. It was completely unfair that someone with so much life was dead. She looked away and toward the packed room. She saw faces she was familiar with: the Porters and of course Olivia with her new lanky boyfriend, but also people she had rarely seen before—the manager of The Rendezvous, the Argent Excursions van driver, the high school football coach whom she recognized from months of watching Chris's practice. These were all lives he had touched. They congregated in small groups; classmates joined teachers and coaches, friends and neighbors mingled separately, co-workers and bosses in smaller numbers talked toward the entrance of the room. The sheer number of people struck her. She had considered herself singular in her relationship with him but looking around, she was embarrassed at how wrong she had been. She was one of hundreds of people who loved him. She walked from the room and out into the warm summer night.

It was Charlotte who came out after her, trying to coax her back in with cliché phrases like "Chris would have wanted you to get through this." What Charlotte knew about what Chris wanted or what Chris had been feeling before he swallowed a handful of Adapin was very little. Bryn told her mother she needed some time to think and was going to take a walk around the block. Charlotte told her not to be long, that the service would be starting in twenty minutes or so.

Bryn set the timer on her phone for fifteen minutes, pressed start and proceeded to walk away from the funeral home. She didn't want to go back—she and about a hundred other people would rather be anywhere else, but fifteen minutes later, she took a seat between her parents in the fourth row of the funeral parlor. She had found the strength in some recess she never knew existed and actually sat through the service.

Mr. Bello was the first to speak. He talked about a renewed relationship with his son that began for all the wrong reasons, but that he cherished nonetheless and was thankful to God for. He talked about Chris's athleticism and the joy playing for the Andover Huskies gave him. In a voice choked with tears, he wished that Chris had been welcomed by his mother's loving arms and walked into eternity. Bryn looked around the room through tearful eyes, noticing everyone was crying. On shaky legs, Samuel Bello returned to his wife, stopping to hug his daughter before he sat down. Chris's sister was going to speak next, and then there would be a brief reading from Corinthians. Then friends and family were welcome to share their thoughts and memories of Chris. With tears streaming down her face and a voice that was gulping for air, Chris's sister began, "As you can imagine, I've been doing a lot of reading about suicide. As a survivor of first my mother's death and now my brother's, I think we would all agree it is an understandable undertaking. Here's what I've learned more than anything and it needs to be shared as I talk about Chris. The primary goal of suicide is not to end one's life, but to end one's pain. He was in a great deal of pain, too much for his young age. A future that had once looked so promising looked grim. We can all speculate, but none of us were in his young and inexperienced shoes." She would stop and start to gain her composure, and then talked lovingly about their relatively carefree childhood and how close they were before their mother died. She talked about their move to Andover, walking to school with one another, the rainy days spent reading comics, a spring afternoon spent watching a bird build its nest outside her room. Bryn was overwhelmed. She had known none of this. Her intimacy, for all its drama, didn't compare to Chris's sister or their father or perhaps a dozen people in that room, maybe including Olivia—she felt like an intruder at a very private affair. She got up to leave for the second time that night and no matter how much Charlotte tried to urge her, she wouldn't go back in that room. She would ask her mother to say her goodnights all around and that would be it. She could make up whatever excuse she wanted. Bryn certainly wasn't going to get up and share any thoughts or memories.

Bryn labored through the week, avoided all phone calls and only came out of her room to eat and bathe. She guessed her family thought she was grieving. She couldn't have cared less what anyone thought. She was hiding and she was going to stay in her hole. Only when Claire was actually holding the bell of the front door with her index finger did Bryn stir from her self-imposed exile. Likely no one else was home to answer and Claire would know she was there since her car was in the driveway. Bryn answered the door in her pajamas. Claire didn't wait to be invited in. She pushed past Bryn and went straight toward the living room.

"Sure, Claire, come on in."

"I don't really care whether you want me here or not."

"I just want to be alone."

"Yeah, I get that, but you're not a grieving widow, Bryn. You were a friend, like a lot of people, like me, like Wally."

"Thanks for being so sensitive."

Tears were welling in Claire's eyes by the time she said, "I didn't come here to be sensitive. I came to tell you to take a shower and get out of the house. My God, Chris's dad is back at work. I think you can pull yourself together enough to get out for a meal. It's not healthy to crawl under a rock."

Bryn hugged Claire and squeezed hard. "What is it? What's wrong? Is this about Chris or something else?"

Claire was visibly shaken. "Can I sit down for a sec?"

"Let's go to my room." As they walked down the hall, Bryn said, "I want you to know I am not crawling under a rock, I'm taking a break."

"Yeah, a week is enough of a break. Anyway, I really need to talk to you."

"So talk."

"Let's get out of here first."

Bryn slumped into her vanity chair. "You know it's funny. What I realize more than anything is we weren't much of a couple you know? If we were, he might have had something to hang around for."

"Bryn, you are not to blame."

"Oh yeah. Tell that to Midnight."

"What about Midnight?"

"He suspected that it was me who planted the meth on Chris and Chris had asked me about it too. He asked me the day before he died. I don't think he believed I didn't do it. I think he felt completely lost and betrayed."

"Anyone would know that you wouldn't do that. You have

to get past this Bryn. Please, I'm begging you for me, please let's move on."

"For you? That's a little selfish, isn't it?"

"I didn't mean it to come out that way."

Bryn wrung her hands. "All I'm saying is I want to take care of all my mistakes, to be there when Chris needed me, to try and understand him and maybe help him. I want to give him a reason not to swallow a fistful of pills. My heart is breaking along with so many other people Chris knew. It is not easy to move on at all."

"We can't go back, Bryn. No one would have ever expected Chris to take his own life over something that seemed so insignificant in the grand scheme of things. No one."

"You think what he was facing was insignificant?"

"I don't mean it that way. He seemed like the kind of guy who could weather that storm, you know?"

"I guess. I just feel so shitty all the time."

"I think a little fresh air might help. I'm not leaving until you get dressed and we head out to do something. I don't care what it is."

"All right, an hour or so to get some lunch and get you off my back."

"Where to?"

"Someplace that isn't close. Let's drive to Tappanook."

Claire toyed with the flowers on the nightstand. She looked perplexed. "Tappanook? Why Tappanook?"

"I've never been there and I want to see it."

"Why?"

"My mother is from there."

"You sure you're not just avoiding people?"

"I'm not avoiding anyone. You're the one who said let's get out, so let's get out and you can talk to me about whatever you need to talk to me about while we drive."

The girls drove out toward Tappanook. A *Welcome to Tappanook* sign showed there were over 30,000 residents in the city proper—a fair-sized town in a state riddled with townships and hamlets. It took them under an hour to get there. Once they were in town, Bryn parked the car near the river-trail and they walked toward what seemed to be the heart of town. They passed a small museum and an art gallery and walked by a few grand, Victorian homes. They passed bars and sandwich shops and settled on a cozy restaurant called the Thistle. It boasted the town's best burger on its outdoor menu. Claire and Bryn both fancied a juicy burger with all the toppings and they walked inside. The Thistle smelled of warm baking bread and frying onions—a scent reminiscent of The Rendezvous. Bryn pressed her palms into her upper lids, erasing the memory, as the hostess asked them if they would like a booth or a table. They opted for a big booth adjacent to the front window.

The moment they sat down, Claire said, "This is kind of a cute town."

"I think so too. It doesn't look like this on Google Maps."

"What does it look like?"

Bryn reached for her phone. "I don't know. It looks kind of worn and tired."

"You don't have to show me. I can see that in places that we drove through on our way into town, but this downtown is killing it."

Their lunch conversation was banal—the town, the people

in the restaurant, the drive in. At two different times Bryn asked Claire what she wanted to talk to her about, but Claire brushed her off, saying it didn't seem like the right time. Bryn's curiosity was piqued, but Claire continued to tell her she'd rather talk about it a different time, so Bryn let it go. Since neither of them knew anything about the town, Bryn told Claire she wanted to go to City Hall to do some snooping into Charlotte's family. She wanted to see if there was any information about her grandparents. She had searched for information through the years, but the results were dead ends.

They asked for the check and walked the short distance to City Hall. The woman at the front desk sent them up to Public Records. Bryn sat at a desktop and typed in "Bolandz." The search came up with nothing. She tried a variety of possible spellings and still got nothing.

"Maybe if we tried your mom's married name?"

Bryn replied, "I think I've tried that, but never got anywhere. We can try again, but I'm not sure if Richard and Charlotte were married when my grandparents died."

"You don't know?"

"What about my family would ever make you think I'd know that one way or the other? You know my mother is not a big sharer. It doesn't bother me as much as it use to, but I think it drives Jack crazy."

Claire stood in back of Bryn and settled her hands on Bryn's shoulders. She massaged them gently. "Jack is the cutest guy ever."

"Yeah, he is kind of sweet, but he's taken."

"I didn't mean it that way."

Bryn turned her head and smiled up at Claire. "Sure you didn't."

"Oh, come on, just search."

Bryn typed "Charlotte Bolandz Wilson" onto the computer screen. They found an obituary for Matthew and Eve Bolanger, who were the parents of Miriam Bolanger and Charlotte Wilson (nee Bolanger) and an article about a deadly car accident, dated June 6, 1997.

Bryn tugged at Claire's fingers still resting on her shoulders and said, "Good call. Now, this is intriguing, Charlotte has a new last name."

Claire pulled out a chair and sat next to Bryn. "I'd say. Did you know it used to be Bolanger?"

"There should be a new word for something mysterious, vague and secretive—we'll call it a Charlotte'ism."

Bryn's grandfather's name was Matthew Bolanger and his wife was Eve Henderson Bolanger. He was born in Chicago, Illinois. She was born in Wilmette. They were married in Milwaukee, where Matthew attended the Milwaukee Trade School, and apparently moved to Tappanook four years later. In the meantime they produced two daughters: Miriam and Charlotte. She read on. Both Eve and Matthew died in a car accident on the same road Bryn and Claire drove in to town on. According to the Tappanook Times, while apparently headed out to do Saturday errands, they were hit by a construction vehicle head-on and killed instantly. They were buried in Polasky Catholic Memorial Park, a local cemetery. Bryn asked Claire if she wouldn't mind if they went to take a look. She told Bryn she'd actually like to go. It was kind of fun in a totally macabre way. GPS guided them about ten miles on a two-lane highway and then a quiet street called Hook Eye Road. The cemetery was off to their left.

It was Claire who spotted the single, large headstone that read simply: "Here lie Matthew Bolanger 1947-1997 and Eve Henderson Bolanger 1949-1997, together forever." There was the smallest Star of David under Matthew's name.

"Claire, do you see that?"

"I do. Did you know your mom is Jewish?"

"That would be a hard 'no'. Anyway, looks like she's half Jewish. Wow, I didn't have a clue." Bryn paused and stared at the headstone. "This is a big secret though. It isn't like keeping the price of Blahniks from Richard."

"Like, what else do you think she's hiding?"

"This is pretty big already."

"That's not what I meant. I only wondered if there were other things."

Bryn took out her cell and was taking pictures as she spoke. "I don't know. There always seems to be something. She's incredibly elusive and I've never really known anything about her past. Who knows what else I might not know."

Claire pulled at Bryn's arm. "There might be something really juicy. Like you and Jack might have an older sister somewhere or something like that."

"Maybe. Who knows? With my mother anything is possible. You'd think I'd be entitled to vital information, but she doesn't see it that way."

"This is something about who you are, though, not just about who she is. I actually think it's pretty cool."

"I don't know how I feel about it. I guess it's cool, but also kind of unbelievable. Let's get out of here. I want to share my snapshots with Charlotte."

"You're going to show her?"

"I think so. It's a good conversation starter, don't you think?"

They strolled arm in arm through the headstones and back to the parked car. Storm clouds were rolling overhead and they could hear thunder in the distance. Bryn complained about a wet drive home, but the rain cleaned the world and Bryn loved the earthy smell a hard rain left behind. She remembered its name from science class—Petrichor. An hour later, Bryn was dropping Claire off.

"Hey, you never did tell me what you want to talk to me about."

Claire shook her head and her eyes moved from side to side as if someone else was around to overhear. "It'll keep. You've had a weird day and now probably isn't the time."

"Well, now you've got me even more curious."

"Nah, I'll tell you later."

Bryn waved as she pulled out of the Porters' driveway. Ten minutes later she was parking her car on the right side of her own driveway, leaving plenty of space for Richard's car. Nothing riled him more than having to park on the street in front of his own house—idiosyncrasy number umpteen. Bryn sat in the car for a long time. She thought about the Franciscan friars who taught theology—Brother Paul in particular. He was funny and startlingly good-looking for a guy wearing brown robes. She smiled about the handful of Dominican sisters who taught mostly language classes, but were deeply involved in extracurricular sports and school fundraising. Sister Stephanie was her favorite. She shared stories about teaching in orphanages across sub-Saharan Africa, her college years as a varsity tennis player at UCLA and her childhood in Spokane. She didn't seem like the type to become a nun. She wondered what they'd think about her newfound discovery. She thought Brother Paul and Sister Stephanie would find it fascinating and she was anxious to tell them about it.

Bryn stood in the foyer and called out. "Anyone home?"

Charlotte replied from the kitchen. "I'm in here paying some bills and closing some accounts. Where have you been?"

"I've been out driving around with Claire. What are you closing?"

"It's not important."

"I want to show you something."

"Be quick. I have a lot to get to."

"I want you to take a look at a couple photos I took this afternoon at a cemetery."

Without really paying attention, Charlotte told Bryn she thought it was a bit macabre to be out taking photos of graveyards.

Bryn pulled out a chair and sat next to her mother. She enlarged the image and put it on the kitchen table in front of her mother urging her to take a look. "I know the story. Claire and I drove to Tappanook and went to public records at City Hall. Then took a little side trip to the cemetery on Hook Eye Road." Pointing to the Star of David below this name, she said, "There is a small Star of David on the headstone under the name of Matthew Bolanger." Continuing to point, she said, "See, right there below his name. I'm fascinated to finally know something about my grandparents. This is an interesting thread in their story and yours, for that matter."

"You may find it that way, but I don't. I feel like my 'story' is no one's business except my own. But, in the interest of avoiding this topic coming up again and again, I'll tell you as much as I know and then I'd like to drop it for good."

"But I think it's important and would like to do some digging beyond what you may know."

"Do you want to hear or not?"

"Sorry. Yes, go ahead."

"Your grandparents were from the Chicago area. From what I've been told, your grandfather was from a relatively prominent Jewish family. I didn't know any of them as a child or in adulthood. Your grandfather was a gifted designer and wanted very much to be an architect. His dream was dashed when he met your grandmother. She became pregnant a few short months after they met and his family wanted nothing to do with his Gentile girlfriend or her Gentile baby. An unwed couple expecting a baby wasn't what it is today and her religion made her completely unacceptable to his parents." Bryn tried to interrupt, but her mother shushed her. "Your grandfather could not abide by his family's decision and was subsequently disowned by them. He would not forget or forgive that. They set out for Milwaukee, where he promptly enrolled in trade school, which they could afford, while your grandmother just as promptly miscarried a boy who would have been my older brother. She went on to have your Aunt Miriam and then me, but she was never the same. Your grandfather could not leave her alone for long stretches of time. Her behavior was erratic and sometimes alarming and anti-social. He quit school, moved to Tappanook and took a job with no responsibility and very good hours so he could care for her and for us. My mother was not what you would call an involved parent. He loved her very much. He loved her enough to give up his dreams. He was completely selfless. They were both killed when I was a young woman. It was a few weeks after your father and I were married. I missed them, but I was glad somehow that they died together." Charlotte folded her hands and looked out the window. "My mother would have been lost either way, in heaven or on Earth; she could not function without him. God did Miriam and me a favor that day. It was hard for us to see that right away, but in time, we both were grateful, but I always missed your grandfather. He was a wonderful man. And that's about all I know, although I vowed that I would never entirely give up myself for another person—any other person."

"It's sad, but it also explains some things for me."

"Explains what?"

"Well, you've never really been engaged with what goes on here—at least not with me."

"That's such crap Bryn. Just because I am not a PTA, pot-luck, play date kind of mother, doesn't mean I'm disengaged. That's not me, Bryn, and it never will be."

"You think that's what I'm talking about? PTA?"

"Then what else? Be clear!"

"For starters, what about my school play? That's a glaring example."

"I told you, I had made prior plans that could not be cancelled and your father was away on business."

"Never mind. Whatever I say, you'll have an excuse and you'll be right and I'll be wrong."

"Oh my God, am I at the heart of all your problems?"

"Oh forget it. I guess I was speculating."

"Well, don't."

"I'm sorry I hit a nerve."

"Let's drop it."

"Fine. All I wanted from the start was some background on my grandparents. They sound like interesting people. It seems ridiculous that I have no clue about them. I don't know why you can't trust anyone with the truth."

"Bryn, it was my choice to make—a choice that I made before Jack or you were born. Can't you understand my wanting to shed my past?"

"Maybe. Maybe there are some things, but not things that define who you, who we, are."

"I did not see it like that and for the record, you are not Jewish. Your grandfather was agnostic at best. I think he saw little point in practicing a faith captained by people who had abandoned him. Your grandmother was a Catholic, which makes you a Catholic. I'd think all the money spent in a private parochial school would teach you something about theology."

"Out of curiosity, does Dad know?"

"Yes, your father knows. It's of little significance to him. He couldn't care less about it. Bryn, it's hard to explain, but I think I wanted to shed my past and become a different person and saw the opportunity to do that when my parents died. I think I was ashamed of them. No, maybe not ashamed, but so different from them. I created someone I like more than the girl I started out as. Everyone except Miriam, who is far away, is dead, so there were no messy tentacles reaching into my past."

"But can't you understand you may have deprived me of something rich about my past?"

"Well now you know."

Bryn turned to leave, but added, "This is a big deal to me, whether you understand that or not."

"Before you go to your room, please remember, Bryn, this is my secret, not yours."

"Well, it's Claire's too. She was with me all day."

"Then please ask Claire to refrain from discussing me. She can stick to her own family. That ought to keep her busy for years."

"Fine, I don't see the harm, but I'll tell her that it's your business."

"Thank you. If you're hungry, we're having dinner a little early tonight. Around six. I ordered from LaScala's."

"Why so early?"

"Because your father has an event at the club and he'd like to eat beforehand. I don't understand why he can't eat at the club, but he doesn't want to do that.

Bryn plodded off to her room feeling wobbly. Things were coming at her fast and she longed to share them with Chris, but then that wasn't going to happen. She had spent the last ten years studying Christianity at a parochial school, looking up to Sister Stephanie and longingly at Brother Paul. She intended to bowl them over with this discovery. There wasn't much detail, but she was going to share it with them anyway no matter what her mother said. She'd start out explaining that it was a kind of confession, which required them to keep silent. There must have been a good deal more about her grandparents and their parents and even their parents before them. What about the love story between her grandparents? He loved her so much that he gave up everything. What about the miscarriage? There had to be much, much more. Bryn had her theories, but they were just that—nothing would ever be substantiated, but she intended to search the Internet until her fingers bled. She knew her mother would never raise the topic again, but it would be fun to poke around all the same.

Bryn called Claire from her room saying her mother asked them not to spread any gossip about what they had unearthed that afternoon. Claire agreed, not really caring about it one way or another. Bryn was convinced, however, that at some dinner or another it would slip from Claire. She would tell Bryn it "just happened" and that it was no big deal. Funny thing about Claire, as long as things were no big deal for her, that meant they were no big deal.

Claire spoke. "Are you still there?"

"Yeah, I'm here, I was thinking."

"Thinking about what?"

"Thinking that this is actually important to my mother that you keep this between us. I'm obviously going to tell Jack, but please don't let me hear a month from now that you and Midnight and Wally were talking and it came out."

"Jeez, sorry for one time we talked about you and Chris. I won't say anything, okay? You're being really bitchy."

"I'm not trying to be. I'm asking you to do something for me. Well, actually for Charlotte."

"OK. By the way, have you asked her if your dad is Jewish? I always thought your last name was English or Irish, but it could really be anything."

"I'm not actually Jewish, because my grandmother wasn't. Would it make a difference?"

"Wouldn't make any difference to me if you were from Mars."

"I have to go. Dinner is on the early side tonight and I don't want to ruffle any feathers. I want a nice, quiet atmosphere to watch a Game of Thrones marathon on HBO."

Bryn thought she might ask her father about the origins of Wilson at the dinner table for the heck of it, but GOT loomed large. Richard was OK, but when he got onto that second scotch he could get mad at the dumbest things. Avoiding all conversation and eye contact seemed like the best path to an evening with Jon Snow. But then to her surprise, Richard was the one to start a conversation, asking her very specifically about her relationship with Chris. Richard always seemed glad there wasn't much of a relationship to talk about, so she sat there and stared at him.

"Bryn, how serious were you about Chris Bello?"

Charlotte jumped in. "Richard, do we have to talk about that terrible tragedy?"

"I'm not talking about his death. I'm talking about his life. I heard something today and I want to get to the bottom of it. I was at the club for lunch with two of my managers and ran into Paul Brandt. He stopped me on the way to the table and asked how everything was at home. I thought the question was meant to be general and meaningless, so I told him everything was fine, but he pressed, which I thought was odd. I don't know the guy well enough to have any kind of long conversation. He told me he heard some gossip and brushed it off at first but then thought if it were about his daughter, he'd want to know."

Bryn sat very still with her fists clenched on her lap.

"I asked him what he was talking about and he said he's heard a story at least a couple times that involved you and didn't feel it was that harmless anymore. Then he said he heard you planted the drugs on Chris in some scheme to spend time with him. Chris killed himself while you kept the secret from Chris and the police." Bryn yelped out "what?" but Richard asked that she let him finish. "According to Paul, there are a lot of people who have their suspicions. He was shocked I hadn't heard the story myself. I told him we keep pretty much to ourselves and don't like to gossip. He assured me he wasn't trying to spread any gossip but really would want to know had it involved his daughter. I told him I'd better get to my table and he apologized for being the one to tell me, but said again, he'd want to know if one of his kids were mentioned in that kind of story. I told him thanks and headed toward the table on goddamn wobbly legs."

Bryn felt dizzy.

Charlotte looked at her with a question mark of an expression as Bryn told them she could never do anything to hurt Chris. She searched both of their faces for comfort, but there was nothing but blank stares.

It was Charlotte who began, "How would people ever get that idea, Bryn?"

"All I know is that I loved—still love Chris with all my heart and I would never do anything to hurt him or his family. If I had known anything about anyone who might have put the drugs in Chris's jacket, I would have gone to the police with that information immediately."

Richard jumped in. "I would certainly hope so, but answer your mother's question. What would ever make people think this?"

The room seemed hot and her head was spinning. She sat quietly to gather her thoughts, but her father asked the

226

question again, so Bryn tried to answer. "Well, we did wind up spending more time with one another and I loved that, but not enough to ever do anything that would ruin his life and mine, because that's what happened." Bryn's voice trailed off. When Chris first died she thought about all the things he did for her and gave her, not tangible things, but the ethereal, and she had given him nothing. A day didn't go by without her looking at his picture. She wore his long-sleeve blue shirt to bed every night. She couldn't let go of anything that had been his.

She began again. "Do you know how many times I drive to the bridge over the Argent River? I stand there and stare at the water going by and I think I'm going to hell for not helping him…or maybe I'm already there."

Richard's voice rose. "What the hell are you staring over the edge of a bridge for?"

Bryn quickly spoke up. "It's not like what you're thinking. The Argent is where Chris and I had our first date, where we first got to know one another."

Charlotte asked her not to be so melodramatic, but Bryn assured her it wasn't for effect. Then Richard said, "Bryn, this whole thing is a mess, but I can't imagine for all the attention in the world from that kid you would ever have anything to do with it."

"But did you tell Mr. Brandt I would never do such a thing? Did you defend me?"

Richard stared at the ceiling with his fingers pressed against his lips.

Charlotte said she didn't think Bryn had anything to do with it either, she was merely asking her not to be so melodramatic. She asked what Bryn wanted to do about the gossip.

Bryn said, "nothing, nothing at all." She knew it would take its course no matter what, but she vowed to confront Midnight and Wally. She suspected they were at the heart of the story's beginnings. She headed to her room while Richard and Charlotte continued the conversation.

"Maybe I shouldn't go to the club."

"What? You committed to going, so you should go."

"Is this your way of telling me you want to be alone?"

"Not necessarily."

"But you do want to be alone?"

"What I want is for people to stop overanalyzing everything I say, but yes, I would rather be alone with my thoughts. Bryn found out about my parents this afternoon."

"How? What happened?"

"She and Claire took a drive to Tappanook and the rest, as they say, is history. I won't bore you with the details."

"Bryn was upset?"

"I guess. She seems upset about everything. More melodrama."

"I think she is pissed off at the world, but this tragedy with the Bello boy is a lot to handle."

"Clearly."

"Well, I'm headed out. Guessing I'll be back in a few hours."

"Speaking of heading out, that reminds me. I'm going to D.C. this coming weekend."

Richard shook his head. "Jesus, this is the third time in as many months. Is your sister going through chemo or something?"

Charlotte didn't dignify the question with an answer. Richard added, "Why don't you take Bryn with you?"

"I don't think she'd have a good time away from her friends. They don't want to be away from one another for ten seconds."

"OK. I thought it might be a nice change of pace for both of you."

As the door closed behind Richard, all she could think about was Mike and the short time she would remain in Andover. She had completed three very important items on her to-do list that very day. She had closed her MasterCard and Bloomingdale's accounts and searched Mike's neighborhood to get familiar with restaurants, stores and coffee shops. Lastly, she phoned Salon 213 to speak privately with her stylist, who seemed happy for her about the decision to leave Andover for good.

Fall

Bryn called Claire to tell her about the conversation with her parents, but got her voicemail. She didn't leave a detailed message—she needed to talk to her about Midnight and Wally and nothing more.

Two days and three messages later, Bryn finally heard from Claire.

"Since when do you take two days to return a call? I thought you were dead."

"I've been super busy."

"Too busy to call me? What is ignoring me about? I haven't talked to you since we went to Tappanook."

"I am not ignoring you."

Bryn's voice was a little shaky. "That's what it seems like. Does the cemetery have anything to do with it?"

"Don't be ridiculous, not at all. I told you, I thought the thing at the cemetery was interesting."

"So let's meet at Starbucks. I have to ask you something about Wally and Midnight."

"Oh, I can't. I have errands to run for my mom. I'll call you later."

It was hard for Bryn to believe, but Claire didn't call her back, so she went to the Porters' home to speak with her and get an explanation. She rang the bell and Wally opened the door telling her to come in while he ran upstairs to get Claire. Bryn said she'd rather wait on the front porch. Wally came out several minutes later and told her Claire wasn't home after all. He looked nervous and jittery and Bryn could tell he was lying. On her way home she tried to put the pieces together. Something had happened between the drive to Tappanook and Bryn telling Claire to keep quiet about the cemetery. The more she thought the more convinced she became that the cold shoulder was about the growing gossip surrounding Chris's death, but it seemed unfathomable. Claire would know better. And then Bryn began to notice the dismissal was not confined to Claire. Everyone was civil, but no one initiated communication with her. It was always Bryn calling or leaving a message or sending an email or a funny tweet or text to girlfriends. Responses were noncommittal at best. It was usually a returned phone call at a time she obviously wouldn't be around to pick up, or a returned email saying "lol" and nothing else. Everyone outside Bryn's family gave her the brush, with the exception of Midnight, and she couldn't talk to him. He had convinced her that he never said anything to anyone about his suspicions and she believed him, but she needed some distance. It was in the way he looked at her, a combination of sadness and hope, like a refugee captured on the pages of a magazine. And she missed Claire far too much to risk her seeing her and Midnight together, even if they were only taking a walk or waiting in line at the movie theater. It would give Claire even more cause to shun and ignore her. Her brother Jack, Richard and Charlotte had become her community. They were little substitute for what was once a large circle of classmates and friends. As the entire lake, adjacent town and even surrounding countryside took up a total of twenty-five miles, she wondered how Claire was successfully avoiding her. It would have required Harry Potter's Marauder's Map not to run into her. She was finally reentering the world after Chris's death. She could go out without feeling guilty, laugh at a joke without feeling like she was betraying his memory and now this new hurt took over. It consumed every inch of her and overflowed into the spaces around her. The silence from Claire was difficult to reconcile. She would try to re-focus on early graduation or the million related items that needed attention, but her mind would drift back to the day in Tappanook—the last day she had talked to her best friend. She began to accept that she wouldn't hear from her or see her. She sat on her bed feeling spent and sad when Jack knocked on her bedroom door.

He poked his head in and said, "What was it you wanted to tell me about Charlotte? I've been so caught up at work, I haven't been around."

"I've noticed."

"Why didn't you text me?"

"I wouldn't know how to explain it in a text. I need to show you something. Do you have time for a drive?"

They drove to Tappanook and the cemetery on Hook Eye Road. During the drive Bryn explained what she and Claire had found out about their grandparents.

They got out of the car and walked to the grave. Jack reacted with a long, open-mouthed stare at Bryn, and then said, "I almost didn't believe you. Goddamn Charlotte. She really is a tight-lipped crazy person." He added that despite the initial shock, he always felt there was something significant their mother was hiding—not her peripheral bullshit, but something that was important. He had suspected her secrets went deeper than lying about her age and her father's employment. He actually thought it would be something scandalous: a conviction or drug rehab. Their grandfather's religion seemed like a ridiculous thing to hide. During the walk and drive back home they talked about many things but mostly, Jack talked about how much he liked going away to college and thought Bryn might thrive with a change of scenery. She was at a crossroads and she could either stay in Wisconsin or move to a new place filled with new people and new experiences. Bryn didn't know what she wanted. This was the first time anyone asked her about what she might want to do. After a long discussion of pros and cons, they agreed sunny Florida might be the first place to look into. So when they arrived home, they began poking around websites for a handful of Florida schools. She kept on coming back to the University of Florida. She liked a lot of what she read about the programs in liberal arts, fine arts and history. She and Jack began making a list of all the things she would have to complete to apply for early admission. She would have to prepare an essay, get her transcripts, decide what she'd want to highlight from her extracurricular activities and several more items. Jack put his arm around her shoulder telling her it was going to be a lot of work, but he knew she was up to the task and figured it would be a terrific distraction for her. Tears welled up in her eyes as she nodded up at her brother.

He put his hand on the top of her head. "What's wrong?"

"Oh Jack, I'm so unhappy and this is the first thing that has felt good, or at least promising, in a long time."

"It can't be that bad."

"There's a lot of bad gossip going around about me and none of it is true."

He smiled and took her hand. "All the more reason to get

outta Dodge. I can see you in Gainesville already."

She could almost feel the warm sunshine on her face.

Bryn decided she would approach her father after talking with her guidance counselor and making sure she had done everything exactly as it should be done. If she had messed something up or skipped a step, she didn't want to open the door for her father to say it was a crazy, disorganized idea. Her guidance counselor agreed a change might be good and thought her chances of getting in via early admission were solid. He would confirm her early graduation via the necessary forms. She decided to hold off until she actually heard back from Florida's admissions department. Then, if everything went according to plan, she would be ready to go during Christmas break.

There wasn't much more to do than wait. She checked the school's website under her password every day and then in late November, there it was. She printed out the note and with paper in hand she knocked on her father's office door. Her nerves were rattled. She didn't know what she would do if he said it was a bad idea or that he would not pay for her to go to an out-of-state school.

She walked into his office with the paper clenched in her right hand. "So, I kind of need to talk to you about something."

"Yes, what is it?"

"I've decided I don't want to go to UW."

"You've talked about going there since you were ten. Why the change of heart?"

"I don't know. I've changed my mind."

"Why?"

"I'm not really sure. There are a few things. I could use a change of scenery for one."

He rolled his eyes. "Really? You have spent years talking about UW and all of a sudden you tell me you don't want to go there because you could use a change of scenery."

"Well Jack and I have talked a little about expanding my search beyond UW and looking at schools with great liberal and fine arts colleges and where the weather is warmer."

"I'm glad Jack's helping you out and I get the warmer weather, believe me, but we have plenty of time to get everything straight before next fall."

She inhaled deeply. "Well, not really. I want to go to the University of Florida and I want to go beginning of winter term."

"That's completely out of the question."

Bryn stood staring at her father's bookcase. "I don't understand why that would be out of the question. I have the credits. I've done really well in school and dedicated a lot of time and effort to activities that made my college application stand out and now I want a change. It's not radical. I'm not saying I want to forego college and move to Budapest."

Richard gave out a long sigh and shook his head slightly.

Bryn added, "I realize tuition will be dramatically different as an out-of-state student, but I would get a job and help make up the difference."

"You'll get a job? Bryn, you've never had a job in your life. It's not as easy as you think and this is about more than a damn job."

"I understand that, but I really want to do this."

"Bryn, I of course want you to be happy, but this is a

sweeping change."

"You say you want me to be happy, but happy in a way that makes you happy."

"Why, because I don't accept that you've simply had a change of heart and thought about moving to a place where the weather is warmer. I feel like there's something deeper here. Is it some boy? Is some boy going there and you've decided to follow him like a lapdog?"

"That's not it at all. Have some confidence in my decision. I swear it doesn't revolve around someone else. It's about me, and what I want."

"I have every confidence in your abilities, but this doesn't make sense."

"You really want to know?"

"Of course."

"And you'll accept and support me?"

"If I can."

Bryn hesitated to gain her composure. "I can't live around here anymore. Everyone avoids me and no one talks to me. Everyone thinks I did something awful to Chris and I need to get away from here."

"But you wouldn't be living here, you'd be in Madison."

"It's the same. It's all Wisconsin and I'd have to wait another seven months, which I don't want to do. This is my opportunity to go somewhere new and meet new people and get away from the gossip."

"So that hasn't blown over?"

"No it hasn't."

Richard got up from his chair and walked to Bryn. He stared into her eyes looking for uncertainty. There was only resolve. He said, "I don't necessarily condone running away from problems or challenges, but in this case, I guess I understand. Go up to your room and let's talk about the details later."

She wasn't sure if she wanted to laugh, cry, scream with elation, or sit and let it sink in, but Bryn began packing her bags that very night. She gently put the few printed photos she had of Chris into a folder and placed it at the bottom of a suitcase. She placed his blue shirt on top of that. Then she began a more pressing assignment—she began purging herself of Claire the way Claire had deleted her. Bryn had accepted the cold shoulder. She had run into her—the cafeteria, the commons, classes—Claire would abruptly walk away. Bryn stopped trying to get her attention. She began with removing Claire from her Facebook, Instagram and Twitter accounts and followed that with her profile information on her cell. The process of erasing her felt one part vindictive and two parts therapeutic.

A few weeks later, she closed her suitcases and hauled them out to her car, along with two boxes that held bed linens, a desk lamp, her laptop and other incidentals for her dorm room. She was set to hit the road. It would take her two days, with one overnight in Nashville, where Richard had arranged for her to stay. She'd be in Gainesville by December's end, a full week before midterm classes were scheduled to begin. She would use the time to stroll the campus, shop for anything else she needed for her room and familiarize herself with her class schedule and the buildings where they were held.

The only person outside her family she contacted was Midnight. No matter what had transpired, she couldn't leave town without some goodbye. She wrote a text that said, "I decided 2 go away 2 school—Gainesville to be exact. Hope you're enjoying Madison and ☹ I haven't seen U during winter break—I'm actually heading down to FL right away." He answered quickly, texting that he was shocked she decided to go to Gainesville and hadn't said anything until she was ready to leave. She quickly wrote a couple of lines telling him she needed a change of scenery, which he completely understood. Midnight said he'd head home over the coming weekend, so they could have dinner and talk about the details, but Bryn told him "no, right away is tomorrow".

Midnight's eyes burned with tears.

Winter

"Wally, can we talk?"

"My God Claire, you look serious."

"It is serious."

"Your room or mine or off-campus?"

"Let's get out. I need to clear the cobwebs."

"OK, let's take a walk around the lake."

Two hours later, Wally and Claire returned to their house. Wally headed to his room to call Midnight.

"Hey, dude, can you meet up tonight?"

Midnight didn't hesitate. "Sure. What time?"

"If you don't mind, I'd like to head to your house. Like in an hour good for you? I don't want to talk here in Grand Central."

"Sure, I'll see you later."

Midnight greeted Wally at the door, having seen him come up the walkway. "Hey man, what's up? You look like crap."

"I feel like crap. I've got something big to talk about."

"Let's go down to the den. Grab a game of pool?"

"Sounds good."

As Midnight twisted the blue chalk over the cue's tip, Wally began to talk. "How's UW?"

"Good. Some classes are pretty tough, but nothing I didn't expect. Hey, you really want to talk about school?"

"No, it's just that I don't even know where to begin because it took Claire two hours to explain it to me and I still don't get it."

"Let's have it."

"I may in part be to blame, but let me start. So, it winds up that Claire has had a crush on you for a long time. God knows I never knew it, but I'm bad at noticing shit like that. We're talking about back in sixth grade, even."

"Yeah, she kind of told me she liked me months and months ago, but it was harmless and she wasn't really serious. We both dropped it in about fifteen minutes. Deep down, I think she knew dating her would be like dating my little sister. I kind of said that to her, too. I was embarrassed."

"I'd be embarrassed too. I always thought she was hanging around because she liked to hang around."

"I guess in some way I was maybe flattered, but believe me, Wall, I can't stress 'harmless' enough."

"Yeah I know, but you won't be flattered by the time I finish. So, despite being besties with Bryn, Claire has always been a little jealous of, well, how you are around Bryn."

"Yeah, I guess, but that's over—adios."

"Maybe not so much."

"No it's over. Bryn has been in Gainesville for a while. I haven't seen her at all or heard from her much either. But you know what? I'm kind of glad for her. It got pretty messy around here with Chris. I called her a few times when she first got down there. The conversations were a little strained—you know, how's school, how are your parents, boring blah, blah, but it's all good."

"It's not so good, dude. "

"What isn't?"

"Bryn going off to school."

"You lost me."

"Look, you know everyone treated Bryn like a leper when gossip started to spread about her setting up Chris. I don't think I necessarily treated her the same and I never even thought she did it. Anyway, it was the reason she decided to go away to school, rather than go to Madison. Remember we saw her that night at El Caliente with her brother and she was dropping little hints about trying to escape all the drama?"

"Yeah, I remember. She actually sent me a text right before she left. I couldn't believe it at first, but what does all this have to do with Claire?"

"Well, I think based on what Claire told me today, she began to ignore Bryn out of guilt and nothing more. Claire turning her back on Bryn... well, I think that was the final blow for Bryn and her wanting to leave this place behind."

"What would Claire have to feel guilty about with Bryn?"

"It was Claire who planted the drugs on Chris."

"No effing way!"

"Yeah, I know. I couldn't believe it either."

"But why? Why would she ever do that?"

"To get Bryn and him back together. Claire figured Olivia would leave Chris when his popularity was sinking faster than the Titanic and she knew Bryn would be there with a lifeboat and she was right. She also thought, and I stress 'thought,' you would be less into Bryn as she became even more involved with Chris and that you would start seeing her in a different light when Bryn became completely unattainable. It's totally screwed up, I know, but clearly Claire is screwed up and despite me wanting to kill her, she never in a million years thought Chris would react the way he did. Shit, she thought he'd never even get close to jail."

"Wait. Wait a second. How did she ever figure out the cops would stop him?"

"She called the police station and told them there was some guy driving erratically. She even gave the plate number. I guess the arresting officer never put two and two together. I mean, why would he? I'm sure she was talking to a dispatcher, certainly not the guy who arrested him, and dispatchers get calls like that all the time. And the tip was right. He was driving erratically." Wally paused and stared into space. "I could kick myself. I remember thinking he was drinking too much and too fast. I felt like for every beer I had, he had two. Shit."

"It wasn't your fault, man. Why is she telling you all this now? It's a little late for a confession, isn't it?"

"Gary Jensen saw her do it and threatened to rat her out if she didn't say something to Bryn. I guess he was spying on Claire up in the bedroom with all those coats. You know how Gary hangs on the fringe?"

"Yeah. He is a kind of fringy guy, but he's all right."

"Yeah, I know, I'm just saying. He's certainly not the guilty party here. Anyway, he went to Claire and said he saw her put the shit in Chris's jacket. He thought it was all kind of harmless, but then Chris gets arrested and then kills himself and ultimately I guess he decided it was time to say something. Then Claire asked him to give her some time to figure out how to tell Bryn and the Bellos. According to Claire he said, and I quote, 'Well, the clock is ticking. I was going to say something right after Bello's funeral, but then it seemed kind of senseless. I can't keep quiet anymore.'"

"This is so screwed up on so many levels. I mean, Chris is dead and that's on Claire."

"I know, I know. It makes me sick to even think about it."

"Holy shit. I think I have to be the one to tell Bryn. I'm

afraid how she'd react to Claire and no offense, dude, but you don't seem like the right person."

"I don't think I am either, which is why I'm here. I think you'd have a better way of explaining it to her."

"Not sure I can actually explain it. Is it explainable?"

"I'm guessing that's a rhetorical question 'cause shit no, it is not explainable. I don't know how to explain something so completely off the tracks. FYI, I've convinced Claire to make it right and tell the Bellos right away. Well, not make it right—that's not what I meant—but you know what I mean, right?"

"Yeah, I get it."

"I'm sure she's going to get into a lot of trouble, certainly with my dad. She'll be lucky if Sam Bello doesn't slap the shit out of her, but I'm tagging along so that doesn't happen. I don't think Bryn will ever speak to her again."

"Man, I'll say it again, this is messed up. What was she thinking with this ridiculous scheme?"

With his voice raised, Wally said, "This scheme, as you're calling it, is not ridiculous, it is selfish and harmful and devious. You make it sound like it was a prank, like she was sneaking out of the house past 2 am or putting marbles in the AC duct at school."

"Hey, don't get pissed at me."

"Sorry."

"Shit, her plot kind of worked for a while. They were back to seeing one another, but once people started questioning Bryn's motives, I think Bello began to question them too. Maybe that was too much for him."

"Mid, don't speculate like that. No one is ever going to

get inside Bello's head and his reaction seemed like an over-reaction, no matter what he was up against."

"That's easy for us to say. I never liked him, but I feel terrible. God, what was Claire thinking?"

"I think she was thinking Bryn and Chris would live happily ever after and so would you and she. When I think back, whenever it came up that it might be Bryn, Claire was always confidently saying it wasn't Bryn that planted the meth. We always thought it was her defending a friend and nothing more."

"I think I'm going to try and fly down to Gainesville tonight."

"Tonight?"

"If I can't get out tonight, then I'll go first thing in the morning. I'm going ASAP and I swear I'm going to try and be as diplomatic and gentle as I can be about Claire."

"Do me a favor and at least talk to Claire before you go. Tell her what you're going to do."

"I think she's going to have to prep herself for some hate from Bryn and everyone in town, for that matter."

"What do you think Mr. Bello will do? Do you think he will press charges? Can you do that? Like, what if there is a wrongful death suit or something?"

Midnight was pacing around the pool table by the time he said, "Man, let's not go there yet. I think your dad may punish her well beyond what she could imagine, though. He is a serious guy and he's going to take this very seriously. I am still having a hard time grasping this, Wally. Shit, someone is dead, really dead, and Claire is to blame. Why wouldn't she go to anyone once it was feasible that Chris would go to jail?"

"I don't know for sure, but I think she was scared."

"She was scared? What about Bello?"

"I know, I know. It's hard to think about because she's my sister. One thing you're right about, Zach is going to go bat shit on her."

"It's weird how nice Mr. Bello turned out through all of this, isn't it?"

Wally rolled the white ball back and forth against the bank of the pool table. "Yeah, I guess so. I think a lot of it has to do with his wife. She is a bona fide knockout, but she is also a nice lady. I overheard my mom talking to one of her friends saying that she is maybe pregnant. I'm sure they're not looking to replace Chris but that might be good for them."

"Nice wife or not nice wife, your family is pretty deep into the shitter now."

"I know. I am mortified."

"I guess it doesn't help rehashing. Sorry. I'm going to talk to Claire right now, but I think I'd rather stop over and do it face to face. I don't want to play tag and then text and then have something come out wrong or be on record."

"That's cool and do me a favor, okay? I am royally pissed at her, but can you be gentle with her? She's going to catch shit from everyone; she doesn't need it from you and me."

"I'll walk home with you and talk to her, but I can't promise going gentle."

Midnight tapped softly on Claire's bedroom door. "Claire, it's Midnight. You decent? I think we need to talk."

"Yeah, come in, Mid."

The room was dark except for a sliver of light from the streetlamp poking through a small space left open in the curtains. Midnight reached for the wall switch and two bedside lamps came to life, bathing the room in soft light. There were clothes scattered everywhere and Midnight smiled, despite himself.

"I know my room is a mess. It's always a mess. I seem to get it all cleaned up and Lili comes in before a date and that's it—clothes everywhere."

He stared at Claire, not knowing where to start or what to say. She was a pretty girl, but he never thought of her "that way." She was always going to be Wally's little sister and nothing more.

He thought back to the day of the University Arts Festival. She had told him she liked him. They both stumbled through the discomfort of that conversation, but she didn't seem devastated, not even hurt. She seemed a little pissed off for a very short time. She had asked if he wanted to stay for dinner for God's sake. There was nothing in her response that would ever indicate this kind of wanton manipulation.

It was Claire who began.

"Midnight, I don't know what to say. I know I screwed up."

"That's an understatement, Claire. Why did you ever let it go so far?"

"I don't know. I never expected Chris to do what he did."

"But even before that. When it went all the way to trial, why didn't you say something?"

"I don't know. I guess I thought everything would still be OK."

"Really? That's what you thought? Chris was in a really bad place and you let him wrestle with that, no matter what you thought or what your intentions were. And even afterward, what about ending Bryn's pain? You let her fall away."

"I thought the gossip would blow over."

"You're a coward, Claire. That's it, isn't it? You were scared and you let it all wash off you and onto someone else. She was your best friend, Claire."

"'Was' being the operative word."

"Do you think you deserve her friendship?"

Claire began to cry and despite the urge to wrap his arm around her and console her, Midnight hung back. He sat on the floor and watched her. It had all been so stupid, so self-ish. Chris was gone, Bryn was gone and now Claire was gone to him as well. He would never see her the way she had once appeared, Wally's cute little sister who loved sports and dance and pop music and practical jokes. A conniving monster replaced her.

Wally trudged back toward their house, Claire at his side. He thought it was a miracle Samuel Bello hadn't killed her. As she was poking around for the words to explain her actions, he thought he might kill her himself. Explaining her motivation about getting Chris and Bryn back together came out as one of the most pathetic things he had ever heard. Was she actually trying to make it seem like this scheme was somehow meant to turn out well for Chris? Wally silently prayed Mr. Bello's interpretation wouldn't be that she was trying to say it was Chris's fault. Yes, it was nothing short of a miracle that he hadn't strangled the last breath out of her.

Wally had called his father earlier, asking that he meet Claire and him at home about a matter of some urgency. He explained they were at the Bellos' house but would be home in an hour. After what Wally considered a million lawyer questions, he finally had a chance to interrupt and simply ask that his dad do him a solid and be there in an hour. It was a toss-up whether he was asking as a matter of actual urgency or whether he wanted someone to know where he and Claire were in case Mr. Bello's axe fell on both of them.

"I can't believe you called Dad to come over and talk about this."

"What did you expect, we'd keep it from him?"

"I'm just not ready to tell the world, Wally."

"Well, you better get ready. What are you thinking, Claire? Do you think this is somehow going to be okay?"

"That's not what I think."

"Then what do you think?"

"What do you mean?"

"I mean exactly what I asked. What do you think of all this?"

"I feel terrible, Wall. I really liked Chris and I love Bryn and she will never forgive me and I'm pretty sure the Bellos never will either."

"Do you expect them to?"

"No, I guess not."

"Well, that's a start. You know Claire, I am getting the feeling you are not getting the weight of this. You are going to have to get a grip about how serious this is."

"I understand that it's serious."

"I sure as shit hope so. Anyway, Mom and Dad will help with where we go with all of it. Don't get me wrong, they are going to be beside themselves over what you've done, but I truly believe they'll try and be constructive as well."

When they walked through the front door, both their father and mother were sitting in the living room.

Zach spoke first. "Wally, what is going on?"

Wally looked at Claire and she back at him. "Claire, there is no way to make this conversation a nice one."

Wally looked at his father and began. "I don't know how much deep background is needed, but Claire's in big trouble over something she did."

Her mother was sitting on the long living room sofa next to Claire and rubbed her hand. She asked, "Claire, what have you done?"

Claire could not speak. The tears began to fall in thick streaks down her face and Wally began again.

"It'll probably help if you let me get through this and then we can take Q&A."

His father scowled at him. "Wally it doesn't seem like the time for sarcasm."

"Believe me, Dad, it's not sarcasm. It's going to be tough enough to get through without interruption."

"Then go ahead."

As Wally went through the story Zach could not remove his palms from his eyelids and just as assuredly he could not move his legs. He wondered if his wife felt the same. Mary seemed as anchored to the sofa as he was to the side chair. At last count, she had muttered "my God" four times.

He finally said, "Why would you ever do this?"

Claire answered. "It didn't seem awful at the time. It seemed like everything would work out."

"Are you out of your mind? It didn't seem awful? How could having someone falsely accused of a serious crime not be awful?"

Claire began to stammer and Mary said, "I'm not sure we're going to get anywhere with the whys or the hows. What are we going to do about it, Zach?"

"My God, I don't disagree with you, but some answers might help me wrap my head around the profundity of it."

Mary jumped in before Zach could say any more. "I think the first thing we have to do is speak with the Bellos."

Wally didn't think that was a great idea, at least not so soon after he and Claire had been there. He thought they might need some time to comprehend everything, but Mary didn't agree and scolded Wally for even suggesting it. They had to be brave enough to face whatever Mr. Bello wanted to dish out. Zach agreed wholeheartedly, saying he was going to call them and ask if they would see him. He suggested Mary stay with Claire and get more details, but she refused, telling Zach she would not let him shoulder the Bellos alone.

Mary and Zach stood on the Bellos' front porch, taking in a couple of deep breaths before ringing the bell. The door opened immediately, with Samuel Bello standing to one side to let them both in. Cathie Bello was sitting in the living room knitting what looked to be a receiving blanket. Mary instinctively looked at Cathie's belly and noticed the small bump. She figured Cathie was probably about four months along. She wanted desperately to say something and have the conversation begin on a happier topic, but she knew it would infuriate Zach and possibly Samuel and Cathie as well. She sat quietly after Samuel motioned for them to sit.

It was Zach who broke the heavy silence. "Mr. Bello, as I said on the phone, it's only today that I found out my son Wally and my daughter Claire were here. Mary and I felt we should come over and try to make some sense out of this. Sorry, there is no making sense out of this, but talk about what exactly happened, due process and of course our culpability."

Mary went to speak, but Samuel began, "I'm not sure I know where to start. At first, I couldn't believe what I was hearing. I didn't really understand your daughter's story or her motivation, or the fact that she did not come forward until now. As you know, Chris has been gone for several months. It's a long time to sit silent."

Mary quickly said, "I believe she was frightened."

Zach interrupted and looked directly into Samuel's eyes. "Samuel, I cannot imagine what you went through and to think that Claire had the information but not the wherewithal to put a stop to everything is unimaginable to me. Even though she is my daughter, I am finding it unforgiveable. I don't give a damn whether she was frightened or not." He turned to Mary and said, "I swear I am not trying to contradict you, but I have to make it clear to Mr. and Mrs. Bello that it is completely irrelevant what she thought. The singular thing that is relevant is what she did and admitting to ourselves and the Bello family that we will never be able to right her outrageous wrong."

Zach pressed his palms to his eyes, this time to keep from crying and then Samuel spoke again.

"My first impulse was to hurt her in some way, like she hurt Chris and like she hurt Cathie and me and Chris's sister. You know, I never believed much in therapy, but Cathie convinced me to go after Chris... well, after Chris passed away. I couldn't sleep. I couldn't work. All I could think about were my shortcomings. I don't know if you know, but Chris's mother took her own life as well. Anyway, you'd have to be some kind of monster not to question your own role in those events. I won't bore you with my time on the couch, but what I quickly saw on your daughter's face was a mistake made out of immaturity and stupidity. In the final analysis I have no desire to hurt anyone the way Chris's death hurt me. I went through the gamut of emotions, even being ashamed of Chris, thinking him a coward for not facing what the world had thrown his way. Then I remembered the words his sister spoke at the memorial service. I remembered what a wonderful young man he was and that shame went away, along with the deep envy every time I saw a dad with a teenage son. Finally, only the love remained. Do I have Chris to hold onto? No, but I have the love just like with his mother, God rest her.

And life renews itself, I am happy to say."

Cathie beamed at him and reached out to grab his hand.

Zach spoke. "You are an extraordinary man, but Claire's immaturity and the idea that she can manipulate people and her surroundings is a reflection on Mary and me. As generous as you are, I cannot let this pass over her like she did nothing wrong."

"That is your decision to make, but there will not be retribution from Cathie or me. We don't want to fill our lives with revenge or retaliation right now. Claire is a young woman and we don't see any sense in ruining her life. She will be allowed to do that all by herself and I don't know if you can prevent that, given her behavior."

"I think the way to prevent it is to have her pay for her mistakes. I don't know where to begin. I've spent the better part of my life as a litigator and this could be contained as a civil matter or have the criminal courts reconnected."

Samuel looked down at his shoes and not at Zach when he said, "I can't help you with that, Mr. Porter."

Mary looked and sounded frantic when she said the Bellos were right. They should focus on the love and not punishment. Punishing Claire wouldn't bring Chris back.

Zach continued, "Mary, everyone is being too generous with Claire and something inside tells me she's counting on goodwill and leniency. Well, not from me. Not going to happen. Samuel and Cathie, we're going to get out of here to go talk. I can't think of the words to say how deeply ashamed I am. Saying I'm sorry seems wanting and bereft."

Zach held the door for Mary and shook Samuel's hand with a firm grip. Mary kissed Cathie on the cheek and whispered, "Congratulations."

The second he closed the car door, Zach said, "We have a lot to talk about."

"Zach, let's not go home right now. Let's take a drive or have a coffee or something to eat. Please, let's do anything except go home and talk to Claire right now. I feel like there is a chasm between the two of us in how we want to approach this."

"Agreed. To start, she is in need of years of professional counseling. I'd like to get to the bottom of what made her tick so we don't repeat it with her younger siblings. God help me, I have an impulse to slap her! My God! What do you say to your kid when she has completely ruined other lives and probably her own in the bargain?"

"We are agreed on therapy and I'm not underestimating your urge to slap some sense into her, but corporal punishment is not the answer and certainly not with Claire. She's too introverted."

"Claire? You think she's an introvert?"

"Yes, Zach. Her public exterior doesn't match what's going on inside. She is not as confident as people would guess in spite of her obvious attributes."

"Jesus, I feel like I've been on Mars."

"No, I think it's pretty common for dads to see something different than moms do, at least when it comes to daughters. You probably understand the boys better than I do."

"No one understands Wally better than you."

"Perhaps."

"Let's head out to the Northrop Inn. We can have something to eat and take a couple hours to hash this out. I'll call Wally and tell him neither he nor Claire is to move a muscle until we get home."

"Well, Wally certainly isn't to be punished or blamed."

"No, I wasn't suggesting that, but I think she needs a chaperone and he's my first choice."

"Ah, okay."

They drove to the restaurant in relative silence, both trapped with their own thoughts. Mary broke the quiet. "God Zach, what are we going to do?"

"Let me answer that with some food in front of me."

They arrived at the restaurant and sat at a secluded table where they figured they wouldn't be overheard. Mary put her napkin on her lap and her hand over Zach's. "So, here we are. What are we going to do?"

"I really believe she needs to be punished if she's to learn any lesson from this and I want her to learn something about her complete lack of judgment."

"I know, and I don't want her to go unpunished, but I guess I don't know where to begin."

"Well, therapy is going to be an absolute must."

"Yes, we've already agreed to that. A professional should handle the emotional side. What do they call that syndrome? I think it's called responsibility deficit disorder or something like that. One of the symptoms, if I remember correctly, is belief that by trying to change others rather than oneself, life can be happier and more rewarding."

"Mary, did you see this coming? Do you know something you're not telling me?"

"God, no. I just remembered that from one of the child psychology lectures the PTA hosts at St. Agnes."

"In addition to therapy my second thought is to remove her from her current surroundings while I think about how to handle the rest of this mess. I'll need to speak with our attorney ASAP. We should look at her browser history as well before she has a chance to fiddle with it—in case we're asked."

"What good would that do?"

"Well, I'd like to make sure we don't have a goddamn Slenderman on our hands."

"I didn't mean that."

"Jesus, are you suggesting we not get legal advice?"

"For goodness sake, no. I meant what good will removing her from home do?"

"Well, in some ways I think that will be easier on her. She'll be able to avoid a good deal of reaction and distraction, but I also see it as part of her punishment. Wally won't be around to hang out with, no company from Lili in their bedroom, no hanging out and watching HBO. She will learn something about isolation and loneliness, which I'm sure Chris was feeling a good deal of as he awaited trial. I think we isolate her in a place like the Dearborn Academy, where there is a strict routine, no frivolities, discipline and lots of options for therapy. Their focus is kids who are troubled and whether Claire cops to it or not, she is troubled."

"You're sure you really want her away from home?"

"It's not what I want that's important, but what I think is best for her."

"But what about friends and family and swimming and her potential scholarship?"

"I don't see any of that happening. Not now. Who knows, maybe they have a swim team." He looked at Mary's vacant expression and added, "I mean, it's not a prison, it's a regular school with regular programs, its students merely have …"

"What, criminal records?"

"No, that is not it at all. They have *issues*—unresolved issues that they're having problems with. That's all."

"That's all?"

"Let's be frank here. If Samuel Bello had decided to press charges, Claire might be facing jail time for obstructing a police investigation or at the very least impeding an investigation. With or without Samuel's involvement, I am not convinced we shouldn't go to the police and the courts right now. The law is the law. Forget that it's kids, forget it's our kid, and forget the motivation and all the other shit. I could lose my license over this. Right now there is containment, but that never lasts."

Mary was ringing her hands and staring at the tablecloth. "But the Bellos aren't going to talk about this to anyone and we can tell Wally it is to be kept quiet."

"It's naïve to think someone else won't know this story."

She didn't reply and Zach continued.

"No matter what we do, it's going to seem awful to Claire. I think we can both accept that, but I don't think we have the luxury of grass growing underneath us. I think we go home and tell her Dearborn is the first step—no arguments, no backtalk and then you and I will decide what's next."

"Agreed."

"Really? Agreed?"

"Yes, I think we should get the check. I can't eat anything. I'm too sick to my stomach. Should we tell her together?"

"Of course."

Mary and Zach made their way home, heads hanging as they walked through the front door and yelled for Claire to get in the living room "now." Claire sat quietly and listened to her father tell her that she would be spending the remainder of her senior year at the Dearborn Academy. She would not let herself cry. She bit the inside of her mouth with her back molars as hard as she could to rechannel her pain. She could barely hear what he was saying about classes and therapy sessions and the possibility of a swim team. He intended to have her registered and packed by the end of the week. He didn't want any protest. He and her mother had made up their minds.

She had lost Midnight and Bryn and now she would be losing Wally and her mother and even him, traitor that he was. What was his punishment for leaving her mother for some woman in his office? No one sent him into exile for that. No one said anything about his complete lack of judgment, but at last count, he'd said it to her six times. Of course what she had done was monstrous. Of course she blamed herself for Chris's death. Of course it didn't matter that she never, ever, ever thought Chris would take his own life. She felt as puny and awful and diabolic as she possibly could. She didn't need her father to remind her. She still had a hard time believing it ever happened. Everything had been going so fast and she didn't know how to stop the momentum. She envisioned a 50-ton bulldozer careening downhill without a driver. She wanted to turn back time. She wanted him alive again. She wanted him with Bryn. She wanted everything to be back the way it was.

Her father's voiced became raised. "Claire, are you listening to me?"

"Yes, I'm listening."

"You don't act like it, goddamn it!"

She looked directly at her father and said she was listening, but trying to take it in and process what he was saying.

Maybe Dearborn would have a swim team and she'd make new friends and she'd see her mother. In his rant, her father had said something about them visiting. She wouldn't say another word. She would simply pack her bags and not show how afraid she was.

The plane to Gainesville took forever. Midnight had to fly through Chicago and then take some vintage Bombardier 20-seater from Tampa to Gainesville. His chest felt like it was going to explode from nerves and bad O'Hare sandwiches. What would he say to her? He didn't know why he was concerned whether Bryn ever spoke to Claire again, but he was. Claire had looked like a beaten puppy by the time he had left her room. He'd been muddled—one minute he wanted to punch her, the next, he felt sorry about everything that had happened and wanted to hug her. Claire's last words to Midnight, as he walked out the door, were "please give my love to Bryn."

"Love to Bryn." He thought it overly optimistic, but the words haunted him on the two-hour flight into Tampa. A woman in the middle seat who insisted on disregarding his personal space pressed him into the window and his knees were in his chest. He was at least three inches too tall for the seat, but he wrestled into a comfortable position and began to doze off. He thought about Crane Lake. Everyone there seemed like a second family, especially the Porters, including Wally's dad. Midnight couldn't hold a grudge against Judge Porter, despite Wally being angry with him about the girlfriend. And more than anyone, he had always loved Bryn. There was something about her that got into him and stuck. He remembered when he first saw her. The sun was bright overhead and sparkling across the lake. He held his hand over his eyes to shield the glare. She was standing and talking to Claire on the front porch of her house. The Wilsons had moved in a few weeks earlier and she and Claire were already becoming bookends. The two were giggling about something, and he could see that broad, easy smile and the dimple in her left cheek, her aquiline nose and that sweet pixie haircut. She had a boyishness that fit her. Claire was taller and traditionally prettier, but Bryn made him dizzy. What he wouldn't give for a do-over. He would have confessed his love for her that very day.

Bryn slammed the exit bar out of Bartram Hall and felt the sunshine and the humidity on her skin. She looked around. She was the only person without a tan. Eighteen years of snow and ice made for a color somewhere between beige and linen-white. It would pass. She had gained a pound or two, but somehow felt lighter. She was less self-conscious. The drama before and after Chris's death was now part of her past. She decided to stop on her way back to her dorm and enjoy some sun under a Spanish moss and do her anthropology reading assignment for that week. She loved the department. Many of the undergrads were male and even though a day didn't go by without still thinking of Chris, she liked being surrounded by a bunch of guys. Girlfriends had proven to be disappointing.

Thinking about one fellow student in particular, she con-templated the face of the guy turning the corner at Newell and walking toward her. He looked like Midnight: dark curly hair, kind of gangly. He had Midnight's walk. Yes, there was some-thing very familiar about the gait. Maybe she was just missing home. Spring break was a few weeks away and she'd make her first trip back home, getting to see Jack and Claire and Wally and Midnight. She prayed Claire and she could mend whatever happened that day they drove to Tappanook, and put it behind them. Maybe whatever had gotten into Claire had thawed. She put her reading assignment down after two pages and found her volume of Hemingway's short stories in her backpack. It was a gift from Chris. If her house were ever on fire, it would be one of the things she'd grab. As the guy was getting closer to Bryn, he began to smile. The glare of the midday sun was making her squint, but as she focused, she saw that it was Midnight. She leapt off the grass. Small bits of the blades were still clinging to the back of her thighs and she took a moment to brush them off. By that time, Midnight had begun to run and was nearly to her. He hugged her tight.

She gave a good long blink and her eyes widened as she grabbed onto Midnight's shoulders and gave them a little shake. "Oh my God, what are you doing here?" She continued to shake her head. Her mouth was open and her smile broadened as she said, "I can't believe you're standing here. Holy shit, it is so good to see you!"

"It's really good to see you too."

"You have completely got to be kidding me that you're here. I kind of thought it looked like you, but then thought, no way. I still can't believe it."

"Yeah I know. Surprise! Here's the thing, I have something to tell you and wanted it to be face-to-face. Is there someplace close where we could maybe go for coffee?"

"There's a Starbucks about 2 blocks away, but tell me now. I can't stand the suspense."

He grabbed Bryn's elbow as they walked and it occurred to her that Midnight was steadying himself, not her. "Just give me a chance to sit down and get my thoughts together." Their pace was brisk and they were ordering lattes ten minutes after their hug.

Midnight started their conversation with the first question that came to mind. "So, how's school? How are you doing?"

"It's good. I like it down here. After all those years in the tundra, it's nice to soak up some sunshine."

"I bet. How about classes?"

"They're good, but it's all still really new. There is a pattern. I hate first-year algebra as much as I did in high school. I thought it would be an easy credit, but as it turns out, I was wrong. I love my anthropology class and my acting class in the general theater department. I might change my major to theater, which would be a hoot for Wally. Remember us in *The Crucible*?" Bryn laughed and added, "He'd be so proud of me. How about you? How's UW?"

"Cold."

Bryn laughed again. "Oh, come on, there has to be more than that."

"It's great. You know me I've never had a problem with school or study. I have a pretty full course load, but no complaints."

Bryn's head was swimming with questions. "And you're here deciding to take a little break before spring break? Not that I'm complaining about seeing you, but that doesn't make much sense. For god sake, what's up?"

Midnight avoided looking at her. "Yeah, I'm coming to that. Wally and I were talking and he told me something we both think you should know, so I decided to come down here. We haven't talked much since you left and I feel kind of bad about that. I tried, you know. I tried to call you a few times."

Bryn played with her napkin and rotated the sleeve on her coffee. "I know and I'm sorry, but the way everyone acted toward me, it was hard to be in touch."

"But I never treated you differently."

"Really? You're the first person to have asked me if I planted drugs on Chris and you should have known better.

You should have been a better friend."

Midnight sat in silence for a moment. "I was wrong, but everything was so crazy and I never said a word to anyone else. You know that, right?"

"I do. Let's drop it, okay?"

"Okay."

Bryn reached for Midnight's hand and squeezed it gently. "So come on, enough small talk. What's so damn urgent from Wally that you'd come all the way down here?"

"God, I'm starting to lose my nerve. I'm here because I thought you'd want to know the truth about something, but now I'm second-guessing myself."

"I am going to kill you! The truth about what?"

"I found out who planted the drugs on Chris."

Midnight could barely hear Bryn as she whispered, "It can't be. It just can't be." She began to cry as Midnight told the story. When he finished, he said they should all try to put it behind them. He didn't know exactly how it would all shake out back in Andover, but thought she'd be better if she tried to let it go. Bryn told him how crazy that was and reminded him that someone was dead. The Bellos would never stop thinking about it regardless of "how it might shake out" and she wouldn't either, no matter what Midnight might think. Midnight accepted that, but seemed annoyed with her and she felt equally annoyed with him.

They walked back to her dorm, talking about what they thought Claire's punishment should be. Bryn thought she should go to jail, while Midnight thought that would just be another life ruined. He thought she should do some kind of public service, maybe with kids who are in trouble or with teens susceptible to suicide.

Bryn stared at Midnight for a long time and then said, "What would Claire know about a troubled childhood or teens on the verge of suicide? My God, I think that is the dumbest thing I've ever heard. Everything about her is privileged—the family, the face, the swimming. If the Porters aren't going to do something I am seriously thinking about doing something on my own—the police should be notified."

Midnight felt any response would come up short, so he said nothing. Bryn was right. Claire wasn't qualified to counsel anyone no less someone in real trouble. He asked if they could drop the conversation and instead go grab a beer. Bryn thought both ideas were good. They went to a supermarket and bought a six-pack of Stella and two bottles of wine and headed to Bryn's dorm room. Her roommate was studying in what they designated as their common area—it consisted of two beanbag chairs and a small crate in a space that measured about four-by-four feet. Bryn asked her roommate if she might give them some privacy and she immediately obliged, saying her boyfriend would welcome the company and the excuse not to study. Bryn grabbed her arm as she was leaving and said, "thanks." She whispered back, "He's cute" and then opened the door. She waved at Midnight, saying, "It was nice meeting you." The door was barely shut when Midnight kissed Bryn. His lips were full and soft and partly open against her lips. Bryn didn't stop him, but she didn't fully respond. She asked him if he wanted a beer and he quickly said yes. He could tell Bryn wanted to change the direction the evening was headed. They sat and watched movies and drank their beer and wine.

Despite agreeing to drop any discussion about Claire, Bryn reached for the remote and paused the movie. "So what about you and Claire?"

"What do you mean?"

"What do you think? She's clearly crazy for you."

Midnight looked straight into Bryn's eyes as he replied. "I never felt anything for Claire. She's like my little sister. That's goddamn obvious to everyone, except for you. I'll tell you one thing, I wish she had come to me with this messed up plan. I would have held her down and knocked her out."

Bryn looked down and began to fiddle with the remote. "God, I wish she had told someone. Chris might still be alive."

"I know. It's hard to get your head around it. I'm sorry, Bryn. I really am. Chris and I weren't friends, but that doesn't mean I don't feel awful about what happened."

Bryn's eyes were welling with tears. "Yeah, everyone seems to be sorry, but it's not good enough, you know? No matter how much times passes, it really doesn't sink in that he's actually dead and now I know it was completely avoidable—that wicked bitch."

She got up to go to the bathroom and staggered. When she came back, she said, "We should go to bed. I don't know about you, but I've got to get some sleep. I'm exhausted."

"I'm spent too."

"Holy shit, we've been drinking for six hours and I have an English Lit class in the morning. I am presuming you're staying here."

"I had planned on it, but not so sure it's a good idea now."

"No, it's fine. No worries."

"As long as you're sure."

"Yeah, I'm fine with it. I could use the company. It's a sad night."

Midnight hesitated for a moment, but then said, "I can go, really."

"No. You should stay."

Despite one brief protestation, Midnight and Bryn had sex in her tiny single bed that night. She didn't care how Midnight felt about her and at that moment, she didn't care how she felt about Midnight. She needed the touch of someone and justified or not, she wasn't ashamed at the idea of hurting Claire. They kissed and fondled and explored one another. Midnight mapped every inch of her and when she got up to get a glass of water, he watched the silhouette of her naked shape walk across the room. He couldn't breath—he thought she was the most beautiful thing he'd ever seen. Before she came back into bed she said "Alexa, play Moondance" and then she pulled back the blanket and slid on top of him. As they sobered, they talked about many things, but didn't bring up Claire or Chris again and that alone made the conversation feel strained. Bryn finally fell asleep resting her head on Midnight's chest just shy of 3 a.m.

They woke late in the morning, both confessing to hangovers. She had already missed English Lit class. Midnight asked that they go get some coffee and maybe something to eat. Bryn suggested The Buttery Biscuit, which was off campus and specialized in hangover food. Bryn looked out the window and toward the countertop diners. She was nauseous from drinking and feeling uncomfortable in the light of day. She searched for small talk and asked Midnight more about UW and how his mom and dad were. She confessed to having a little crush on his father when she was younger. Midnight

smiled and said he thought his dad was a great guy. Still looking to fill their occasional silences, she asked him if he was
still seeing Nora.

"Nora and I have never been anything but friends."

Bryn smirked. "I bet that would be news to her."

"No, I don't think so. Nora and I were always authentic
with one another. We weren't going to be a long-term thing
and you may not believe it, but she was fine with just hanging out. It's actually one of the things I really like about her.
She's super mellow. I thought you knew, especially now, that I
always hoped you and I could, well, be together."

Bryn didn't know what to say.

Midnight broke the silence. "Bryn, I think it's time we
clear up some things."

"I don't think there's anything to clear up. It's kind of like
how you feel about Nora. That's how I feel about you—we're
friends."

"Then what was last night about?"

"I don't think I really knew what I was doing. I think I got
carried away in the moment."

"Oh come on. You knew exactly what you were doing and
who you were doing it with. Don't act like you didn't."

"I think I needed to be with someone, anyone."

"That's a horrible thing to say to me. Anyone? Really? I
never thought I'd say it and I've forgiven you for many things
in our past, but I feel like you've become a different person
and not necessarily a nice one."

Bryn was ashamed to look Midnight in the eye and stared
down at the table. "I don't know what you're talking about.
What have you ever had to forgive me about?"

"Don't pretend to be so confused. One thing you did drives me crazy. I can think of three times off the top of my head when you and I had made plans to go somewhere with the group of us and you called at the last minute to cancel because Chris had called you when his work schedule changed. It always left me raw."

"I don't remember ever doing that."

Midnight shook his head. "Well that's convenient."

"Even if I did do that, it isn't that big a deal."

"See, that's what I mean. It is a big deal. It's a big deal to do that to anyone and if the reverse happened, you'd be whining about it. You know, I've always loved the gentleness and quietness about you. I liked that you didn't need to be part of any stupid cliques and that you didn't need to look like the latest pop star. Instead you kind of dress like a politician's wife. You're smart and funny and well, all those things don't seem to matter so much now that you said I might as well be any stranger."

"I always thought we were friends and nothing more."

"Well, don't worry; like I said, I don't feel much for you anymore. I think you're kind of nasty and just a so-so lay."

Still not meeting Midnight's gaze, it felt like minutes went by before she said, "Nice, really nice thing to say. Oh one other thing. No matter what you think, I'm calling the Andover police to tell them about Claire."

Midnight threw his fork on the table and got up to leave. Bryn grabbed at his sleeve and he stopped. "Where are you going?"

"I'm headed to the airport."

"Do you at least want a ride?"

"Nope. I can get myself to the effing airport."

Bryn watched Midnight stand at the curb staring at his phone. She didn't want him around and figured he didn't want to be around her either. He was giving too much advice about putting the past behind and moving on. She didn't want to put those days behind her. The sad truth was that she wanted to put the previous night behind her. Someday she might put things into perspective, but she wanted to be sad and angry and she wanted Claire to pay for what she did. She couldn't have cared less whether Midnight thought she was nasty or not.

Midnight's cell was buzzing as the plane touched down. It was Wally. He thought about ignoring him. He couldn't talk about Claire or Chris or the Bellos anymore. He wanted to not talk about any of it for the rest of his life, but Wally was his best friend and he couldn't bring himself to press "can't talk right now".

"Are you with Bryn?"

"No. I left her this morning."

"Shit."

"Why?"

"I wanted you to hold off on telling her. While you were with Bryn, my parents were with the Bellos. I had a long conversation with my dad a little while ago and he'd like as few people to know as possible."

"Well, what's done is done."

"Shit, my dad wanted the whole shit show to stay between us and the Bellos while he got some things straightened out with his lawyer and some judge and somebody else who I can't remember. I've been trying to get you for the past few hours."

"I'm sure I was in transit."

"You weren't down there very long. What happened? How did Bryn handle it?"

"It's a long story. I'll tell you when I see you. Let's just say, not very well. Maybe you could drive back to Madison with me. I have to get out of here and back to school."

"Did you expect her to handle it well? I didn't."

"No, I guess I didn't, but I expected the time with her to

be better."

"Let me see if I can borrow my mom's car and then I could drop you off and drive back. You can tell me about Bryn and I can tell you about my parents. Unbelievably, Zach told me, well he actually told Claire, but I overheard him. The Bellos have no interest in pursuing anything with the courts or the police. Sam Bello should be canonized. My parents feel like the Bellos are wrong though, and the court must be involved. I can tell my mom and my dad feel helpless."

Midnight headed out of the airport—his shoulders tightened up to his ears. "That's pretty much how I feel too."

The morning temperature was hovering at 30 degrees and it looked like a late-season snow might be on the way. The sky was the color of slate and the air felt moist and heavy. Zach's hands were shaking as he locked his bike to the stand outside the courthouse, but it wasn't because of the cold. He was scared. He had talked with Mary and then sat with Claire to tell her his intended course of action.

He and Mary thought it would be best for Zach to speak with the Bellos again, then with his lawyer and go from there—meet with the prosecutor, Judge Merck, and then maybe the police, depending how the first conversations went. He thought, based on his prior conversations with the Bellos, he could assure his attorney there wouldn't be any civil complaint, but he was going to ask them again. Containment however; was already slipping from his grasp. Jon Wright knew all the details and he intended to tell Bryn Wilson and there was the kid who saw Claire in the first place, and threatened her with exposure. There would be no way to hide what had happened or keep it between them and the Bellos. And, even if he could hide it, he wasn't sure he ever would.

The one good thing he saw coming out of a situation he found hopeless, was realizing how much he loved Mary. They had been spending a lot of time together for all the wrong reasons. He had been a fool and a cad and prayed she'd take him back. He felt it might be the only way he and Mary could weather what was ahead for Claire—doing it together. He loved his daughter and it made him sick to think what she had done to someone else's life and her own, but his natural instinct was to protect her even if that meant him taking the fall. As he steadied his hands and looked up into the grey sky, he opened the door to the courthouse.

The first people he saw were Samuel and Cathie Bello. They were seated on a long bench outside one of the courtrooms. Zach had asked them to come. At first they declined saying they didn't want to rehash any of it. They had quite enough of talking about it, but Zach urged them. He explained it was the only way to put it all behind them. Judge Merck would not make a decision without speaking to both of them.

They sat with Zach's attorney talking about what he expected the judge to ask, what he was going to say to the judge and how he thought the proceedings would go. After a short time, they were summoned to meet with the judge and the public prosecutor. Zach's attorney explained what had happened the winter before, beginning with Chris's innocence pertaining to the drug charge and Claire Porter's involvement. Looking toward the Bellos, he assured Judge Merck they had no interest in any civil action or wrongful death suit. He explained that a considerable amount of time had passed between Chris being arrested and his suicide. Ms Porter had no reason to believe Chris was suicidal. There were no extenuating circumstances which pointed to that end. Yes, during that time, Ms Porter could have come forward. Her actions were those of a reckless adolescent and then she became frightened. He assured the judge it was not an excuse, but as the months went on, Ms Porter's anxiety grew to the point of being debilitating. He added that Claire Porter's therapist from the Dearborn School could come in to discuss this point further if the judge saw fit. Zach's attorney knew it was a novel area of the law where nothing was clear-cut and little case law existed, so he left it to their judgment how to proceed.

Judge Merck directed his first questions to Sam and Cathie Bello. The judge wanted to make it clear that it was within their rights to proceed with criminal action against Claire Porter or a civil case where a financial judgment could be rendered. Samuel Bello hoped that for the last time he'd explain he didn't have any interest in ruining any more lives. Then the judge asked Zach Porter a few questions about what he intended to do with his daughter. Zach explained her daily therapy sessions and registration at Dearborn, but conceded he did not know what the therapy team would recommend for Claire after graduation, which was fast approaching.

The judge told him he would confer with the prosecutor and let them know their decision the following morning. He didn't see any reason to have it draw on any more than it already had. He looked at the sad faces surrounding him. He pushed back from his desk and shook his head, murmuring what a senseless chain of events it had been.

Spring

Bryn skipped going home for spring break, but it was nearing summer and she planned the first trip home since leaving five months before. She hadn't been in touch with any friends or acquaintances and remained silent about Claire's role in Chris's death. Her last connection to home had been that breakfast with Midnight, which hadn't gone well. When he stood at the curb scheduling a ride, she wanted to go out and talk to him, but she sat frozen in the booth, thinking about all he'd said to her. It hadn't been very nice. His ride came and he threw his backpack into the back seat. She watched the car for a good thirty seconds, thinking Midnight would turn around. He never did.

She had tried to convince herself that Midnight was not important to her and that she was glad about his departure and lack of contact. She'd repeated the events of that day to her roommate on several occasions, stressing she wanted to put the whole thing behind her and forget about Midnight. Her roommate said, "For someone who wants to put it behind her, you talk about it a lot. As Shakespeare said, the course of true love never did run smooth, or something like that."

"True love? I don't think so."

"I don't know. You did sleep with him and he's awfully cute."

Bryn laughed. "I'm not sure that's the criteria for true love, but it's a long story, so I won't take you through it, because I like you."

Her roommate folded her arms and smiled. She said, "I

have all the time in the world."

Bryn began at the very beginning. She met Claire the summer before third grade and they had instantly become friends. For all Claire's silliness, Bryn was more sensible. Claire was athletic and energetic. Bryn was more delicate and passive. Bryn supposed she was the yin and Claire the yang, but no matter, they grew into sisters by the time they reached their teens. They shared everything with one another—their deepest secrets and personal dreams. Claire's house was like her home. They studied together. They went to the same school. They liked and disliked the same people. They spent less time with one another when she had started dating Chris and things changed a little bit when she knew about Claire's crush on Midnight, but the important things were all the same. They remained inseparable. Bryn ended the story of her ten-year friendship at what Claire had done to Chris Bello.

"Wow. I'll tell you one thing, it sounds like she deserves payback."

"She does, but Midnight isn't the way to get it."

"For what it's worth, he likes you. I could tell."

"And that makes it all right? I don't know. That seems like pretzel logic to me. And, if you had heard some of the things he said to me, you'd question how much he likes me. He did once, but not so much anymore."

"Hey, I was here for about ten minutes at the most, but I saw the way he looked at you and I say he's got a lasting thing for you. I think you have to examine your feelings for him, because I don't know you super well, but I don't think you'd sleep with someone you didn't care for at all."

Bryn sighed. "We were pretty drunk."

Two weeks before the end of the term, Charlotte called Bryn to tell her she and Richard were getting a divorce. She asked Bryn to take a look around the house during the summer break for anything she might want to keep. They were doing a quick sale with everything included. Furniture, appliances, artwork—everything was going. There wasn't a grain of remorse in Charlotte's voice. Initially Bryn couldn't believe what she was hearing. Despite the arguing and the long silences that followed, her parents had been married a long time. It took a moment to regain her composure and ask a couple of questions. When did they decide to split? Did anyone else know? Once she had gotten off the phone and wrapped her head around it, she was actually glad for both of them. She thought they would be happier without one another. She came close to asking her mother if someone had taken her father's place, but decided against it. She figured there probably was someone and in their small town Bryn probably knew the person. She wasn't keen on getting any details. She'd find out soon enough on her return home for summer break.

The sign on the highway read, Andover Junction, 32 miles. The thought of taking the turnoff made Bryn nervous. Her stomach was upset and her palms were sweaty. The miles rushed by and in less than a half hour she was taking the exit toward home. Her mother greeted her. Her father was not there. In fact, Charlotte told her he no longer lived there. He had moved to the country club condos adjacent to the golf course. Bryn could almost picture him in a smoking jacket, cigar in hand, sipping scotch—the James Bond of Wisconsin. She asked her mother what the rush was on selling the house and Charlotte informed Bryn she was moving to Seattle on July 1.

Bryn was shocked. "What? Seattle?"

"Yes, Seattle."

"I'm afraid to ask, but why Seattle?"

"Well, I met someone on an airplane, of all places, when I went out to see my sister in D.C. and he is from Seattle. He works for the Seattle Mariners and you know how much I love baseball."

Bryn sat, shaking her head. "I don't know that at all. I don't think I've ever seen you watch a game."

"That doesn't mean I don't love it."

"It actually does kind of mean that."

Charlotte stood with her hands on her hips, looking exasperated. "Oh, forget about the baseball aspect of it. We began a long-distance relationship several months ago and have decided to live closer to one another."

"Are you planning on marrying this guy?"

"I have no idea, but I want a fresh start."

"Well, now the quick sale and quick split make perfect sense."

"Despite the conclusion I'm sure you're jumping to, my relationship with Mike is a small part of your father and I splitting. Your father and I have been on the road to ending our marriage for a long time. I think you know that."

"Yeah, whatever."

"It's hard to explain and may be impossible for you to understand given the privilege you grew up around, but I envisioned a different life for myself than the one I wound up with and I dislike that dismissive *whatever* tone."

"I think I understand perfectly. You never really wanted kids and you never really loved dad. You wanted to trot around the globe in first class, but you're the one that made up this life."

There was silence between the two of them. Charlotte stared out the kitchen window and finally said, "I don't really want to or think I should have to explain myself to an eighteen year-old, but I love you and I love your brother in my own way. I'd be lying if I said all those things were untrue. I was never sure about children or parenting, but once you came along, I loved you. Did I want to live in a small town in Wisconsin? No, but there have been lovely times here, too. You paint a bleak picture."

"Well that's always how I saw it. I was a lonely kid, with little involvement or support from you, or dad for that matter. You have never really been interested in my life over your own and I'm not sure if being the wife or girlfriend of some baseball guy is going to give you what you want."

Charlotte continued to stare out the window and Bryn stared at her back.

"I am not completely clueless, Bryn. I know what you're saying. I can't make up for what you feel you've lost, but I feel like we gave you everything."

"Well, you would be wrong and I wasn't looking so much for things."

Charlotte turned around to face Bryn. She looked angry, but she sighed. "We can go in endless circles about that. The bottom line is I can't stay here anymore and I'd like you to be happy with my decision."

Bryn sat with her chin poised in her left palm, staring at the kitchen wallpaper.

Charlotte pulled out a chair and sat next to Bryn. "Bryn, I know you've had a rough go of it for the past year or two and I know your father and I haven't helped much."

"No, you didn't help at all."

"Frankly, we didn't know how, but all I want for you is to be happy too. It's all that really matters."

"Yes, everyone says that, but it's kind of bull-shitty and it's not easy."

"No, it's not always easy."

Bryn pushed back from the table. "I don't think I can talk about this anymore."

Charlotte got up from the table as well and walked over to the cupboard next to the fridge and began inspecting the contents. "Fine. Have it your way. Over the next couple days, go through every room and take anything you want. Start a pile and I'll figure out how to get it to you, and put a sticky note on any furniture you may want."

"Fine."

"Are you going to see Claire while you're here?"

"I'm sure I'll see Midnight or at least try to. I'm not sure about Claire—I've heard through the mill that she was packed off to Dearborn for the rest of her senior year."

"Well she's back at her parent's house. There's a lot of whispering about her going away to school when she was four months from graduation. I can't imagine what she did to be sent to a reform school. I never much cared for any of them and don't want to quarrel with you about it, since you love

Mary Porter so much, so that's all I'll say."

Bryn said it so softly that her mother could barely hear. "You never cared for Claire?"

"Not especially."

"That's sad. She adored you."

"That's so odd. I never got that feeling. Anyway, there's a good deal of speculation that her departure to Dearborn had something to do with the Bellos. Apparently, Mary and Zach Porter have been spending a good deal of time with them and they were never friends before Claire went away. Oh, and speaking of Mary and Zach, Mrs. Wright told me they're back together."

Bryn was so happy for both of them. She blurted out, "Oh my God, I am so glad they're back together!"

"Mary never struck me as much of a catch, even for that nut Zach Porter."

"She's a wonderful person and so is he."

"As I said, I know how fond you are of her—so many virtues."

"Yes, they both have many virtues. I have to get rolling. I have a ton of stuff to take care of, but I do have something I wanted to tell you. I'm thinking about transferring to Madison in the fall."

"Where did that come from?"

"Florida's not bad or anything, but I think I want to be where old friends are."

"You better let your father know. I'm sure there will be costs."

"If I can get the transfer, it should be cheaper in state."

"Well as long as it's not Seattle, I don't care. I'm looking for some time to work on me."

Bryn left the house without replying. Her mother was hurt-ful. *I'm looking for some time to work on me.* Really? Her own mother didn't want her around. There should be an exam to be a parent followed by a really tough practical home test where a social worker and psychologist are on hand to grade parenting scenarios. Bryn felt like starting the car and driving it directly through the den windows and straight through the kitchen, pinning her mother against the stone countertops. Despite the urge, she got in the car, backed away from the house instead of into it and headed to her father's new apartment.

She made herself calm down while driving. She had to ask her father about UW and didn't want to be huffing and puffing. She walked in calmly, glanced around and commented on how nice it all looked. She tried to keep it lighthearted and searched for some neutral ground before jumping to the topic of trans-ferring. He asked about her friends and she admitted she hadn't seen or talked to anyone, but confided that Midnight was on her list, even if she had to drive to Madison to see him. She explained that they'd had a fight when he visited her months earlier and it all felt kind of like unfinished business. She had spoken terribly to him, and he to her, and they were too close to let a rift become a chasm. And speaking of Madison… there was her segue. She told her father she was considering a trans-fer at the beginning of the fall term or midyear at the latest.

"What the hell is so pressing about Madison?"

"I've been thinking about it for a while. I think it's a better school. Well, better for me. I like the arts programs at Gainesville, but have been doing some research and there's an interdisciplinary program at UW that would help me figure out my main focus."

"Really? I thought Gainesville was suppose to be so perfect."

"Well don't get angry."

He had been rearranging some books on a shelf next to the TV, but stopped and sat next to Bryn on the sofa. "Well, I'm thrown, since your going to Gainesville seemed so crucial—great programs, great weather, and now a few months later, you tell me you don't want to be there anymore. I hate that wishy-washy shit."

"I know, I know, but I've learned more about available courses in that time and everything was so awful here last fall. Things are better now and I want to be closer to home. I miss it here."

"Miss here or miss someone here? You can't bring that Bello kid back, Bryn."

Despite expecting his look of disapproval, she told her dad she had loved Chris. He surprised her when he said he hadn't necessarily disapproved of Chris. He had thought Chris was an okay sort of boy, but was concerned she was getting too serious and might make an irreparable mistake with her life. He regretted treating Chris poorly and that regret deepened on hearing about Chris's suicide.

Richard didn't look at Bryn. He stared down at the floor and said disliking the Bello family was really about Chris's dad and that he had been shocked by Samuel Bello's greeting when they met at the memorial service. They had never been friends—quite the opposite. He guessed it was the solemnity of the moment that required they shake hands and greet one another.

Bryn asked what would ever sour her father's opinion of

Mr. Bello. He shook his head, saying he didn't really want to talk about it, but that made Bryn insist even more. Mr. Bello had been so kind. She wondered why anyone would dislike him.

"What would you have against Samuel Bello? Do you even know him?"

"I don't know him well, but your mother did."

"Really? Chris never told me that."

Richard awkwardly grabbed for Bryn's hand. "I'm not sure Chris knew. After his wife killed herself and before he and Cathie married, Samuel and your mother saw a good deal of each other. The Bellos had lived in town a long time, but were newcomers to the lakefront. Actually, now that I think about it, it was not long after we moved here. Your mother was quite the welcome wagon."

"That can't be true."

"It wasn't much of a secret, Bryn."

Richard got up and stepped back to the bookcase.

"Please tell me the truth about what happened. I don't think anything about mom could shock me."

He continued to stare at the bindings along the shelf, but began to speak. "Let's just say when he asked Cathie to marry him, it tore your mother apart. We were never really able to piece our marriage back together." Richard paused to reflect and then said, "I think I tried, but sometimes I'm not sure I tried hard enough. There may have been something satisfying for me about her being dumped. We were never the same after that."

"Did Jack know? About Mr. Bello?"

He turned and looked back at Bryn. "Yes, I believe he did. I'm sure he heard the gossip at school and other places."

"Well, that explains some of their issues."

"Some things, yes, but they're complicated. I always thought I'd come to understand their contempt for one another—or hoped their hostility and animosity would come to a magical end, but no such luck. Maybe I should have intervened, but I don't think it would have done much good. I guess I'm rationalizing. How about we change the subject?"

Bryn let out a sigh. "Okay, I guess."

"Have you seen the new boyfriend?"

"Is that changing the subject?"

He laughed. "Entertain my curiosity."

Bryn stared at her father for a moment. She hadn't seen him laugh in a very long time. "No I haven't seen him. Has he been in town?"

Richard moved toward the liquor cabinet to pour himself a scotch then looked at his watch and stopped. "It's a little early even for me." He paused. "I don't know. I thought maybe he was at the house."

"Not that I know of."

Richard looked down and took a small piece of lint off his shirt. "I did see a photo that was obviously left out for me to see and without any ego, I don't get it. He does not seem your mother's type at all."

"She has a type?"

"I'd like to think it's someone who is tall, smart, witty, masculine. But this guy is short and looks like his face has been punched a couple times. I don't get it. Maybe it's the sports thing or baseball players in general."

"What?"

"There was Wheeler Davidson."

Richard went on to tell the story of how he and Charlotte met and Bryn was reminded that Wheeler Davidson had gone to Purdue on a baseball scholarship.

Bryn saw a smile brush across her father's face—maybe happier times, happier days. She stood and took in the room. "It's a curious story. I've never understood her well and the story of your meeting doesn't shed any light for me. She's secretive and aloof. Oh my god, the whole thing about her parents is one glaring example."

"I know. I always thought it was a stupid secret to keep. In hindsight, I don't think I understood her that well either. Not even back then. But there was something about her that I immediately fell in love with. In my youth and foolishness, I thought I could change her."

"And what did you want to change about her?"

"I'd want her to love me for something besides my money."

"That's a terrible way to feel."

Richard reached for the scotch bottle for the second time and poured himself a drink. "Yes, it is."

"Would you ever take her back? I mean, if she came back, would you take her back?"

"I don't really know, but I'd like to think I wouldn't. I hope I'd have enough self-respect to tell her to go to hell and then move on with my life, but I'm not sure. We have a lot of history, so it's hard to be black and white about it. I'd like to think I'm happier and better without her, but I get lonely and lazy about making an effort to get out there. I vow to go onto a dating website or join some singles club. Instead I get in from the office, make myself a drink, stare at the fridge hoping dinner will materialize, then order food in, go through emails, watch some TV and go to bed."

"How about the weekends? What do you do?"

"Golf. Christ, I don't know what I'll do in the winter."

There was a long pause before Bryn said, "So, I think I'm going to head back. She wants me to go through every room and every closet and let her know what I want. Is there anything you want me to save for you?"

"No. Nothing there feels like it belongs to me. You know we don't have to talk about your mother or me."

"No, that's not it. I really have to get moving. I have some unfinished business with Claire and I need to call Midnight too. I want to tell him about my plans and UW. Actually, you never said it was okay. We wound up not talking about it much."

"You promise me this is about what UW may be able to provide that Florida can't and not a whim? If you can promise me that, then I guess it's fine. At least you can start the process and see if a transfer is even feasible. It certainly would be a financial win for me. UW would save me a boatload of money."

Bryn headed to her car feeling sad. She didn't feel like her mother's new life would work out for her, she didn't see any evidence of her father's working out for him and she wasn't at all sure if leaving Florida would work out for her. Maybe it was a whim—she had been winging most of what she said about interdisciplinary studies. She needed to see Midnight.

Bryn couldn't enjoy the walk to the Porters' despite sunshine and a warm breeze that was making the weeping willows move in unison like a water ballet along the road. She had rehearsed what she would say to Claire, but wasn't sure any amount of rehearsing would help. Bryn wasn't even sure why she had initiated their meeting. Bryn guessed Claire knew she was home from Florida, but Claire had made no overture to see Bryn. That alone wasn't very promising. Midnight had told her Claire's ridiculous story back in the spring, but now that Bryn was home, she had to hear it from Claire—why, why, why would she ever do something so reckless?

Wally saw Bryn coming up the walk and answered the door before she could even press the bell.

He gave her a warm, tight hug. "It is so great to see you. How long has it been? You look great."

Bryn smiled and gave him a small peck on the cheek. "Thanks. You look good too. You always look good." She backed away from him, but continued to smile. "It's been a while since I saw you. I left in late December, so that's around six months ago and I didn't really see much of you before Gainesville."

"Yeah, and I'm sorry for that. How's Florida?"

"Oh, it's okay, but I actually think I'm going to try and transfer to UW."

Wally made his way into the living room with Bryn tagging behind. He took a one-handed hurdle over the back of the sofa and relaxed into the cushions. "In Mad Town?"

"Yeah. Florida has been good but I miss the bleak, endless,

bone-jarringly cold winters."

Wally laughed saying who wouldn't miss six straight months of freeze. He was mid-sentence when there was a thud on the stairs. Both Bryn and Wally turned toward the noise. It was Claire. She had dropped a plastic water bottle and was stooped to pick it up before it rolled down the flight. Her hair was in its usual topknot and her eyes still glistened with a hundred different colors, but she looked paler and thinner than when Bryn had last seen her.

Standing as quickly as he had sat, Wally said, "I have to get going. I'm due at work pretty soon and I know you have a lot to talk about. Bryn, it was great seeing you and don't be a stranger this summer."

"It was great seeing you too. Thanks."

Claire finally spoke. "You want to come up to my room? I straightened up this morning, which means there's some visible floor space."

Bryn didn't react to Claire's attempt at being funny. "Sounds fine."

They took their usual places. Bryn sat with her back pressed against Lilli's bed while Claire plopped herself onto her twin mattress, lying on her stomach with her elbows bent, jaw line fixed into her palms. She began, "God, think of all the times we've been up here listening to music or doing homework or reading gossip about rock stars and actors."

"We have spent a lot of time here. It makes me sad."

"Why?"

Bryn shook her head and stared wide-eyed at Claire. "Why? Well, shit. Let me think. All the plans we talked about haven't exactly turned out, have they? God, all the times we talked about Chris." Bryn's voice trailed off. She couldn't look directly at Claire, when she asked, "Why, Claire? I don't get it."

Claire began. "No one understands when I try to explain what I did and why and it's hard for me to articulate. You have to believe all I wanted was for you and Chris to be together. I never imagined he would kill himself."

"Yeah, I'm guessing no one would foresee that outcome, but why the drugs? If you wanted Chris to come back to me there had to be an easier way than a criminal conviction. We're talking about Chris. He was your friend. You had known him as long as you've known me."

Claire put her face into her mattress and mumbled something Bryn couldn't hear.

Bryn began again. "Why don't you try your best to explain it to me, because I've been without a clue and I'm guessing I'm not alone. I've wrestled with the leap between you wanting Chris and me back together and your elaborate scheme to get him back into my arms. I don't get it. No sane person gets it."

Claire reconstructed the conversation she had with Mr. Bello almost word for word. Bryn, like everyone, asked why Claire hadn't come forward when Chris was going to trial. Claire told Bryn how afraid she'd been and how she thought everything would still turn out well.

Bryn interrupted. "Whoa. What do you mean turn out well?"

Claire reminded Bryn that she and Chris didn't really get together until the trial had begun once Olivia was out of the picture. That's when her plan seemed to be working. The two of them had been spending much more time together. She went on talking about Bryn regularly at Chris's house and the two of them going out in public again. She continued to tell Bryn how scared she was, but she failed to say anything about what the effect coming forward would have on a potential swim scholarship. As she repeated the edited, less selfish version of the story to Bryn she could make herself believe the idea of losing all chances of a scholarship hadn't ever entered her mind.

Bryn interrupted her. "Claire, I can't help how angry I am, but more than anything I get the feeling you're annoyed that everyone isn't on board with this craziness."

"You're right! I am annoyed. I'm getting tired of explaining myself. I did something terrible, but I thought I was doing something for the right reasons and I attempted to tell you. I did."

"When?"

"That day we went to Tappanook."

"What are you talking about?"

"Remember I said I had something to talk to you about?"

Bryn shook her head in disbelief. "My god, Claire, you should have tried harder. I think you told me it could wait. Chris was already dead! Wait? Really? Wait how long, Claire?"

Claire put her face into her bedspread and in a muffled voice said, "There was no turning back. The damage had been done and after that day I couldn't look at you anymore without being reminded of what I did."

"So instead of facing your responsibility, the better idea was to ignore me?"

Claire came up for air and looked at Bryn. "I guess."

"Well, no, it's not guessing."

"I feel awful about everything Bryn."

"Do you? I think it's too big of a thing to just *feel awful*."

"But what more can I do?"

"I don't know Claire. I don't know." There was silence between the two of them, but Bryn looked up at Claire. "And you're telling me this was all about Chris and me and had nothing to do with you and Midnight? Did you think about your potential swim scholarship when you decided to conceal what you did?"

Claire almost choked on the air she was breathing. She hadn't mentioned her NCSA post or potential scholarships, but Bryn knew her too well. All Claire said was, "Midnight was like an afterthought, I swear."

"You know, Midnight and I talked about friendship a while back and he convinced me of some things. I swear I wanted to forgive you. I wanted everyone to forgive you, no matter how hard I thought that might be. But listening to you now, I don't believe you for a second. If you had admitted it was about you, things might be different right now. If you had copped to how selfish it was and how insane it was, then this talk might have changed how I feel. I never, ever thought I'd say this, but I can't even look at you and I certainly don't want to associate with you. You are not my friend."

"But I swear I did it *because* you're my friend. You're my only real friend and I wanted you to be happy. You talked about him all the time. Being with Chris was the thing that made you happy."

Bryn couldn't hear any more. She left Claire's room, walked down the stairs and found Mrs. Porter in the kitchen.

She gave her a hug that would have to last them both a lifetime. To be out of Claire's life meant she remove herself from the entire family. She closed the front door behind her and her childhood with it. She began the walk home.

Claire heard Bryn leave. She thought about going after her, but there was nothing more to say. She lay back on her bed, staring at the ceiling. She thought everyone should be moving on. It had been a year since Chris died. She had been punished—had to endure the Dearborn Academy, which had no swim team, and months of therapy with a doctor who smelled like Listerine and Sharpie ink. If it hadn't been for her mother's insistence, she'd still be in his stale office at Dearborn. She was continuing therapy, but not in that dreary place. She was forced to listen to her parents' scripted discussions about narcissism, middle child syndrome and affective disorders, but at least she was home.

She hadn't been able to express what happened that Valentine's night well enough and Bryn hadn't stayed long enough for Claire to try and be clearer. She would have told her about seeing Chris with Olivia and watching Bryn leave defeated. She would have tried to make Bryn understand that yes, she wanted to be with Midnight, but that wasn't why the idea came to her that night.

The night of the party, after Bryn left, she walked down to the lake brooding about her parents and Bryn and Chris. She sat on the pier with the party noises behind her thinking about how hard it was to love someone when they didn't love you back. And then the idea came to her out of the crisp night air. She could make everything work out for Bryn and figured if it worked in her and Midnight's favor that would be a bonus.

A sort optimism set in and she popped up from the pier and headed back to the party.

She'd seen a couple of sketchy characters at the party. One guy in particular named Jerry Newsom had been arrested a few years earlier for dealing drugs. He had dropped out of school and gotten into trouble on a couple occasions. She would approach him on the chance he might have something to sell her that she could plant on Chris. She was pretty positive that a guy with a record wouldn't come forward after Chris was arrested to say he had sold drugs to a minor and there might be a connection. She had seen Chris come in wearing his letter jacket. She remembered it because it seemed too lightweight for the weather, so she knew which jacket was his, and it was easy to get the drugs into the lining—it was thin and slightly threadbare. It had been just as easy to watch Wally and all his friends, Chris included, down beer after beer until they started to get a little drunk—not sloppy, but certainly tipsy. And it had been easy to phone the police too. She walked the two blocks to the Trading Post and used an old pay phone that stood in the parking lot like a dinosaur. When the dispatcher asked for her name and location, she simply hung up. If Chris didn't get stopped by the police, then no harm done. If he did, Bryn was the girl who stuck like glue—Olivia was not. Bryn would be the person Chris could count on if he was in trouble.

She knew of course that Chris and Bryn would be furious, but they would forgive her. Time would pass and they would forgive her and they would be together. But then it all went to pieces. The charge had been more serious than she figured and his attorney hadn't been great. The cop came off looking like a combination of John McLane and Aragorn. Chris came off like a nervous felon. Then as the trial dragged, summer came. She had overheard her mother's phone conversation. "I couldn't feel worse for Samuel. First his wife, now Chris." Claire understood at once—Chris had killed himself. She ran up to her room taking two stairs at a time. She slammed the bedroom door behind her, barely making it to her bed before collapsing. After the funeral she had resolved to go to Bryn's house and tell her what she had done, but she never had. She got scared and so ashamed that she never said anything. She couldn't even look at Bryn after that. Her stomach twisted into tight knots whenever she saw Bryn's name on her cell. She felt sweaty and shaky when she saw her in the hallway at school, and would make up some excuse about swim practice if Bryn spoke to her, or walk away before Bryn could catch a glimpse of her. And as the time passed, she grew more and more terrified of being found out.

Months had passed since Chris's death, and Bryn had already been in Florida over a month when Gary Jensen came up to her as she walked out of the gym late one night, her backpack feeling heavier than the weight of the world. He looked lost in thought as he walked toward her. When he began to talk, her life exploded like a supernova. It turned out that Jensen had been across the hall from the room where the coats were and had seen Claire go in the room by herself. He had looked through the open space between the half-closed door and the doorjamb and had watched Claire put something in Chris's coat pocket. When Gary heard about Chris's arrest he figured what Claire had done, but never said a word. He didn't want to get involved. Even after Chris's death he continued to stay silent, but his conscience was torturing him and he decided he couldn't stay quiet any longer. He wanted to tell

Bryn, but Claire dissuaded him and had asked that he give her some time to first tell the Bello family and her own parents.

And now the people she loved knew what she had done. Lili didn't want to share a room with her. Even Wally began to look at her differently. Every time she caught his eye she saw nothing but sadness. She hadn't seen Midnight and knew she wouldn't. She actually felt his contempt crawl across her skin like a chill when he left her room the night before he went to Florida. Her mother and father argued about her and it was always the same argument—her father thought she should return to Dearborn, her mother was adamant she stay home. The stress was aging them both.

She couldn't begin to make anyone understand she hadn't meant to harm Chris. She really hadn't.

Bryn called Midnight and left message after message until she felt ridiculous. She spent a fair amount of time after spring break writing lists of pros and cons about him, with the pros winning by a landslide.

Months had passed since Midnight had made the trip to Gainesville to tell her about Claire's involvement in Chris's arrest. She still toyed with the idea of telling anyone who would listen what Claire had done. Her talk with Claire had only strengthened that feeling, but then what good would it do? Wally and Midnight would be furious with her and she cared more about their opinion than retribution at that point.

She bristled at the idea that while she spent so much time thinking about Midnight he might have been busy finding a new girlfriend—some fabulous UW co-ed who was smart and sexy and adorable and thought Midnight was adorable too. She probably called him Jonathan. He would shed his past like a snakeskin to make a future with her, and his nickname would be the first thing to go—something that attached him to Bryn.

She committed to using the upcoming days to go through the inventory of her childhood home, as she had promised her mother she would do. She'd make an early appointment with the registrar's office in Madison to discuss a possible transfer before filling out the forms online. She didn't want to waste too much time if they weren't accepting more applications or if her credits wouldn't transfer. Most importantly, she would hunt Midnight down. She needed to explain things much better than she had in Florida and she hoped he would listen.

A couple days of calling and getting his voicemail passed, but she finally caught up with him playing hoops at the park. They agreed to meet for coffee after he had a shower and changed.

They sat sipping iced coffees. He listened politely, nodding his head and committing to "right, I see," or "yeah, I hear you." She talked about her feelings for Chris and how hard the past year had been. She asked for his forgiveness for treating him badly in Gainesville and said she hoped they could pick up their relationship again. She told him she'd given it a lot of thought and that there must be something to salvage.

There was a long silence. Midnight sipped at his coffee and looked down at his cell. Bryn let him think without interruption, but finally said, "So? Say something."

He asked her if she was finished and she said that yes, she was. He looked over toward the counter and then slowly back at Bryn. His face was blank. "You know what, Bryn? Go to hell." Midnight explained that he wasn't the guy who followed her around like a puppy anymore, waiting to see if she wanted him to beg or sit or stay. He had wanted her to be in his life more than anything in the world, but they were never on the same page. He asked whether she could pity him the way she pitied herself when she chased after Chris—Chris, who had responded to her with little more than a cold shoulder most of the time, or a brief conversation only when he felt like it. Then he cut her off before she had a chance to answer. He got up, left the coffee house and headed toward the lakeshore. Without looking back, he lifted his hand to give her a backward finger. He did not turn around.

She sat there alone, considering how she would make it work.

He was angry with her, but he'd get over it. She would figure out a way to see him on campus. She'd find out his class schedule and take them or audit them without credit, if necessary. He wouldn't be able to ignore her and he would warm up to the idea of being with her. And then, as she watched Midnight walk away, getting smaller and smaller in the distance she thought about that ridiculous plan, her own self-worth and supposed she wouldn't be seeing Midnight again. As she headed toward her car, a gust of wind came across the lake and the memory of Davis Brummell blew around her. Davis had drowned two years earlier. Some of the events surrounding his death seemed vague and disordered, but some of it was very clear. It was her mother and brother arguing about Davis that brought her to Chris and with a wince she thought about how she had pursued him the same way she thought about chasing after Midnight. No, she deserved more and so did Midnight. She would return to Gainesville after all. Her father would hit the roof, but she'd reason with him. She had begun to make new friends. Her roommate was terrific. She was completely engaged in so many of her classes especially her theater work and she loved her professors. The weather was warm and inviting and above all, she could be herself, whoever she turned out to be. She wouldn't be Claire's less attractive friend anymore. She wouldn't be the girl desperate for and dumped by Chris, or the girl constantly at odds with Midnight. She would always love them: Chris and Midnight and Claire. She would also carry the deep sting of loss and rejection associated with them, but it was time to navigate her own path.

Epilogue

Mary Porter stood with her hands resting on the handle of the vacuum cleaner, staring out the living room window. Fall was in the air. Little bits of color freckled the oak that stood in their front yard. She was lost in thought. There was an unusual quiet in the house and she contemplated putting the vacuum away and picking up the best seller she had been reading. As she stood thinking about housework hooky, a police car pulled into the driveway. There were no sirens or lights flashing and Mary expected the officer was using their driveway to turn around, but then Zach's car pulled in behind it. She wiped away tears as Zach spoke with the policeman outside. She knew why he was there. Despite all their late night talks about keeping Claire's crime from the police, she had always known Zach would never be able to hold up his end of the bargain. His silence ate away at him. His sleep was restless, he lost weight, he lacked concentration. She had imagined this day—the shouting at one another, the accusations flying, but instead she was calm and there was an odd inner peace. She had known Zach Porter since she was a young girl and she loved him for all the qualities that made this day inevitable.

Two days later it was Midnight who told Bryn. She was in the Gainesville campus library when she saw his name on her phone. She texted him that she was in the library, but she would call him ASAP. She gathered her notebooks and her textbook, stuffed them in her backpack and raced out of the building.

His voice was the same and she suppressed the butterflies

she was feeling. She opened their conversation asking how he was and he told her he was fine and that school was good. In what sounded like a deeper voice he said, "Bryn, I'm sorry about this past summer. I want us to be friends. I don't want us to screw that up."

"I want that too. I've missed not being friends."

"Yeah, me too."

There was a long pause and Bryn asked if Midnight was still on the line. She thought the call might have broken up or they somehow lost a signal and got disconnected. Midnight cut in. "I'm still here. I was just thinking about something. It seems like I'm always bringing you weird news."

"Uh oh. What's up?"

"Well, Claire has been arrested."

"You have got to be kidding me. That's crazy! All this time passing and now she's arrested."

"Did you say something to the police?"

"I never said a thing. I know it's hard to believe, but I really did let it go."

"That's what I thought. I just wanted to make sure and God knows I do not want to talk about it anymore. So, are you coming home for winter break?"

"Coming home for winter break? Are you kidding me? You don't want to talk about it?"

"Not for right now, okay?"

They spent an hour talking about school and their classes. Bryn talked about the play she was rehearsing and Midnight told Bryn he was actually considering medical school. They spoke about Bryn's father's new girlfriend and what wound up being her mother's ex-boyfriend. And of course, Bryn asked about Midnight's dad before they said goodbye and made plans to see one another that coming winter.

Acknowledgments

Like most novels, if not all, this is a labor of love. Many people, through their kindness and encouragement, kept me going through the process. In no particular order, let me begin with Dessa, Nora, Pamela H, Dana, Aimee, Bryce, Matt H, Brett, Javier, Ken E, Sharron, Ed Z, Egan, Lisa T, and my wonderful, supportive brother Tom and sisters Lori, Tara and Lorna, and of course Vicki and Greg.

A special thank you goes out to those people who first read the book and practiced patience through the necessary edits. Your input was priceless, your praise, adrenaline—both carried me through the final miles toward publishing.

I am grateful to all the beta readers and especially to Katie Willson and Anna Willson for taking the time to read the book despite (crazy) busy schedules while still providing sensitive, generous and helpful feedback.

Special thanks also to Melanie Hogue, for her sharp pencil, kind words and wit.

Discussion Questions

1. Like the river is to Bryn, what are the places that evoke the most significant memories for you?
2. If you could revisit one place, what would it be?
3. A boy drowns at the very beginning of the book. Discuss the significance and metaphor.
4. People, lots of friends and/or acquaintances, family and community, surround Bryn. Talk about her loneliness. Why is she so lonely?
5. Bryn's brother Jack creates and instigates many issues with his mother. Do parents play favorites, despite telling every child they are loved equally? What do you think of Richard standing by or even siding with Jack against his own wife?
6. There are many broken relationships throughout the story, who is the one person you would most like to repair a relationship with?
7. Sneaking out of the house in the middle of the night was a pretty harmless prank. Have you ever done anything like that? Do you regret it? Did it have consequences?
8. Claire is a complicated young woman who can't get out of her own way. Do you believe her actions are selfless or do you see her as manipulative and narcissistic?
9. How do you feel about Charlotte? Should she be pitied or understood for having her own moral compass whether we agree with it (or not)?
10. Whose side did you take in the locker room confrontation between Midnight and Chris?

11. Bryn finds more than a distraction in her school theater group. She's having fun and she's happy. Chris shows up uninvited on a really important day for Bryn. Have you ever tried to take someone away from something they loved because it was diverting too much attention away from you? Have you ever tried to pull someone away from something because you were jealous of their commitment to something/someone other than you?

12. Does your sixteen-year-old self feel confident?

13. Do you believe Chris was duplicitous with Bryn or is he just a friendly person?

14. Crushes are complicated and (sometimes) wonderful. Who was your first crush on?

15. Do you think we are born with confidence or is it a learned personality trait?

16. Do you have lifelong friendships?

17. How difficult is it to try and see the world through someone else's eyes?

18. Do you think your family keeps secrets and perhaps tells lies?

19. If you were Bryn, would you have escaped to Florida or continued to live in a toxic environment hoping it would get better?

20. Bryn's relationship takes a big step when she and Chris sleep with one another. If Bryn had a more engaged mother, do you think Bryn would have gone ahead with the plan to consummate the relationship?

21. Did you see how Chris felt trapped? If not, can you see it from a 17-year-old's eyes?

22. Midnight is a great guy. He is tangled up with Bryn and

doesn't see his way out. His father gives him pretty good advice (and fair warning) about Bryn and her feelings. What advice would you give Midnight?

23. As Bryn grows a little older, the relationship with her father is evolving. How have your most important relationships evolved?

24. Do you think Charlotte can ever be happy or contented? What about Richard and the other adults in the story? Is the ground Zach and Mary stand on shaky? How about Samuel and Cathie?

25. Tappanook is a nice little town and nice place to grow up, but Charlotte completely closes the door on her upbringing. What do you think this is about? Religion? Class? Reinvention?

26. There seems to be ever-growing cache of communication devices and with it increasing opportunities for bullying. Is ignoring a friend/fellow student a form of bullying?

About the Author

Carol Lansen spent many years employed at advertising agencies working with movie studios and TV networks, but always wanted to be a novelist. After a series of stops and starts, she finally sat down to write her first novel, Whispering Pines. She grew up in pastoral Wisconsin surrounded by lakes and forests and farmland, as well as extraordinary (sometimes quirky) people, many of whom influence her writing. She lives in Southern California with her rescue dog Oliver, where she is busy working on her second novel, proving that you can be who you set out to be, even if it takes longer than you thought.

Please connect via spumoni books at spumonibooks@gmail or you can find Carol on Instagram @CarolLansen or Carol Lansen Author | Facebook

If you like the book and feel like you want to tell others, please leave a review on Amazon or other social media—always helpful and fun to see.

photo: Michael McNellis